I0729233

FORREST WOLLINSKY VAMPIRE HUNTER

THE BEGINNING

LEONARD D. HILLEY II

Copyright © 2016, 2019 by Leonard D. Hilley II

ISBN-13: 978-1-950485-07-9

All rights reserved.

No part of this book may be reproduced in any form or by any electronic or mechanical means, including information storage and retrieval systems, without written permission from the author, except for the use of brief quotations in a book review.

❧ Created with Vellum

For Christal, as always, with love.

UNTITLED

"Folks might consider this my autobiography, but it's actually my resume."
—Forrest Wollinsky, Vampire Hunter

ucharest, 1888

THE WIND HOWLED like an awakening banshee as it swirled and lashed around our snow-covered cottage nestled in the barren trees at the edge of the forest. I was only eight years old, but it was the harshest winter in my one hundred and thirty-odd year memory.

My father had been gone for several days, which wasn't unusual. Mother had said that he was hunting and should return soon, but the blizzard had set in with a fury, burying the roads, fields, and the forest floor beneath several feet of snow. Wherever he was, he'd be stuck for quite some time.

Snowdrifts lined three sides of our meager cottage and the snow-storm had barely started. The outside layers of snow helped insulate our rugged home. The warmth of the fire felt like the heat of summer, making it almost easy to forget about the freezing howling winds outside.

The hearth fire crackled softly under a black bubbling pot of rabbit stew. Garlic cloves were strung together above a basket of dried yams.

We had enough food to last out the week, which made me wonder why my father had chosen to hunt during the worst of the blizzard.

My mother sat in her creaky rocker and was sewing a new coat for me from rabbit hides. Only eight, I was as husky and tall as a young man in his teens. It seemed that I outgrew my clothes about as quickly as she could make new ones.

While she sewed, I sat near the fire and sharpened a long curved dagger my father had given me. He had traded fox hides for the blade, and I expected to soon use it whenever my father returned with his kill.

A slight pause in the winds caused my mother to stop rocking. She leaned slightly forward and cocked her head to the side. The curious frown on her face caught my attention. I set down the whetstone and rose to my feet.

A gentle rapping at the door was faintly noticeable since the winds had quieted, and probably would have gone completely unnoticed had they continued to whistle. But there it was again.

Rap-rap-rap.

A bit bolder, but not overly pronounced or with desperation.

With my dagger gripped in my hand I eased toward the door. Confusion furrowed my mother's brow. She set her quilt aside and held her scissors to her side, ready to help fend off whatever danger awaited outside that door.

Stepping to the side of the door, I lifted the metal latch that secured the door and eased it against the door panel, careful to be silent.

Rap-rap-rap.

Without fear, I grabbed the large oval handle and yanked open the door. A whoosh of cold air sprang forward, sucking out our much-treasured heat.

On the path directly outside the door, the snow was stained crimson beneath the gray overcast sky. A trail of blood cut farther down the path into the forest. Large heavy snowflakes dropped, steadily trying to erase the blood path. No other tracks were in the snow. No bandits or attackers were visible amongst the snowy tree trunks. The bloody path ended at the door where the body lay.

A desperate weak hand shook, reaching up for me.

"John!" my mother shouted, running across the room to the door.

In terror I stared down into my father's haunted eyes, barely recognizing him. His face was battered, and his eyes were swollen nearly shut. Blood caked in his graying beard. His useless legs twisted behind him. How far he had crawled or how he had managed to do so with the amount of blood he had lost? It was a mystery then, and remains so even to this day. By every means he should have been dead, long before he got to the door, but his stubborn determination enabled him to ignore his pain and fight to pull himself back home.

I sheathed my dagger and grabbed his nearly frozen hand, heaving him out of the snow and across the threshold. Mother quickly closed and secured the door when we were safely inside.

My father's cold hand fell from my grip and a huge sigh gushed from his mouth as he lost consciousness.

"Father?" I asked, dropping to my knees in front of him. Blood trickled from his nose. I glanced toward Momma. "What happened to him?"

"Get him to the bed," she said, wiping away tears.

Placing my hands beneath his underarms, I lifted, pulling him up enough to wrap my arms around his chest until he was upright. His body was cold, but the heat of his leaking wounds stuck to me. I cringed. So much blood. I fought tears. He was dying. Had to be. Nothing lost so much blood and survived.

My father wasn't a massive man, like he and my mother always insisted I would become. He actually weighed less than I and was several inches shorter. In spite of his stature, he was a crafty fighter, capable of defending himself against men twice his size. Stout and thinly muscular, he had incredible strength and feared no one.

For once, I was proud of my abnormally large size and his lack thereof. I hefted him and walked toward the bed, his boots scraping the wooden floor as I moved. Gurgling sounds rumbled in his throat.

"A bear?" I asked, looking at her. "Was he attacked by a bear?"

Mother brought a pail of lukewarm water and set it by the bed. She shook her head and tore strips of cloth.

I eased my father onto the bed and laid him back. He gasped and groaned in pain, but his eyes never opened.

"Strip off his coat," she said. "His boots, too."

I quickly obeyed.

She peeled back his shirt, revealing long gashes across his chest and abdomen. The lacerations were too narrow to be from bear claws, but the cuts were dark and deep. Older white scars were visible. On his chest above his heart was the singed outline of a cross. Two puncture marks near his shoulder were swollen, bruised. Two dark dots.

"What did this?" I asked, pointing at the wound. My fingers almost touched the marks, and she slapped my hand away.

"No!" she gasped.

"What kind of animal could do this?"

Her dark eyes were hollowed from fear. She was paler than normal and seemed more delicate.

"Mother, please tell me what did this to Father?"

She took a damp cloth and washed blood from his nose and beard. With another cloth, she washed his forehead. Tears heated her eyes. She spat out a word with complete contempt as she whispered, "Vampire."

My chest tightened. Anger rippled inside me. "A vampire attacked him while he was hunting game?"

"No," she replied. "He was hunting the vampire."

"Why?"

"It is his calling, his duty. Magistrates and governors seek him out to kill vampires. They pay in gold and silver coins."

I stared at my father's frail body. His chest rose and fell with shallow breaths. "Why has he never told me?"

"To protect you."

"From what?"

"Them."

"Vampires?"

She nodded.

Frowning, I asked, "Why would they wish to harm me? My schoolmates tell tales that are quite scary. I'd never venture into one of their lairs."

"You're like your father, but you're too young. In time you'll be as fearless as he."

"Too young for what, Mother?"

"To train to hunt the vampires."

My eyes widened and fastened upon my father's incapacitated body. He was barely alive. The possibility that he would die during the night was greater than the chance of him surviving his injuries. I didn't think I was foolish enough to pursue the fanged demons of the night. Trained or not, hunting vampires was destined to become a short-lived profession.

"His legs are broken," I said.

She nodded. "I know."

Tears streamed down my mother's cheeks. She cried quietly without calling attention to herself. I took a damp cloth and pressed it against one of the lacerations across my father's stomach. I hoped the pressure might stop the bleeding. Some of the cuts were scabbing, but the two puncture wounds pulsed softly, in rhythm with his faint heartbeat. It was unnerving to witness, as if the injuries were alive, feeding off of his body.

While I held the cloth, her eyes widened. She rushed from the side of the bed and ran to black water pot near the hearth. She was back in seconds.

"What's wrong?" I asked.

Momma was too frantic for words. She turned my father's head to the side, pried open his mouth, and black blood oozed out. She took the damp cloth and inserted it into his mouth with her finger. She swirled her cloth-covered finger around the inside of his mouth like one washed a dish. When she pulled out the cloth, it was saturated with more of the dark blood.

"Is he bleeding that badly?" I asked.

She shook her head. "It's not his blood."

"What?"

"Under the bed," she said softly. "Get the box."

I lowered to my knees and peered under the bed. I grabbed the handle and pulled the heavy suitcase box out, scraping the floor loudly.

I lifted the heavy box and set it on the edge of the bed.

"Open it," she said.

I did.

Inside of the box were several sharp wooden stakes, a wooden mallet, a silver cross, glass vials filled with powder, and more glass vials filled with clear liquid. My mother took one vial of the liquid, read the label, and popped the cork. She walked around to the other side of the bed.

"What are you doing?" I asked.

"The puncture marks have to be purified and cleansed. Or your father will become a vampire."

"How?"

"The bite somehow causes the victim to turn. Don't ask me how. Your father would know but—" Her voice broke into sobs.

I wanted to tell her that he was going to be okay, but I couldn't tell a lie that convincingly. His condition was severe. No way to deny it.

Then the revelation gripped me. I suddenly realized his injuries were intentionally far worse than I had imagined. The vampire who had inflicted the damage upon my father intended for him to die so that he, too, would become a vampire.

"What's in the vial?" I asked.

"Holy water."

"That will cure him?"

Mother replied, "If we can fully cleanse the wound, it's possible that we can save him. But, it's painful for him to endure. In his weakened condition, the cure might well kill him."

"And if that should happen?"

"You will have to drive a stake through his heart. I can't . . . I simply *can't* do it."

Stunned, I looked into her eyes with uncertainty, questioning. She nodded solemnly. I knew the depth of her love for my father prevented her from killing him, even if he were to turn, but I wondered if I was capable. Could I drive a stake through the heart of my father? In the matter of age, I was still a boy, struggling with a problem that only an adult should have to consider. I had to shoulder the responsibility but how?

CHAPTER 2

$\mathcal{M}$y father struggled to breathe, to hold onto life, while my mother tended to his injuries. He was a proven fighter, having survived the war and carnage of twenty years before, and now a vampire had struck down his entire valor in a singular battle.

As I stared at my unconscious father, I thought about what my mother had instructed. Could I do it? Being as he would no longer be my father, but instead a monster, I knew my answer. I could drive that stake through his heart to save my mother because I'd be killing a bloodthirsty monster. *Not* my father.

As long as I was able to keep that in the forefront of my mind, I'd carry it out. But an instant of doubt could easily shatter my resolve, making me cower, hesitate, and that was enough of an opportunity for any vampire to capitalize upon.

Growing up in Romania, the legend of vampires weren't unknown. Exaggerated, yes oftentimes, that was true. But, every child my age knew the stories from the time of Count Vlad, the crazed blood-lusting and heartless ruler. We knew where *not* to go. The legends weren't fables. Evidence portrayed that vampires existed and thrived upon the unfortunate that happened to enter the haunted forests after sunset. Dead bodies, with the same punctured wounds as my father's, were victims by the kin of what my father had sought to kill. The bloody war had been a feasting ground for them.

"Forrest," my mother said softly, dislodging me from my mind wandering. "Place your hands upon your father's chest. Hold him down while I pour the holy water into the wounds."

Walking to the edge of the bed, I didn't see any reason to hold him down. His frail body held onto life by a single thread. He barely breathed. He had lost so much blood. In my brief moments of hesitation, her eyes grew fierce and her brow grew rigid. I knew if I waited another second, she'd smack the back of my head with her hand, so I placed my hands against his chest but didn't apply a lot of force. He had suffered enough without me pressing my weight against him.

Mother tipped the vial. A stream of holy water struck the left puncture mark. Steam rose and the hole bubbled. My father bolted upright with such force that I stumbled backwards, having to readjust my footing to keep him from knocking me down. Where had this incredible strength come from?

He growled and gnashed his teeth. Foam frothed at the edges of his mouth. His wild eyes were dark like a wolf's. I pressed my weight against him, but his stiff body resisted. His hands went for the bottle of holy water. My mother moved back, keeping herself out of his reach.

"See?" she said with a scolding tone. "*This* is why I told you to hold him down."

I grabbed my father's hands, pressed them against his chest, and leaned forward with my entire bodyweight, lying upon him until he was prostrate. She poured more holy water onto the same hole. The darkness of the bite mark drained until it was almost light pink. Then she poured more onto the right bite mark. Steam rose and liquid bubbled. My father stiffened slightly from the pain, but his strength was gone. He merely gritted his teeth with a small groan before finally becoming limp.

After she emptied the one vial, she retrieved another one and repeated the procedure, even though there was no obvious reaction when the holy water seeped into the wounds. She took some salve, coated the bite marks, and pressed a cloth against it.

"What now?" I asked.

"We wait."

"Do you think he will turn now?"

Her eyes were saddened. "Doubtful. I believe the bite was the freshest wound on his body."

"And that's good?"

She nodded. "Less time prevents it from getting deeper."

"Prevents what?"

"Whatever abomination that causes a man or woman to turn into a vampire." She took her scissors and cut the sides of his pants legs. The leg bones were bent in multiple places. She cringed. "Son, go to the woodpile and gather some long narrow strips of wood, so I can splint your father's legs. Make sure that they're strong and sturdy. It's doubtful that he will ever be able to walk again, but I must try."

I wrapped my heavy coat over my shoulders, took the wood ax from beside the door, and looked back at my father stretched back on the bed. Tears burned at the edges of my eyes. They did not brim from sadness, but from sudden growing rage.

Easing open the door, a fierce wind hailed its greeting, flickering our candles. Sharp sleet stabbed at my face. I grabbed my scarf and tightened it around my neck. I stepped out into the blizzard and jerked the door closed behind me. The forest looked darker, like the sun had already set. Had we worked with my father until nightfall?

I didn't think so.

Snow-covered trees usually made the forest brighter, even after sunset. Evil grew like a thickness. I sensed eyes watching me, immediately wondering if the vampire that had tried to kill my father was nearby. Any hungry vampire, or predator for that matter, could have easily followed the path of my father's blood. The scent, unnoticed by me, probably still hung in the air directing bloodthirsty beasts toward our cottage.

Heavy snowflakes continued to fall, making the bloody packed path to our door less visible. The forest was eerily quiet. No birds flittered or chirped. The sparrows and doves were most likely bedded inside the great firs where the needles protected them from the snowstorm. The only audible sound other than the wind was the rapid beating of my heart and my hampered breathing.

Few things ever brought fear to me, even when I was eight years old, because I realized I had the protection of my parents. But with my father so near to death, that protection was on the brink of vanishing forever, and it would then be left to me to protect my mother and provide for our needs.

My mother clung to the hope that she could patch him up, but knowing my father, if he lost the ability to walk, he'd die even if he survived the severity of his other injuries. He wasn't a man capable of enduring confinement. He labored hard, was a hunter and provider, and often traveled on foot for days at a time to find work. He'd deteriorate quickly if all he could do was sit in a chair. His will to live would be snuffed.

The woodpile at the edge of our cottage was buried beneath several inches of snow. Long shiny icicles hung from the sides of the roof. With quiet steps, I walked toward stacks of cut firewood. As I neared, something caught my eye.

A shadow moved between two massive trees. Whatever it was had left no tracks in the snow. My hand tightened around the ax handle. Not necessarily an appropriate weapon to fight a vampire, but what did I know? My father had never trained me, and all I knew were the supposed rumors of how vampires died.

Taking a deep breath, I bravely stood at the woodpile and raked the layers of deep snow off of the crudely cut logs. With all of the snow, finding narrow stripped pieces of wood wasn't an easy task, especially while I was watching the trees with my peripheral vision. It was probably easier, if not quicker, to find firewood of the appropriate length and split them into narrow slats.

Brushing away snow, I grabbed a nearly frozen log and propped it on a wide snow-crusted stump. As I brought up the ax, the shadow moved between the trees again, but paused long enough for me to see its strange eyes before vanishing again. I held the ax above my head, frightened to lower it, and watched the tree for further movement. Stiff as a statue I waited.

Suddenly my attention was turned, not toward the trees where the shadowed creature had passed, but toward the black cloud swirling above the forest several hundred yards away. This was no normal storm cloud. In fact, it wasn't a cloud at all. Whatever it was, it was filled with life, as it made strange chirping and shrieking sounds. Sounds unlike any I had known at that point in my life.

Dread filled me. I was afraid to completely turn my attention from the unseen beast on the other side of the woodpile, but this black ominous cloud was a greater threat. I was what the darkness therein sought. It was coming for me.

The sound of the breathing cloud increased as it swarmed and changed shapes continuously as it moved through the treetops. Ignoring the invisible beast I lowered the ax and turned to face the menacing shrieking shadow. As it neared, I realized it wasn't a cloud as one imagined a cloud to be. The chirps and shrieks indicated it was a flock of winged creatures.

Birds?

No.

After their sharp pointy fangs became visible, there wasn't any question of what they were.

Bats!

Over one hundred bats spiraled and flitted toward me, gnashing their little mouths with their sharp razor-edged teeth. They formed a long line and headed directly toward me.

Perhaps I was temporarily paralyzed with fear, or simply too stubborn to budge, but I held my ground. I didn't flinch, nor did I swing madly at them with the ax. All the while they wailed with high-pitched cries. But not one of the bats struck me. Instead, they parted around me, and lofted upward to avoid splattering themselves into the side of the cottage before they shot back in the direction they had come.

They weren't retreating, but on their unsuccessful attempt to get a fearful reaction out of me, they regrouped into their cloudlike appearance over the trees and watched me momentarily.

Their chirps and shrills silenced. The quiet of death hovered over the forest. Even the invisible beast chose not to move.

The dark cloud of bats descended slowly to the snowy ground, assembling themselves in an odd way. Stunned, I watched, remained silent, and held the ax firmly with both hands.

Where the bats had assembled, a man wearing a black cloak emerged. He was the bats, and they were he. It didn't seem possible, and yet, it was.

The tall man's complexion was pallid, a near bluish-gray, but he held the arrogance of a wealthy aristocrat; owing no one allegiance and expecting knees to bow at his arrival, which was something I refused to oblige.

Death loomed in his eyes that gauged toward me. I met his gaze and felt immense power tug at me, trying to lure me, to hold and control me, but still I didn't budge. His brow hardened. I felt his anger and detestation because I didn't succumb.

No one had ever told me that looking into the eyes of a master vampire was the most dangerous thing a mere mortal could do. I held no knowledge of how direct eye contact could enslave an individual to such a vampire's will. His inability to charm me became an instant challenge. My ignorance at that time should have doomed me to live my eternal life as an undead servant.

In his first step toward me, I evaluated him. His haughty posture and mannerism were completely out of place where we lived on the outskirts of the city. The wind ruffled the edges of his cloak. His crimson vest was fastened with bright gold buttons. A white silk shirt and black silk tie were also a part of his attire. He held prominence elsewhere, even as a vampire, which made me wonder why he'd bother appearing here where peasants, gypsies, and serfs lived in utter misfortune.

He shifted his feet and moved his right hand. He bore a cane I had not noticed a second before. His right hand gripped the golden ball at the top of the cane. He produced a fine top hat in the other and set it upon his head. Long sharp fingernails protruded from his hands. Drops of blood dripped from each of his jagged nails.

Again, I looked at his face. His skin was withered. Gazing into his eyes once more, I sensed his power but didn't yield. He gnashed his teeth and snarled; blood was on his teeth and lips.

My father's blood.

I don't know why I had immediately assumed such, but later discovered that it was true. This vampire was the one that had attacked my father and tried to kill him. Father had nearly died because of this undead fiend, and at that particular moment, death seemed inevitable.

"You, lad," the vampire said, "are a fool. Dare you challenge me?"

His smooth voice flowed gracefully and with elegance, demanding submission without any obvious threat or the hint of severe repercussions for refusing to become compliant. His coaxing velvety tone should have drawn me to him, but for some reason I resisted without a fight or protest. I simply stood and stared into his piercing eyes. The longer I looked at him, the more hideous his features became. Whatever power he possessed to maintain his attractiveness was weakening and his handsome guise slowly faded. In my eyes, he was nothing more than a standing corpse with shriveled skin, fresh from a long buried casket.

A wave of energy flailed in my direction but parted around me in the same way a river divided and flowed to each side of a massive stone. The intenseness in his eyes glowed. His anger grew. The bones in his face contorted, making him appear less human and slowly he seemed to be transforming into a rabid animal. By his gaze, I sensed his hatred toward me, that he wanted me dead, and that he was preparing to attack and kill me. But for some reason, he never advanced.

"Defiant fool," he said with a harsh glare. "You did not answer me. Do you think yourself more privileged than those of the social status above you? If not for us, you'd not have the crumbs that fill your belly. Surely, your father has taught you to respect your elders, especially those of us who rule over you."

"Sir," I replied. "I do not recognize you, nor the position you *deem* recognizable outside of our forest where we live, upon which you're presently trespassing. If it's groveling and ring-kissing you seek, seek it elsewhere. I hold no allegiance to you, nor will I ever."

The man's brow rose, his eyes widened, and spittle formed at the sides of his mouth. "Trespassing? You insolent child, I'll have you know I hold the deed to the land upon which your cottage stands. I *own* the entire forest."

His pale hands formed into fists. I expected him to rush forward to kill me, but he did not. His attention fastened upon the door to our cottage and back to me, as if he wished to sprint past without any added interference from me.

"You're the one who almost killed my father, are you not?" I pointed a stern finger toward him. "That's his blood on your hands and mouth."

The vampire flashed a dominating grin. "How old are you, lad?"

"Eight."

His eyes widened momentarily. "Your wisdom far exceeds your age. Oddly, you look much older. Based upon that, I'd think you were lying, except I can discern the truth. You have told the truth; therefore I will not hide my intent from you. You deserve nothing less than the truth in return. Indeed, you are correct. This is your father's blood, and I've come to end his miserable wretched life."

His eyes again flicked toward the cottage door, perhaps calculating the distance. Before he moved, I took three quick steps and stood before the door, blocking his direct path. Uneasiness reflected in his eyes.

"Step aside, lad. Allow me passage into the cottage, and I'll make his death quick. There's no need for you to die as well."

Quick?

My eyes narrowed. I had no idea how far my half dead father had dragged himself through the freezing blizzard to get home, but there wasn't anything *quick* about his death, even if his life ended now. He had endured much pain and suffering in his struggle to return to us. He had only survived because he was too stubborn to die. And then again, perhaps he had lived because he wished to identify his assailant before death claimed him.

In a physical confrontation, I wasn't any match for this vampire or any vampire for that matter. I lacked the knowledge and skills necessary to kill a vampire. I'd die quickly, regardless of how aggressively I fought back. I held no doubts about that. But I refused to be subservient and step aside so he could kill my father. I was prepared to die first, if that were the case. I didn't fear death like most children, and I wondered if my lack of fear was what made him hesitant to approach.

In the blink of an eye, he withdrew the sword hidden inside his cane. The blade gleamed, and a smile of triumph widened on his face. "Blood spills tonight. I will feast upon you, your father, and your mother after I dice all of you to pieces."

The invisible beast I had forgotten about between the trees moved like a blur, his wild shadow spilling across the snow as he ran straight toward the vampire. Right as the shadow stopped in front of the vampire, a bright blinding blast of silver light flashed with the strength of the sun, forcing me to shield my face with my hand and turn away.

The vampire shrieked with frightful fury.

When the light lessened enough for me to look, a cloud of bats filtered and scattered through the forest, too disoriented to fly in close formation. Some struck tree trunks. Others spun endlessly in circles. All retreated farther into the forest.

Another figure stood in the place of the vampire. He regarded me with an inquisitive stare. Unlike the vampire, this man wore rugged clothes beneath a heavy wool coat. A tattered hat rested upon his head. His drab clothes allowed him to blend in with the tenants encamped throughout the forest and on the outskirts of Bucharest. Based on his appearance, one might take him for a trader passing from town to town, except he had no wagon or horse or any pack filled with wares for trade.

His greasy black hair flowed wildly down his shoulders. Thick unkempt sideburns covered his dark cheeks. His brown eyes gleamed like a hungry wolf, and shifted slightly, cautiously as he took in his surroundings. He was on alert, perhaps searching the trees for the vampire's return. The only valuable thing in his possession was the long silvery cane that he leaned upon. Even in the faint light as daylight slipped away, the cane shimmered like silver ice.

I reached behind me to grab the door handle.

"Wait," he said sternly. "You and I need to talk."

CHAPTER 3

"Are you Forrest, the son of John Wollinsky?" he asked in a thick accent. His voice was deep, intimidating, but he lacked the haughty nature the vampire had displayed.

"I am."

"What power do you possess to terrify a master vampire in the way that you just did?"

"None."

"None at all?"

"None that I know of. Why? Who are you?" I asked.

"Jacques Amanar. I'm here to help your father, provided I'm not too late."

The name held no recognition for me. I gazed past him, toward the trees where the dazed cloud of bats had fled. "The man who turned into a cloud of bats was a master vampire?"

"I can answer your questions later, but please, let me see your father first, so I can heal him. I fear we have little time."

Doubt must have shown in my eyes. Since I didn't know him, or exactly what he was, I was skeptical, not knowing if I should trust him. After all, the vampire's purpose was to kill my father. How could I know what this man's true intent was?

"What are you?" I asked.

"A friend."

"I do not know you."

He gave a gentle smile, which didn't seem foreign to the wrinkles around his mouth. "Forrest, your father and I have been friends since we were your age. I do not wish his death to befall him on this day."

In spite of his rough exterior, his odd eyes held honesty and no sense of hostility. He had also confronted and attacked the vampire, with what exactly I wasn't certain. The vampire had fled, and that really was the most important factor.

Backing toward the door, I reached for the door handle. He waited until I eased the door open before he approached. Once across the threshold, he removed his hat, gave a slight bow, and leaned his silver cane against the wall.

Momma rose from the side of my father's bed. Seeing this man, she rushed across the room and embraced his neck tightly, sobbing. "Jacques!"

"Olivia," he replied softly. "I wish my arrival came with better news. I'm so sorry."

"You know him?" I asked.

Momma pulled back from hugging Jacques, looked at me with tears in her eyes, and nodded. "He's an old friend."

"Was John bitten?" Jacques asked, approaching the side of the bed.

"Yes," she replied.

My father's pale face was covered with a sheen of sweat. Were his swallow breathing not visibly evident, I'd have thought him dead. Never had I seen him weak or sick at any time prior.

Jacques took the oil lantern from the side of the bed, leaned closer to my father, and peeled back the cloth bandage to examine the wound where the vampire had bitten him. "Ah, good. You've already cleansed the wound with holy water."

Momma nodded.

"Appears you have purified the wound. No fear of him turning during the night. His other injuries are worrisome, and he still stands in Death's shadow. His legs—"

"Forrest, where are the wooden splints?" she asked.

"I—"

Jacques shook his head. "We had an unexpected visitor outside, which prevented Forrest from cutting them."

"Who?" she asked. Her nervous eyes glanced toward the door.

"The vampire who almost killed John," Jacques replied.

"He's here?"

Jacques shook his head. He winked at me. "Gone, thanks to Forrest here. The vampire fled through the forest, but it doesn't mean he won't return."

Dread filled Momma's eyes. "Do you know which vampire?"

"Baron Randolph," he replied.

She gasped. "The baron is a vampire?"

Jacques frowned. "John never told you?"

"No."

"*Perhaps he didn't know*," he whispered, so only I could hear. Then he looked at Momma. "The baron is a master vampire. I'm surprised Randolph ventured into the forest at all when he could have sent his descendants in his stead." Jacques looked at me. "Has your father begun your training?"

I shook my head. "I didn't even know my father hunted vampires."

"No?"

"No."

Jacques was silent for several moments. "You have so much you need to learn, but there is still time."

I didn't know how to respond. I certainly didn't think I was old enough to hunt and kill vampires. Looking at my father, who apparently had fought them for many years and was near death because of one, I didn't know that this was a vocation of my choosing.

His eyes studied mine. For some reason, it felt like he could stare into my soul and read my thoughts. He smiled reassuringly. "The baron has fear of you, lad. Great fear. If your father has not started you with the proper training to hunt and kill these demons of the night, did he perhaps give you a gift . . . a blessed pendant or trinket?"

"Nothing like that," I replied. "But he did give me this before he left."

I pulled my tarnished dagger from its sheath.

Jacques grinned and extended his strange fur-covered hand. "May I?"

I offered the dagger, hilt first. His eyes studied mine with wonderment, as if I knew some secret. The lack of knowingness in my eyes and my confused expression indicated that I did not. Carefully, quite cautiously, he took the dagger by the hilt.

"Marvelous," he said, holding the lantern near the hilt. "Never lose this blade."

"What is so special about it?"

"The engraved inscription is a spell from the olden country. This, young man, has been blessed by a gypsy witch."

"I didn't know a dagger could kill vampires."

"They cannot," he said in a whisper, handing the dagger back to me. Seriousness narrowed his eyes.

I frowned, staring at the blade, suddenly seeing the carved runes etched into the bone handle and immediately understanding their meaning. "Then what use has it?"

He patted my shoulder firmly with his hairy hand. "The reason the baron never came any closer to you was because of this dagger."

"Why? If it cannot kill him, and I'm only a boy, why fear me with the blade?

Jacques lowered into a squat and rested upon his haunches. Soft laughter rumbled at the back of his throat. His deep voice was soothing when he spoke. "Because you could harness control over him. And if he's under your command, all of his vampiric children are also under your control. Should you stake and kill him while he's under your power, all of his minions turn to dust. They will die. I believe your father fought to make his way back home because you have the blade. The importance of that, I shall tell you later. At this moment I must attend to your father's ailments."

His rich brown eyes regarded me with keen interest before he turned his attention toward my father once more. He reached inside his coat and pulled out something wrapped in thick parchment from his interior pocket. "Olivia, take these dried roots and seep them in hot water to make a tea."

Momma took them, nodded, and hurried toward the fireplace.

"Should I go cut those splints?" I asked. "So we can set his legs?"

"No. That may not be necessary."

I glanced at my father's twisted legs. The severity of his injuries brought sympathetic pain to me. Aches radiated up my legs as though my legs were the ones broken and every nerve screamed its protest that I was standing. I closed my eyes and winced.

"I can't see how he managed to survive long enough to get home."

Jacques gave me a side-glance. "Your father is a strong man, Forrest. Incredibly strong. His willpower got him here despite his injuries."

"How can he recover from this that he might walk again?"

"The tea first," he replied.

"If he went to kill the baron, why didn't he take the dagger with him? Couldn't he have used its power to destroy the master?"

Jacques smiled grimly and shook his head. "The dagger you possess looks to be made specifically for you. It would have done your father no good. You see, your father paid the gypsy to enchant it. I believe he planned to begin your training once he returned home."

"Why would he attack the master alone?"

"To be honest, I don't think he intentionally went to kill the baron. He might not have even expected the baron to be there. There's an even stronger chance that he didn't even know the baron is a vampire. Nonetheless, your father's experience and wisdom are too great for him to make a direct attack on a master vampire alone. A true hunter is never that foolish. John had probably targeted a feral vampire and during his pursuit he unexpectedly crossed paths with the baron."

My father groaned and writhed in his pain-induced coma.

"What's a feral vampire?" I whispered.

"One that has recently emerged from the grave. Such newly turned vampires are often disoriented and overly aggressive. They need to be fathered into their new lifestyle. Nurtured. Otherwise, they carelessly draw attention to themselves from their brutal attacks. Vampires have only survived throughout the centuries by maintaining discretion. Quite possibly the vampire your father had sought to kill was the new undead child of the baron."

Momma returned with a decanter of steaming tea.

"Olivia," Jacques said softly. "Soak the tea in a cloth and then gently squeeze out the liquid into John's mouth, only a little at a time so he doesn't choke. Make certain he drinks as much as possible."

She nodded.

"Forrest and I will retreat closer to fire for a while. Once the herbal tea gets into John's system, I will proceed."

CHAPTER 4

The small flickering fire popped and crackled softly inside the hearth. Even though Jacques had never requested, I filled a bowl of rabbit stew and handed it to him. He nodded his appreciation.

He sat back in the rocker and cupped the bowl beneath his nose. He took in a deep breath of the stew's aroma. Steam rose off the bubbling liquid. He tipped the bowl and gulped a scalding mouthful, chewed momentarily, and swallowed without a wince or grumble from its immense heat. Then he took another gulp, seemingly unaffected by its blistering heat.

"Are you a vampire hunter, too?" I asked.

He shook his head. "Not in the sense that you and your father are."

"But I'm not a hunter."

Jacques pointed a finger at me and grinned. "Ah, but you are. It's evident to your father and it is to me as well. Your mother sees it too, but you'd be hard-pressed to ever get her to admit it since you're her only child. Mother's are selfish like that."

I frowned. "You've only just met me. How can you predict that I am a hunter?"

"It's more than obvious."

"How's that?"

He studied me for about a minute. "You revealed to the baron your age. Eight years old?"

I nodded and shrugged. "So?"

Jacques laughed softly. He turned up the remaining contents of the bowl and drank them down. He set the bowl beside his chair.

I rose and reached for the bowl. "Would you like more?"

He shook his head and motioned for me to sit back down. "I was watching you in the forest before the baron arrived. Upon first sight of you, I'd have thought you much older, too. Certainly not a young boy. And your speech, your wisdom . . . I dare say, are far greater than any other lad your age. There's a reason for that."

"What?"

"Every so often a hunter is born with the power and knowledge of a hunter from the past. Mind you, *not* the reincarnation of one's spirit, but more of the intellect, the prowess, and agility. You were blessed with these traits, born with them, so use them wisely."

"I still don't understand how you can be so certain."

"Forrest, no child grows at the rate your body and mind has. Regardless if a child ate abnormally large amounts of food every single day, he still couldn't achieve what you are without it having been destined to him. He'd simply be an overly plump child, no more the wiser, either. May I ask you a question?"

"Sure."

"When the baron stood threatening you, why didn't you run?"

"I wasn't afraid of him, odd as that may sound."

"He was keenly aware of your lack of fear. Even after he drew his sword, I doubt he'd have had the courage to rush toward you."

"Because of the dagger?" I asked.

Jacques shrugged. "That and he probably thought your father had trained you. He feared you'd end him right there."

"But you are the one that frightened him away," I said. "With that blast of light."

"That wasn't to protect you. The baron was simply wasting my time. I needed to get to your father and that pompous bastard was theatrically upstaging my arrival."

"Did he know you were close by?"

Jacques shook his head. "Doubtful. His attention was solely focused upon you."

"So he will think the light was my doing?"

He grinned. "Yes. He will be confused for quite some time, which works to your advantage while your father recovers."

"How did you do that? Make the light?"

"For now, that remains a secret."

"When you mentioned that you were a hunter, but not like my father and I, what did you mean?"

Jacques glanced toward my father's bed and rose. "In time."

He hurried across the room. I followed.

He glanced at my mother. "Were you able to get the liquid down?"

"Most of it," she replied.

"Good. It's time to begin."

Bruises mottled my father's flesh from his ankles to his upper thighs. The angle at which my father's feet were turned indicted that his lower leg bones were broken. His upper thighs were unnaturally bent. He had been tortured slowly. Battered and beaten with a blunt object. How he had managed to escape his attacker was beyond me.

Jacques took my father's right foot in his hands. He twisted sharply. Cracking and popping sounds made me cringe. Momma covered her mouth and turned away; tears spilled down her cheeks.

My father didn't move, nor did he make any sound at all.

Jacques lowered my father's foot and reached for the other one.

"What are you doing?" I asked.

"It's part of the process," he replied.

"Hasn't he been tortured enough? I thought you said that you were his friend."

Momma turned toward me. "*Forrest!*"

"It's okay, Olivia," Jacques said calmly. "Forrest, if your father is to ever walk again, the bones must be reset. Otherwise, they will not heal properly."

"But you're hurting him," I replied.

"No. The tea is a strong sedative, numbing his pain and putting him into a near death sleep. Trust me, he doesn't feel this. He's not even aware that we're in the room."

He twisted my father's left foot with another sharp jerk, which brought more sickening sounds. Sweat beaded Jacques' brow. Tears brimmed at the edges of his eyes. I held no further doubts about how deeply he cared about my father. He was doing what was necessary, and it pained him as much as it did Momma and I to witness it.

After lowering my father's left foot to the bed, Jacques moved to the side of the bed and readjusted the bones in my father's upper thighs. "Instead of wooden splints, I suggest wrapping his legs with tight cloth and tying secure knotted strips of cloth around the girth of his legs about every four inches. He's not going to be moving for some time yet to come."

My mother nodded.

From his lower coat pocket, Jacques removed a jar of salve and opened it. He took a large needle tucked into my mothers spool of thread and pricked his finger. He squeezed his finger until large drops of blood beaded. He held his finger over the open jar, allowing several drops of blood to coat the top of the greasy ointment. He sealed the jar and vigorously shook the contents before handing it to her. "You need to apply this to all of his cuts and abrasions each morning. He won't wake for hours, if not days. If it's no problem, Olivia, I'd like to continue my conversation with your son outdoors. It has been wonderful seeing you again."

Momma walked to him, hugged him, and kissed his cheek.

Jacques walked to the door and grabbed his silver cane. He put his top hat on and pulled the door open. A strong cold blast of snowy wind flowed past us. "Are you coming?"

I nodded and followed him back out into the blizzard. Darkness had settled in. Night surrounded us. But the brightness of the snow prevented us from being engulfed in the complete shadow of night.

The wet snow made soft scrunching sounds as we walked down the hidden bloody path where my father had crawled. The cold bit at my cheeks, and I missed the warmth of the cottage. Jacques seemed unaffected by the quick transition.

"What is the purpose for adding your blood to the ointment?" I asked.

He grinned.

"Another secret?"

Jacques cocked a brow and replied, "One I will gladly share, provided you can handle the truth."

From the moment he first appeared in the forest, I sensed some type of mysterious power surrounding him, perhaps even paranormal strength. "I doubt I could ignore my curiosity of not knowing. It would distract me from the things I need to learn."

He laughed. "I mentioned that I am also a hunter."

I nodded. "But not like my father or what you believe I shall someday be."

"I added my blood to the ointment because of its healing capabilities. I have the mark of the wolf."

I frowned. "You're a werewolf?"

Jacques nodded. He studied my eyes, awaiting my reaction. I'll admit that the revelation wasn't too surprising, given the excessive thick coarse hair on the backs of his hands and the sides of his face. The extreme swiftness he had displayed in the forest intrigued my curiosity as well, but I had never heard of tales about werewolves that were able to cloak themselves with invisibility.

Living in Romania where supernatural beasts and creatures thrived, not only in legends but also in the dead of night, I was mentally prepped to expect the unexpected. I never had any intention of roaming the countryside looking for any of them, but I understood the likelihood existed that one day I would stumble upon a supernatural creature. But two in one day—a vampire *and* a werewolf—not even the best Tarot reader or diviner could have predicted that.

"But your blood," I said. "Will it—"

"Infect your father?"

I nodded.

"No."

"The stories I hear tell otherwise. How can your blood not taint his?"

"Forrest, you live in the remnants of a war-torn country where superstitions are more powerful than most religions. The transforming agent is in the saliva, not the blood. However, the properties of my blood hold a healing capability that I cannot explain. I assure you the ointment will quicken the rate at which your father heals. Not instantaneous, as we'd all like, but at weeks instead of agonizing months."

"So you were bitten by a werewolf?"

"No, by a wolf," Jacques replied. "Long ago, when your father and I were exploring the rugged terrain in the valley near Dracula's Castle we became separated when a pack of mammoth black wolves rushed toward us."

Chills, not brought on by the freezing winter air, rushed down my back. The hair on the back of my neck stiffened. "Mammoth wolves?"

"Massive beasts. Twice the size of regular wolves. Legend has been told that these once belonged to Dracula."

"Do you believe that?" I asked, intrigued.

Jacques eyes narrowed, and he nodded. "I have no doubts about it. For after I was bitten, I hid inside a cave where I suffered from fever and delusions. I emerged a day or so later and searched the path where your father and I had been separated, hoping to track his footprints. Everything about me had heightened. My sense of smell, hearing, sight, and touch were incredibly brighter, keener. My hunger became more aggressive as I held greater cravings for taste, especially meat."

"So your senses allowed you to find my father?"

He shook his head. "Close. I was on the right path. I smelled his scent, odd as that might sound, but remember a werewolf's sense of smell is magnified. As I cut through a trodden path that ran along the river's edge, I was unable to keep tracking him."

"Why?"

"I became enslaved."

"By whom?"

"A vampire. A grandson of Dracula."

"How is that possible? Dracula is dead? Isn't he?"

"No," Jacques said sternly. "He's very much alive. Just not in Romania."

I opened my mouth to speak, but he interrupted me.

"I know, legends tell of his demise, but a word of caution. Legends are filled both with truth and deceit. But one thing is true. The mammoth wolves were subservient to Dracula's offspring and their commands. By proxy, so was I. The pack of great wolves encircled me and prevented me from running. Then the vampire compelled me, drew me to him, and bound me to do his bidding for almost a year. I became one of the mammoth wolf pack."

"For a year?"

He nodded. "During the time of the full moon, he chained us inside iron barred dungeon cages to prevent us from escaping. He knew during our transformations when we became half-man and half-wolf that he held no power over us. That was the time when we held greater power than he. He feared I'd kill him, which I plotted daily. I wanted freed of his control. I wanted to rip out his heart.

"After nearly a year, I had assumed your father was dead. Perhaps the wolves that had pursued him had chosen to kill him instead of forcing him to live under the same bondage as the rest of us. In a sense he had been spared. But I discovered he was alive."

"He came back? Why?"

"Curiosity, I suppose," Jacques replied. "He later told me that he had thought the wolves had killed me. He returned to look for clues, but he came prepared."

Layers of snowflakes clung to us, covering our heads and shoulders. The cold no longer bothered me. I was too enthralled by his tale to consider heading back inside.

"What do you mean?" I asked.

"Your father told others in town about the giant wolves that roamed the base of the mountain where the castle overlooked and how he feared I was dead. He attempted to hire several hunters to return with him, as he said that he couldn't live with himself without having absolute proof that I was either dead or alive. At times he sensed I was alive, and at others, he felt no connection to me at all. The constant uncertainty haunted him.

"But none of the hunters were brave enough, regardless of the high bounty he had offered. Another man spoke with him in private and showed John his scars. He had been one of the pack members that had broken loose before the cage door was locked. He warned John that the wolves were actually werewolves, and there was the chance that I was one of them. If he didn't want to accidentally kill me, the man told him to abandon the thought of killing the wolves. That day was what changed your father's and my life forever."

"Why?" I asked.

"On that day, he discovered what I had become, and that was also when he decided to kill his first vampire."

"What happened?"

Jacques smiled. "That's all of the tale I will give you. Have your father tell you the rest. It will give him something to do while he is bedridden. The ending of that story is partially evident, as we are both alive and breathing. Your story is unfolding before you. You're a vampire hunter."

"But what if I don't want to become one?"

"Your destiny chooses you, and not the other way around. Besides, even though you are young, I perceive that you're not going to be content allowing the baron to live after what he did to your father."

I thought about that. He was right. The baron had chosen to inflict as much pain upon my father as possible instead of simply killing him. Feasting off my father's suffering had been a game for him. How many others had suffered similar or worse fates due to this monster? His sadistic nature needed to end.

I nodded. "The baron's reign of terror will end. I will see to it. That's a vow I intend to keep. The dagger my father gave me will ensure my success."

"A word of caution about the dagger."

"Okay?"

"While the dagger can enslave the master to your bidding, never enter his lair thinking you'll be the conqueror. It will be your death and doom."

"Why?"

"All he needs is to stay outside of the dagger's power perimeter and have his children, his undead minions rip you apart. Remember, the dagger cannot kill a vampire, nor will it control a *lesser* vampire. Only a wooden stake through the heart or decapitation can kill them."

Jacques shook himself and tapped the side of his top hat. Wet snow flung off of him. He extended his hand. "It was good meeting you, Forrest. I'm certain in the not so near future that I shall hear your name spoken in awe in many taverns and whispered in fear at cemeteries after sunset. The undead shall fear your name and the sight of seeing your shadow darkening their path will terrorize them."

"Before you leave," I said, shaking his hairy hand. "How did you know my father was near death?"

He grinned. "He and I took an oath and became blood brothers, back when we were no older than you. We were born under the same moon to mothers who were sisters. We each know the burden of the other."

"You're my cousin?"

"I am. Keep a keen eye on your mother and father during his recovery. Their safety depends upon you. Keep the dagger on you at all times, as it will repel the baron should he return. I'd advise you to keep one of your father's stakes handy as well. I'm certain you know much about vampires from the legends, that they travel and seek their victims at night."

I nodded.

"The master arrived at your cottage before the sunset, or did you not notice?"

"I thought it was darker than it should have been, but I didn't think it was past sunset."

"It wasn't," Jacques said. "Remember this. When the sky's heavily overcast during a blizzard or a horrendous thunderstorm, a master can emerge from his lair unharmed to seek his prey, as the sun doesn't rule the sky."

"Thank you," I replied. "For tending to my father's injuries, your advice, and for making the baron run away."

"Another tidbit of advice I leave with you. Age is the best instructor, for over time you gain experience, sometimes through your errors, and sometimes due to no fault of your own. But there's no greater teacher than your own mistakes, just be certain that none of them are fatal ones.

If you're outmatched or outnumbered, there is no shame in retreat. Dying leaves you without a rematch." He tapped a finger to the side of his head. "Use your wits. Study your enemies. Find their weaknesses. The last thing we hunters need is for one of us to become one of them."

"I wish you could stay longer."

Jacques smiled and nodded. "We shall meet again, Forrest. I have no doubts. You'll be trained and even stronger than you presently are. But it will be misfortune that brings us together again. So, be safe and wary at all times."

"Be safe in your travels."

A second later he vanished through the forest. I thought about his last warning. Uneasiness crept inside me, more for the uncertainty of what was coming than any fear. Misfortune . . .

CHAPTER 5

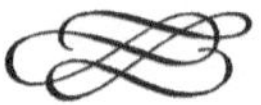

After my werewolf cousin vanished into the night, I stood and watched the large swirling flakes plop, building higher. I thought about the things he had mentioned, about *me* becoming a vampire hunter, or rather his insistence that I already was. Regardless of what ambitions might have swayed me otherwise, my destiny had spoken this day.

My father's broken body, his struggle to drag himself home when he should have already died, and standing my ground against a master vampire, defiantly protecting our home—these events molded my mind, revealing to me that I was born for one reason: to hunt and kill the ungodly bloodsuckers.

I had a lot to learn yet, but over time I discovered that some hunters didn't distinguish in what they chose to hunt. Some sought to kill all vampires. Others stalked and killed werewolves. A few championed killing both, as they regarded both to be the direct spawns of the devil. Dependent upon the circumstances, I'd kill a hunter in favor of a werewolf if such choices needed to be made.

Jacques was the reason I vowed never to hunt a werewolf since he was my blood relative. Besides, werewolves and I held a common enemy. We were allies. From what I gathered from my cousin, werewolves enslaved by a master vampire wanted to be released from their captor. Attack the vampire, and there was a good chance—not a definite guarantee—that the pack would turn on their master. However, loyalties ranged at different levels.

I entered the cottage. The heat clung to me, melting away the thick layer of snow covering my clothes. I shed my heavy coat, hanging it on a spike stuck into the wall. I unbuckled my boots and set them beside the door. Momma had enough to fret about without the bothersome task of cleaning up unnecessary water pools on the hardwood floor.

My mind wondered with all of this information Jacques had blessed me with. Merely a wad of spit in the vast angry sea, but it was vital knowledge for me to retain. While my mother sat on a stool at the side of my father's bed with her head wearily laid on the hard mattress, I dragged a chair and placed its back against the door and sat down. I was determined not to sleep through the night but instead to stand guard.

My mother whimpered softly until she finally dozed off with her head next to my father's hand. I drew my dagger and held it in my hands, studying it in the faint glow of the bedside lantern and the soft fire flickering inside the hearth. The wood ax I propped to the side of my chair.

Jacques had said that the dagger couldn't kill the master or any vampire, but since decapitation could, I favored the ax for my weapon for the night. Should the baron return, I expected he'd sense the dagger's shield at the door as he had when I stood at our cottage door refusing to let him pass. Even if he returned, I didn't expect him to charge at the door, but should he return with his faithful, undead offspring, they were the ones I needed to be concerned about.

After Momma had been asleep for over an hour, I rose from the chair and retrieved my father's hunter box where she had taken the holy water. Six crude notches had been carved down one side of the box. I guessed that was the total number of vampire kills my father had made. I glanced toward him with a different sort of admiration. I had always viewed him as a hero, a soldier who had placed his life on the line by fighting in the Great War for what he believed important. But knowing he had fought against the most dangerous, unholy night creatures to save others from becoming enslaved undead minions, gave me pride to follow in his footsteps.

I unlatched the two silver clasps and lifted the top of the box. The various items inside intrigued me and already seemed to be a part of me.

Jacques had mentioned the wisdom of a past hunter had been bestowed upon me, and I no longer doubted it. I held one of the stakes. Excitement rose inside my chest. An unleashed vigor to drive the stake through the aged ribs of a vampire and pierce its withered heart drew my impatience. The baron's face came to mind. Anger surged inside of me. Vengeance.

My heartbeat hammered. Renewed energy radiated, giving me a desperate need to rush through the forest and hunt down the baron, his minions, and kill them all. Their desperate shrills before their deaths whispered at the edges of my ears. The aged scent of grave dust wafted beneath my nose. Watching them shrivel in their final moments made me giddy inside.

I urgently fought against my self-restraint, but finally acquiesced, putting the stake into its proper slot inside the heavy box. The moment I put the stake back, the harsh adrenaline impulsion waned. It was then I noticed that I had been salivating as my senses overloaded, feasting upon fulfilling my duties as a vampire hunter. After wiping the drool from the sides of my mouth with the back of my hand, I lifted the next item.

The silver cross.

The blistered cross outline on my father's chest matched this particular cross. This one must have been his spare. No telling where the other was now or why the outline remained a permanent design on his skin. Only after my father awakened could he reveal the story behind that, as well as the other pertinent confirmations for which my curiosity demanded answers.

Beneath the silver cross rested a tattered bible. I thought the combination of the two items a bit odd since none of my family attended cathedral services, and yet my father faithfully carried these holy relics in spite of our pagan beliefs. But, perhaps he had his reasons.

From the legends I learned that vampires were unholy, ungodly creatures, cursed forever without the hope for redemption. We children had been told that the cathedral property was sanctuary or hallowed ground. Vampires could never set foot upon such territory, but later I learned this wasn't always true. Jacques had been correct in saying that all legends contain both truth and deceit. This legend was one of them.

During my century-plus years hunting vampires in the farthest reaches of the world, I have miscalculated and made mistakes based more often upon what legends deemed true. At eight years of age, during the innocence of my learning, I held the church sanctuary sacred property from the undead monsters until deadly events unfolded that proved otherwise. That, however, is a story for a later time.

In the early morning hours, I held and examined each item inside my father's hunter box. While the full knowledge for each individual weapon was not entirely revealed to me, occasional disturbing visions and images disrupted inside my mind. Often these bursts of insight were so disconcerting that I pressed my weight against the door to reinforce it, ever mindful that my father was still under attack.

There was a connection between the contents and myself. I sensed the drawing power, how this destined link prompted my young mind with necessary information. And although this knowledge solicited me, I wasn't foolish enough to refuse the fact that while I might understand what each proponent within the hunter's tools represented and how they might be used, I was still not properly trained to act quite yet. I wasn't seasoned. I lacked experience. To rush off into the night with the box was quite possibly my immediate death, regardless of the urgent push inside my soul to exterminate these unholy demon soul leeches.

Slowly I closed the box, reflecting on its contents and again of the knowledge Jacques had bestowed unto me. It was then when other questions that had plagued me for the past several months were finally answered.

All of the children living in cottages inside the forest met three days a week for schooling. We met in an abandoned building that had remained unoccupied after the Great War. Since no one had ever reclaimed it, our parents agreed it was a suitable place for us to be taught.

From the time I was enrolled, I had been the largest child there. Even the children in their early teens were smaller than me. I was shunned because they were frightened by my size, which is understandable. I've always been intimidating to other children, usually upon first glance, and without even trying. It didn't help that my mouth curved partially downward, like I was unhappy or angry all the time. My brow was also firm, even, like a frown. People often misread me, thinking I was an angry child. But my father always corrected them, saying, "Trust me. You'll *know* when he's really angry."

A couple of my teachers didn't know how to view me, but a few of them I intrigued. They marveled at my incredible knowledge and often held discussions with me like they would with other adults, never talking down to me. I found it strange that the some of the history books we were assigned to read—books I'd never even read before— weren't new information for me. What I sometimes read seemed famil- iar, like old news. We didn't have any books at home, so I wondered how I already knew the information. When I did happen upon new tomes filled with new information, I devoured them and retained what I read.

My teachers eventually told my parents that there wasn't any need to have me continue schooling, as there wasn't anything more they could teach me. I didn't begrudge their decision, even though at the time, I had recently turned eight years old. To be released from the school because I was too smart should have been the greatest compliment, but it stung. For I was already alienated by the other children because I was differ- ent, and now, the teachers, some of which had treated me with the utmost respect, were also excluding me from a social group I longed to remain a part of. Over time, other groups would do the same thing but for different reasons altogether. Thus was the life of a vampire hunter, to be solitary and nomadic, never truly having a home because our duties to eradicate the undead required us to seek them out. But for the several months after I was dismissed from the school—up until I met Jacques—I questioned *how* it was possible for me to contain all of the knowledge that set me apart from the others; information I shouldn't have known.

Jacques had told me that wisdom and knowledge of a former hunter had been given to me. His revelation was what I needed.

I glanced toward my father's bed. It creaked slightly as my mother rose, slipped onto the bed next to my father, and positioned herself to the edge of him, barely touching, careful not to hurt him.

When she fell asleep again, softly snoring, I stood and covered them with a heavy quilt. Her hand clutched desperately to the blanket beneath his arm, identical to the hope inside her heart that he'd ever be with her. I watched them sleep for several moments. The bond of their love was incredibly strong. For whatever reason, I knew such love from a significant other was something I'd never find during my lifetime. Why this foreshadowing knowledge pierced my mind, I don't know. Maybe it was to ease the burden early, to prepare me for my constant predestined roaming. The less baggage one had, the less grounds for an attack from a bitter enemy. Not to say that love is a burden, certainly it had never been for my parents, but when an enemy sought to cause the most agony, they struck where it hurt the most—those closest to your heart.

I left them lost to sleep and headed to the hearth. Little flames flickered. Quietly I placed another split piece of firewood onto the fire. Embers rose. A gust of heat greeted the log, licking at the sides of the wood.

I couldn't afford to let the fire extinguish during the night. This was the last chunk of wood inside the cottage, which was why I had delayed placing it into the hearth. I hoped that it lasted until morning. I didn't want to scrounge through the snow-covered woodpile while it was still dark without someone to keep watch over the door. With an armload of the firewood I wasn't able to open the door, so I'd have to leave the door cracked open. During that time who knew what might sneak inside the house? In addition to that thought, I realized I was defenseless while carrying wood and vulnerable to attack. The one piece of wood had to do until morning's light.

CHAPTER 6

$\mathcal{M}$orning came without incident. No violent attacks occurred during the night. After my confrontation with the baron the day before and his disoriented departure, I hadn't expected him to return anytime soon anyway.

I did expect him to be plotting, not only to kill my father, but my mother and myself as well. He seemed the type. I held no doubt that it was attuned to his pompous nature. Aristocrats, governors, and members of royalty were seldom forgiving to those who didn't respect their title or prominence, often viewing the person as an unruly enemy. An enemy that must be imprisoned or publicly executed.

The fire was near death, so I pulled my heavy coat over my shoulders, wrapped my scarf around my neck, and slid my hands inside sheepskin gloves. I glanced toward my parents before opening the door. My mother had, during the night, placed her hand on my father's chest, subconsciously checking for his heartbeat I supposed. His chest rose slightly and fell. He was alive, for which we were thankful, and I couldn't wait for him to awaken. There was much he needed to explain to me; things he should have already told me, so I needed him to survive in a much different way than my mother did.

Easing the door open, I faced a knee-high wall of packed snow that had accumulated overnight. The frigid wind swirled with less snow than the evening before. I trudged onto the snow bank and tugged the door almost closed. Snow clung to the sides of the trees, revealing the direction the night wind had blown. The forest was eerily silent, other than the occasional sound of snow clumps dropping from the trees and thudding onto the snowy forest floor.

Before heading toward the woodpile I searched the surrounding snow for footprints of any sort. Not finding any, I was somewhat relieved. Still no full sunlight, but at least the thinning clouds forecasted a coming break in the blizzard. The less ominous skies meant, at least from what Jacques had told me, that the master vampire would not risk leaving his lair during this day. The sun would eventually shine, making vampires seek the darkness of their tombs.

Wearily I tramped my way through the deep snow to the woodpile. I needed sleep, but chores needed attended to before I could do so. I hefted an armload of frozen firewood to the cottage door and leaned my back against the door, pushing it open.

Momma aroused, perhaps at the noise of the whistling cold wind rushing across the threshold or the clumsiness of my heavy footsteps when I stepped down from the snow onto the hardwood floor. She eased from the bed and met me at the door. Once I was inside, she closed the door.

I lowered the armful of firewood at the side of the door, but no matter how hard one tried, there was never a quiet way to release a heavy bundle of wood onto the floor.

When I rose, I turned to apologize, but she placed a warm hand against my cheek and smiled. Her endearing smile caught me off-guard because she had endured such heartache the evening before, which still hung heavy on her heart. But a mother's smile, one mixed with love and pride, was enough to make a hardened heart relax.

"You're so much like your father," she said softly. She rose on tiptoe and kissed my forehead. "And . . . you've grown so quickly. Your age is a deception because I fear, you'll soon be leaving us."

Momma walked past me, grabbed the miracle salve my cousin had left, and went to apply it to my father's cuts and abrasions. I had to admit, in the glow of the lantern, his wounds were remarkably smaller. The salve was working.

"Momma, why would I leave? I'm still a boy."

She plunged two fingers into the salve and scooped a generous portion out of the jar. She smiled but didn't make eye contact as she applied the ointment on Father's wounds. "Your father has known since your second birthday that . . . you held a different path than a normal child. I sensed it too, though I've often tried to deny it. But Jacques, his purpose here was not just to pull your father back from the brink of death, but to do something your father should have done already."

"What is that?"

Momma's eyes flicked directly toward mine. "Reveal to you what you are."

Chills ran up my spine. Her hushed tone when she spoke those words were rigid, almost cold, like she had been cheated and robbed by a higher power at the blessing—or curse—I was born to bear.

"But Father is a vampire hunter, too."

"Not in the same way as you." Tears crested in her eyes as she whispered. She turned her attention to my father again. "Your father had chosen to hunt them after discovering what they did to Jacques. No higher power had chosen him for the task. He took the path, but what you are is everything he wishes he could have been."

The sadness in her eyes, the slight detest in her voice—not directed toward me, but at whatever authority responsible for predestining me—made me want to reassure her that I was still her son and always would be.

"Momma, I still have not been trained."

"And your father is paying the price for not doing so."

I stared at my father. "You think *this* is his punishment for not teaching me? *Momma*—"

Her jaw tightened. Fury set in her eyes. "How could it be anything else? We both refrained from openly admitting what you are. We wanted to . . . we hoped . . . by ignoring the obvious that it might alter. But you cannot change what Fate demands."

"Momma—"

"Go, put some wood on the fire before it goes out."

I nodded and went to the thawing woodpile beside the door. I tapped melting snow off of two logs and carried them to the hearth. The fire hissed when I placed the damp cold wood onto the remaining coals. While the low flames attempted to dry the wood, I glanced over my shoulder. My mother continued nursing and dressing my father's injuries. I supposed her attitude was a way for her to deal with her grief. It was part of her emotional healing process.

She had been predisposed to tears and her anguish the night before, to clinging desperation while she slept, and this morning anger to thwart succumbing to her inner sadness and despair.

I blew into the growing flames, igniting the white coals to roar slightly, releasing their heat. I snapped a few dry kindling twigs and added them. Once the fire had raised enough to where I didn't fear it would go out, I stirred the remaining stew in the large black pot. Barely enough to last us a day.

I grabbed my rifle from the wall rack and made my way to the door. I was exhausted. Never had I stayed awake throughout the night before. There never had been any need.

Her nervous eyes gazed at me. "Forrest, you should get some sleep. Hunt later?"

"I'm going to check the traps first. Should I see rabbits or squirrels, I'll shoot them and bring them back. Then, I'll sleep."

Before I opened the door, I took the hatchet instead of the wood ax from beside the door. The ax was too cumbersome to carry far distances, especially when I needed both hands for the rifle. Occasionally a trapped animal became frozen to the ground or in the ice. After the past few days of heavy snow, I didn't want to risk the chance I'd need something sharp to cut the animal loose and not have anything. Besides, the hatchet fit perfectly inside the inner pocket of my heavy coat.

I glanced back at Momma as I opened the door.

"Be careful," she said softly.

Words she'd never said to me before.

CHAPTER 7

$\mathcal{B}$ecoming a man was something that generally occurred over a decade and a half. I was slightly beyond the halfway mark, age wise; however, the frailty of my youthful innocence was about to vanish forever, only I didn't know its approach, nor did I recognize its closeness. The mental transition from a child to an adult can be abrupt. Sometimes one never saw the moment they crossed over.

The heavy blizzard snow hunkered down most folks. Any wagon roads were impassable, even for those riding on horseback. Few people ventured outdoors unless absolutely necessary, which was why I had never anticipated seeing anyone else out on that horribly cold morning.

About a hundred yards from the cottage was a narrow brook where my father and I kept our traps set. The brook was frozen solid but remained the only water source for wild game. There was a slim chance that I might find something in one of the traps, and if so, it was better than traipsing through waist-high snow, hoping to frighten a rabbit from its nestled bed.

Snow crunched underfoot. My weight caused me to sink up to my thighs with each step I took. Once I was in sight of the bramble that lined the creek bed, I stopped. Two men talked to one another nearby. They were outside of my view, so I guessed they were walking along the edge of the frozen brook. Their voices indicated they weren't far from where our traps were set, but their accents indicated they weren't one of the locals.

Trapping was common in our country, especially during the harsh winter months when an animal's fur was thicker. There's unspoken etiquette amongst trappers, and that was, quite simply, to never steal from another man's trap. Not only was it illegal, but also when caught, the perpetrator stood the chance of being shot and killed by the man being stolen from. Seldom was the owner jailed or fined for protecting what was rightfully his.

Of course the dangers were also there for the trap owner, should the thief hold no qualms in adding murder to his agenda. Even though the Great War had been over, the unrest remained. For some, they viewed any threat as a legitimate reason to kill. To me, death wasn't worth the hide or meat of an animal.

Before I approached the bramble, I listened. The two men seemed calm, discussing something between themselves. No malice or heightened anger exchanged in their voices, so I approached the brook and stopped beside a massive tree.

This tree was the landmark my father and I looked for when coming to the brook. For one, it was the largest tree, making it easily identifiable, and the other benefit was its massive roots formed a natural set of steps down to the water.

Placing my left hand against the tree, I took a wary first step onto the snow-covered roots. The icy slickness caused me to slightly stumble, but I rebounded by planting my left root against the edge of the next root. My movement and sudden gasp didn't go unnoticed by the two men standing a few yards downstream.

By the time I descended the tree-root steps and stood at the frozen edge of the water, the two men were closer to my vicinity than I wanted them to be. Having a rifle didn't make me feel safe.

"You there," the one said. "These your traps?"

I nodded, looking down at the traps. I was surprised they weren't buried beneath the snow. The curve of the bramble on the bank had caught the heavy wet snow, acting like a lean-to, and formed a slanted roof to force the snow to fall to the outside of our traps. Neither of the traps had caught anything and both remained ready to snap should something step upon one.

With an even gaze I studied the two men. They were a little taller than me, but neither matched my shoulder width or weight. They wore rabbit fur hats with flaps that lowered over their ears. Their long bushy beards were black, mixed with gray, and flowed to their waist. Their heavy overcoats were made from wolf hides. The heavier of the two men carried a tied bundle of wolf hides, beaver pelts, and deerskin over his shoulders. In appearance alone, they looked wilder than the animals they were hunting.

They were hunters, but I sensed they were more than regular game hunters. Power leapt from them, as if greeting what I had felt last night while looking through my father's vampire hunting box. While they should have been kindred spirits with my own, I sensed something darker about these two men. Something I detested and something that needed culled out and destroyed. My newly found wisdom warned me that these men intended to do my family great harm. The quicker I got them to leave the area, the better.

"This blizzard makes small game trapping sparse," the man said.

"Looks like you've had some luck," I replied, glancing to his bundle of hides.

He chuckled, combing his wiry beard with his hand. "Our game doesn't require traps. Just good accuracy."

I noticed the rifles they carried. My father had one similar. One he had used in the war before I was born. Their accents betrayed them as well. They weren't from Romania, but I couldn't place their country of origin. I never had dealt with people from outside our forest and the neighboring hamlets. They must have traded for these rifles, as I doubted they had fought on either side of our war. Of course, mercenaries held no boundaries of country or any morals at all.

"You live nearby, boy?" the other man asked, glancing toward the path beside the massive tree from which I had come.

Although I had physically been gifted with my massive stature, my hairless face gave away my adolescence, as I had yet to sprout any facial hair.

Since these two made me uneasy, I didn't answer his question. The less information about me, the safer my father and mother were.

"What brings you along this way?" I asked. "The brook water's frozen. The nearest hamlet is several miles back in the direction you came. Nothing any closer upstream, either."

"My brother, Guise, and I were tracking a large wolf last night before the snowstorm became too severe for us to continue traveling." When this man spoke, there was gentleness in his speech. He seemed affable and much friendlier than his appearance foreshadowed.

Guise frowned at me. "You see any wolves near here?"

Guise was different than his brother. His aura was dark. I sensed he was untrustworthy and out to gain money anyway he could, regardless of what it entailed.

I shook my head. "From the wolf hides your brother totes, it looks like you'd do better hunting wherever you killed those."

"The wolf we hunt has a bounty upon it. Right Wes?" Guise said with a sly grin.

Wes nodded.

"Who'd put a bounty on a wolf?" I asked.

"It's not a normal wolf," Wes said. "It's one of those cursed beings that turns from a man into part wolf and man. Baron Randolph has offered a generous amount of gold for its hide."

My eyes widened as the shocking news pulsed through me.

"Ah," Guise said. "You've seen it?"

"No," I replied, but my reaction had already given me away. That was another problem of being a youth. Learning how to maintain stolid facial expressions took years to master, but in an instant I had revealed a vital secret by my uncontrolled emotional reaction. Despite any further arguments on my behalf, there was no way I could convince these men otherwise.

"Don't lie to us," Wes said. "We tracked this creature down the edge of the creek last night."

"And with all of the snow overnight," I said. "Any tracks have long been buried."

"All but one," Guise said, pointing at the tree roots.

When I had stepped down the embankment, apparently I had dislodged loose snow from one of the steps, which revealed a massive wolf print that stretched partway into a human's, and the clawed toes pointed uphill. Had it been Jacques? Doubtful. He was wearing boots, and to the best of my knowledge, he had not shifted into a beast.

Between the two brothers, Wes was calm with friendly eyes and seemed the most sensible. Guise kept a constant crazy look in his gaze and was probably less predictable. I didn't trust him and liked him even less.

"Where did you see it?" Wes asked. "When? Last night?"

"Wes, the tracks head in the direction the lad has come from. My guess is we follow his tracks through the snowy forest, and we'll find the werewolf."

"Or perhaps, the lad *is* this wolf we seek," Wes replied. "There is something odd about him. I sensed it the moment I saw him."

Guise frowned and stepped toward me, sternly peering into my eyes. "He's different, but he's not this creature we seek."

"Seems too bold in his stance to only be a young man," Wes said.

I stepped back, toward the root steps, trying to get my distance. Accuracy with a rifle was nearly impossible close up, should I be forced to defend myself and I hoped I didn't have to. The thought of killing an undead vampire didn't bother me, but I was certain killing a human, even in self-defense would affect me psychologically for some time to come.

I was aware of my direct surroundings. I knew the land terrain quite well, and much better than either of these brothers. However, in any other season, I could have used this to my advantage and quickly escaped from their presence, but not in the dead of winter.

Running was completely out of the question. The brook was slick frozen ice, and the bank was covered by waist-high snow. I had no quick way to escape.

They must have realized I was looking to get away because both men simultaneously aimed their rifles at me.

"Drop the rifle, lad, while my brother and I sort this out," Guise said.

"You said that the bounty was given by Baron Randolph?" I asked, not lowering my gun.

"Yes," Wes replied.

"Did he solicit you directly?"

"No," Guise said, frowning while he stared into my eyes. "We read of it on a poster in a tavern near the center of Bucharest."

"I see. So the reward has been offered for some time now?"

"I suppose," Wes replied, looking to his brother. "Why do you ask?"

I shrugged. "More for my benefit than yours."

"How's that?" Guise asked, eyeing me with skepticism. "You know the baron, do you?"

"He actually paid my family a brief visit yesterday, before the worst of the storm set in," my eyes held renewed boldness, as what I said was indeed the truth.

"Did he now?" Wes asked, lowering his rifle.

Guise lowered his weapon, too. "Why would he call upon your family?"

"He requested to see my father, but my father is ill. My cousin saw the baron off on his way, though."

The brothers exchanged uncertain glances with one another.

I held my rifle with both hands but not in a threatening manner. "Why would vampire hunters be seeking gold from a vampire to kill a werewolf?"

"What?" Wes asked, his eyes slightly widening as though he'd seen an apparition.

"Which surprises you the most?" I asked. "That I know you're both vampire hunters, or the fact that the baron *is* a vampire?"

The brothers were visibly shaken.

I smiled at them in a rather taunting way. Both revelations had caught them unaware, and I managed to conceal that it had me as well. Having access to the knowledge of a previous hunter held great advantages, but there was also familiarity coming to my mind that gave apt awareness to certain things I shouldn't have known.

"Who are you, boy?" Guise asked.

"I bear a name you won't recognize."

"Are you a vampire hunter as well?" Wes said. "Surely you must be, to identify us."

Guise glanced at Wes. "He seems to be, brother. How do you know the baron is a vampire? That's never been told anywhere in the taverns, and even we've not heard it."

"Do you think I'm lying?" I asked.

"You don't seem to be," Guise replied. "But how did you get such knowledge?"

"You've never met him in person?"

They shook their heads.

"Well, if you did, you'd know it immediately," I said. "I'll make a deal with you."

"What kind of a deal?" Guise asked.

"You want information about the werewolf that you're tracking?"

"I told you, Wes! He *knows* where it is!"

"Do you or do you not?" I asked.

"Of course," Guise said.

Wes no longer looked so certain.

"I will give you that information but only in return for one thing."

"What's that?"

"The baron wears a ruby ring on his right hand. Drive a stake through his heart and bring me the ring. Then I'll give you the information you seek about the werewolf."

The last thing I ever intended was to give the brothers any clues that eventually led to Jacques. He was family, and I'd fight to protect him. There were several reasons why I had made the insinuation. For one, I didn't believe they'd have the courage to pursue the baron and if they did, there was a greater possibility he would kill them than the other way around. Should they happen to be successful in killing the master vampire, he wasn't even *wearing* a ruby ring, so they had no evidence to bring back to me. But mostly I believed they'd stop hunting the werewolf altogether due to the repulsion of taking money from a vampire. Their true calling was to hunt vampires instead of werewolves.

Wes paled. "What if he isn't a vampire? You're sending us to kill a man of nobility. You realize the penalty we'd face for murdering him?"

"Can you not detect a vampire?" I asked. "A true vampire hunter has the ability to discern their presence."

"Why didn't you kill the baron yourself?" Guise asked, trying to tilt the challenge back at me. His complexion had lightened somewhat, too.

"The opportunity escaped me. He vanished into the forest before I got the chance. Besides, I'm much younger and less experienced than the two of you. And the baron is a *master* vampire. Such would require someone with better hunting tactics. Unless, of course, you don't possess them? How many vampires have the two of you killed?"

"As a team, six," Wes replied. "Apart, none. It's safer to hunt as a pair."

"I don't doubt that. Were any of those master vampires?" I asked.

Wes shook his head. The more he thought about what I had said, the sicker he appeared.

I gave each of them looks of disappointment, even though I had no kills notched on the side of a hunter box like my father. One day I would, and the number of vampires I killed would be greater than my father or these two men combined. "Perhaps that's why you've chosen to hunt werewolves instead? They're easier to kill?"

"They are *not* easier!" Guise said, anger rising in his voice. He paced slightly, like he wanted to rush at me, but my size kept him from doing so. "You, boy, are quite insolent, making such assumptions. Your father should have taught you better manners."

I shrugged. "The baron seemed to suggest as much last night, too."

Guise glared at me. If he expected an apology, he wasn't getting one.

I shook my head and gave an even smile. "Taking gold from a master vampire is a disgrace to all vampire hunters, is it not? Nothing could ever persuade me to be *bought* by a vampire."

"Bought? How dare you make such an accusation," Guise said.

"What accusation? Just moments earlier you told me who was paying the bounty. I told you what he really is. So, you kill this werewolf and take the hide to the baron, he pays you. The baron's a vampire. Did I miss something?" Such philosophic rebuttals were why several of my teachers had enjoyed talking at great length with me, and they probably missed my departure from the school. The brothers . . . they weren't as impressed.

Guise narrowed his eyes. I could tell he was struggling to find a solid reply, but nothing came quickly; not that I expected any fast retort from him based upon all of his previous conversation with me.

"From the moment you both spoke, I recognized that you're not from this region," I said. "Your accent betrays you. What country are you from?"

"Britain," Wes replied.

"You're presently hunting near the heart of Romania, where there's never been a shortage of vampires since the Impaler's reign. And as vampire hunters, you're tracking a werewolf? Perhaps you seek the bounty in order to sail back to your mother country because you don't like being *surrounded* by vampires. But, there is one more thing I can tell you about this particular werewolf that might be of genuine interest to you."

"And what would that be?" Guise asked in a disgusted tone. He looked like he wanted to take a leather strap to me.

"He'd be far harder for you to kill than the master vampire."

The craziness in Guise's eyes settled, replaced by a slight tinge of fear and hesitation. He was clearly uncomfortable, and Wes was even in worse shape.

"Do we have a deal?" I asked.

The studied me in silence for several minutes.

"Look at it this way," I said. "You could request a meeting with the baron and find out whether I'm telling the truth about what he is, if you still have a sliver of doubt. Simply insist that you wish to talk to him about the werewolf's bounty and want to negotiate the terms. Surely he'd invite you into his chambers. Once inside, you'll know the certain truth. Unless . . . you're not seasoned enough to face such a vampire."

I could tell by Wes' reaction that he didn't want to undertake a visit with the baron, but my mocking challenge perturbed Guise, giving him a rise of anger. He probably felt it necessary to prove they could defeat the master. Regardless of Wes' apprehension, he'd never let his brother go alone. Blind loyalty.

"And after we bring you the ring, you'll give us more details about the werewolf?"

I nodded. "You bring me the ring, and I'll know that you're capable of facing the werewolf. Otherwise, there's no need for me to send you directly into harm's way."

Guise turned to Wes and said, "Let's go talk to the baron."

Wes nodded, but I was certain that I heard him swallow hard.

Guise pointed a stern finger at me. "You best not be withholding the truth from us."

I feigned an innocent expression, which is quite difficult given the downward shape of my mouth. "I've told you what I know."

He stared hard at me for a few more moments.

I don't think it crossed his mind how badly he was being duped. It never dawned upon him that if he killed the baron, who'd pay the bounty for the werewolf? No need for him to worry about a ring that didn't exist because he'd kill the banker that held his potential reward.

I never really felt bad about misleading Guise, but I didn't like adding Wes to the casualties. But at the ignorance level Guise governed supreme. He wasn't mentally adept to be a hunter because his actions to discern an ally from an enemy weren't properly scaled. For the first few minutes after I had encountered them, I had thought my own life was in jeopardy, that he considered me an enemy, which indicated he was also a danger to innocent people.

Perhaps Guise had suffered some head trauma during a war or when they had hunted down an actual vampire, but at least I had managed to get them off of Jacques' trail for now. Besides, the true vampire hunters didn't need the added embarrassment of having any association with Guise. He tarnished the reputation of what a vampire hunter should be. As they walked away, following the frozen brook, I wondered if it would be the last time I saw them. It was.

Later I learned that the baron and his minions had torn them to shreds in such a way there wasn't any possible chance to turn them. Apparently the baron didn't want the humiliation of having Guise live an undead eternity inside his lair. But wherever Guise went, Wes surely followed.

Perhaps even the baron detected the lack of stability Guise displayed.

I held no internal struggle in sending the two hunters to attack the baron. After all, he had attacked my father first. I was merely offering a counterattack, which to all rights I was entitled, and from my perspective, we would now be even. And should they be successful and kill the baron, so much the better.

But what I didn't know for quite some time later was the baron had used these two hunters to his favor. Unlike he had failed trying with me; the baron compelled them and drained vital information, and learned that I had been the one that sent them to kill him. The news made the baron detest me even further. I became his mortal enemy that he was determined to destroy, which was probably the real reason he had butchered them. His fury toward me was something he couldn't contain and torturing them with agonizing death, helped release his pent up rage.

Even though I had betrayed the two hunters in favor of protecting my family; being young, I had never properly weighed the consequences. Doing so had been a costly mistake, one I had not anticipated. One for which would change and haunt me for as long as I lived.

Since the traps were empty, I spent a half hour trudging along the bramble edge of the creek, scaring out fat rabbits that gave us food to last several more days. Then I slept, but not peacefully.

CHAPTER 8

Two weeks passed before my father finally opened his eyes for the first time. He was weak, frighteningly thin, like a skeleton with wrinkly skin stretched over the bones. Momma had only been able feed him spoonsful of broth and herbal tea while he had slept, but never too much at any given time. When we helped him sit up against the headboard the first thing he did was demand solid food.

His beard was combed and neatly trimmed. Momma had fussed over him like a daily ritual, singing softly to him and holding his hand, seldom leaving his bedside.

Momma rushed toward the hearth to fix him a plate.

Luckily the snow had receded and a trader's wagon was able to bring wares along the road that cut near our cottage. I traded rabbit and raccoon hides for a large block of aged cheese, a stale loaf, and some yams. We had a deer roast cooking on a spit in the hearth from my morning hunt the day before. Momma sliced off a hunk of the meat and brought it, some cheese and bread, and a small cup of wine.

Swallowing his first few bites was difficult, as his throat muscles were constricted from lack of use. He nearly choked a couple of times. But his hunger pushed him forward. I knew that I ate a lot, but I'd never eaten with such a ravenous smacking display.

Pulling a chair to the side of the bed, I watched my father eat. In so many ways I was thankful he had survived and now was awake. I had questions, lots of questions, but I didn't believe it appropriate to ask them so soon. I wondered how much he remembered of that evening when he had dragged himself home, almost dying outside our cottage door.

He smacked sloppily as he ate.

Momma brought him water after he finished his wine.

His eyes brightened as he looked at her. With a mouthful of food, he asked, "How long have I been asleep?"

"About sixteen days," she replied.

He stopped mid-chew, stunned, and shook his head in disbelief. He tried to move his legs and couldn't.

"Easy," she said. "They've a lot of healing yet to do."

"They're broken?" he whispered.

"Severely," she said.

Father glanced toward me. "I imagine you helped me inside?"

I nodded.

"It's good that you're such a hearty young man," he replied, slowly chewing the remaining food in his mouth.

"Jacques was here," I said.

He turned his head sharply toward me. "Whatever for?"

I looked toward Momma.

"You'd have died had he not come," Momma said softly.

"But how did he know I was injured? Or where we even lived for that matter? He's never visited us here before," Father said.

"He told me that you're blood brothers," I said.

"Did he now?"

"Yes, Father."

"And did he fill your head with any other senseless rubbish?"

"*John!*" Momma said sternly.

He waved her off and glanced toward me with a cold hard stare. "Well, did he?"

Regardless of my incredible size, I immediately became childish in manner whenever he gave me that stern look. There was something about a father's hardened stare that makes a son revert back to his inner child. I was almost fearful to reply, as he seemed to be at some sort of odds with my cousin, something Jacques had never hinted about. In fact, the conversation I had with Jacques had indicated quite the opposite, that they were close like brothers.

"Come along son, tell me. Out with it."

"He told me what I am destined to be," I replied with a slight cringe.

Father took the edge of his bed sheet and wiped his lips. He picked away crumbs that rested upon his beard. "And what are you destined to *become*, young man?"

"A vampire hunter," I replied. "Like you."

He shook his head. "No, *not* like me."

"You're not denying it, are you? You know. It's why you gave me the blessed dagger."

"You showed Jacques the dagger?"

"Yes," I replied.

"And how did he react when he saw it?"

"He was careful in how he handled it."

"I suppose so. The blade is silver. Silver harms werewolves. I suppose he revealed *that* to you as well?"

"He revealed he was a werewolf. He said nothing about the silver."

Father halfway grinned. "Jacques spoiled the surprise, did he? What a rotten rascal our cousin can be."

My inner tension lessened, seeing my father refrain from his faux anger. I nodded toward my mother. "I suppose so, but Momma told me, too."

"Oh, so now the two of them told of your birthright? In cahoots, are they?" He ruffled my hair and gave a broad grin. "And they allowed me to *miss* it! Oh, Olivia, I'd have loved to seen Forrest's face when he first heard the news."

Momma sat on the edge of his bed and took his hand. "You very nearly died, John. Were we not supposed to tell Forrest?"

"Olivia," he said, "Jacques was correct in telling him. I should have done so already. What's done is done."

Momma smiled. "According to Jacques, Forrest stood his ground against Baron Randolph right outside the cottage that night you almost died."

Father's eyes widened and his mouth gaped. "The baron *came here?*"

I nodded.

He pushed himself forward, but his legs prevented him from moving.

"John," Momma said. "You're in no shape to get up. You'll only injure your legs worse."

"Has the baron returned?" he asked, glancing toward me with desperate eyes. "Since then?"

"No. He hasn't. I've checked the snow for tracks each morning. I don't sleep during the night. I sit against the door with the wood ax."

His pale face was covered with sweat. He looked at Momma. "My hunter box. Get it."

I reached beneath the bed and dragged out the box to save her the agony of trying to lift it. The box was quite heavy. I set it on the edge of the bed. The mattress sagged beneath its weight.

"These are tools I need to explain to you, Forrest."

"I've looked at them each night while I sit against the door."

His eyes narrowed. "Do you know what each is for?"

"Most all of them. I stopped holding any of them after the first night."

"Why?"

I explained how emotions and impulses washed through me, almost demanding me to head out in the night to hunt the vampires.

He took one of the wooden stakes from the box and handed it to me. "Here."

I was hesitant to accept it because of the hunting impulses that had plagued me from the first time I picked it up.

"Take it. Make sure you have it when you're sitting at the door each night. An ax can be a great weapon, but you have to have a lot of room to make an accurate swing. Stakes are weapons used in close proximity and easily concealed."

I took the stake from his hand.

"Getting any premonitions from it?" he asked.

I was, but not as strongly as before. Perhaps it was due to it being daytime? I nodded.

Father nodded and glanced toward Momma. "He's a true vampire hunter like we suspected. You're better prepared than I, son."

"Jacques told me that I'd have pre-knowledge and guidance, which is how I interpreted the information given to me when I held each weapon and tool in your hunter box."

"Yes, it's something I wish I had been blessed with. It doesn't help your fighting abilities because those are skills you have to practice to hone, but sometimes you get insight to a person's aura to sense their worth and true nature. Some, I'm told, get forewarnings against setups or baited traps. When the baron came here, what did he want?"

"He wanted me to allow him to finish killing you."

"What stopped him?" Father asked.

I shrugged. "I stepped in front of the door, holding the wood ax and told him to leave. Jacques had yet to announce himself to me. He was in the trees near the woodpile. Jacques believes the baron didn't attack me because of the dagger."

"So the baron knows about the knife?"

"He never saw it. I think he sensed the power of the witch's runes. He tried to compel me, but he couldn't."

"He never attacked you?"

I shook my head.

"And why did the baron leave?"

"Jacques produced a blinding light that disoriented the baron. He fled immediately afterwards."

"That old trick?" Father said, smiling and shaking his head.

"You *know* how he did it?"

He nodded. "Did he have his silver cane?"

"He did."

"Jacques has a medallion on a chain around his neck. Whenever he strikes the tip of the cane to the medallion, it produces that reaction. He got them from an alchemist years ago."

I frowned. "You said that silver harmed werewolves. How does he hold the cane?"

"It's not silver. It's a metal discovered south of the equator. Much sturdier than silver actually and lighter."

"May I ask you something, Father?"

He nodded.

"Did you seek out the master and try to kill him?"

He shook his head. "No, son, I'm not that foolish."

"Could you tell me what happened?"

He looked at his legs for several seconds. "I don't having any pressing plans."

"So you'll tell me?"

Father lifted his plate covered with crumbs and handed it to Momma. "Most certainly, provided your lovely mother will bring me a hearty second helping. More of that venison, if you don't mind, my dear?"

She smiled. We were overly happy that he was awake and hungry. But I was also happy for selfish reasons. I wanted to know what had happened to bring my father into the presence of the master vampire. I needed to know. Jacques had told me to study my enemies. My father held a firsthand encounter. Perhaps in his rehashing of the events that had unfolded, the baron's weaknesses might be exposed.

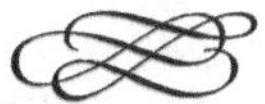

CHAPTER 9

Even though we were modestly poor, as were all of the other forest inhabitants, my father was a man who maintained proper etiquette in diction, in dress, and in his manners. If not based upon his wealth, he was an eloquent statesman to a fault.

Of course, that was *before* he had suffered two weeks of constant sleep with only broth and tea as sustenance. Now his eating manners had become porcine. Never had I seen this man devour food with such drive, loud smacking, and any disregard for proper eating utensils. The sounds coming from him disgusted my mother, and I have to admit, even myself.

Reflecting back on it, though, I believe his stomach had hijacked his brain, commanding no pause in ingesting as much food as possible. After all, he was a man that had nearly died, not only from the physical mêlée against the vampire, but afterwards, he almost wasted away due to starvation.

Father ripped a huge corner of the loaf with his teeth and chewed. His cheeks bulged, but that didn't deter him from adding bits of cheese as his chewing decreased the size of the bread.

I waited.

I'd have never understood a word he said while he chomped such huge bites. It was finally after his third full plate when his eating enthusiasm waned. He still looked like a skin-stretched skeleton, other than his immense bloated stomach.

Having waited patiently in the chair beside his bed for as long as it had taken him to finish eating, I bluntly asked, "What happened?"

Father took a cloth and gingerly wiped his mouth, manners returning. "Once you get older and have killed a few vampires, villagers will seek you out sometimes hoping to hire you to slay a vampire."

"There's no way to remain anonymous?" I asked.

He smiled. "I suppose *I* could have, but . . . it's highly unlikely that *you* will keep your secret from the public's knowledge."

I gave a slight nod. "Jacques said about the same thing. Why is it different for me?"

"You were born to become such a hunter. No birthmark or any such thing like that, but you're blessed with size, strength, and keen knowledge. At an early age, mind you. Your schoolmates sensed you were different. Several of your teachers talked to me, questioning and marveling about your intellect, but I never divulged any revelation. For one, you're still too young, and your mother, ah, she refuses to accept it."

Momma shook her head. "That's not entirely true, John. I'm getting better about it. But when you think about a child fighting against cursed undead beasts that might be centuries old in knowledge—"

"Right you are, dear," Father said. "*Child.* Ah, yes, getting back to the details of my dilemma, son." He paused, pointing his finger for emphasis. "Often the one hiring you is a relative of the vampire they wish you to kill. Such was the case with this one. In fact, it was one of your teachers that had hired me."

"It was?"

He nodded.

I wondered which teacher, but thought it best not to ask.

"Seems his boy, who was your age, had come home with bite marks on his neck. They tended to the wound, as best they could, never suspecting the bite to be anything serious. They certainly never thought the bite to have been from a vampire."

My only teacher with a son my age was Gustaaf Popescu. His son,

Bodi, was the tiniest one in class, looked rather mousy in appearance, and was always small and quiet. In fact, he was the only child in class that actually liked me. Perhaps it was because we were so different from everyone else and on the opposite ends of the size spectrum. Plus, I never allowed any of the other children to pick at him, either. That was a positive for anyone incapable of protecting himself.

Now that my father was telling me about what had happened, I remembered that Bodi was absent from class about two weeks before they dismissed me. The last week, Popescu had taken leave. It made sense now, in quite a painful way. I had assumed a nasty sickness was going around, as several of the other students lacked attendance during this time as well.

Frowning, I asked, "What was he doing that he might encounter a vampire?"

"Boys his size are hired by the granaries to kill rats in the cellars. When you don't have much money, that's not labor any parent would turn away. It's not a hard job and the reward is quick. If a child is good with a slingshot, they can kill a bagful of rats in about an hour. In exchange, they receive a sack of grain equal to the weight of the rats. For the granary, it's cheaper to do that than let the rats continue to flourish unchecked."

"So they thought a rat had bitten him?"

Father nodded.

"Why didn't the boy remember what had bitten him?"

"The cellars are dark, but a vampire can compel a young child quite easily, making him forget ever seeing the vampire or being bitten."

"When did they realize the bite was from a vampire and not a rat?" I asked.

"Later in the night there was a disturbing, loud sound in the child's bedroom. When they went to his room, they noticed the boarded windows were wide open and cold air filled the room. With a lantern, they noticed a new bite on his neck and the boy's mouth was filled with dark blood. His skin was blue."

"He was dead?" I asked, feeling remorse for Bodi.

"They thought he was. In a sense, he really was. Apparently the vampire drained his blood enough to stop his heart, but the blood in the boy's mouth was that of the vampire. That was what turned the lad into a child of darkness. According to the father, he was getting ready to wrap his son in the sheet and await the last rites from a priest, but when he neared his son, the boy's eyes snapped open. Fangs sprouted in his mouth."

"So quickly?"

He nodded.

"How?"

Father shrugged. "Your teacher and his wife are fortunate to be alive. The boy didn't attack them. He hissed at them and fled out window into the night."

"Why was the vampire's blood in Bodi's mouth?" I asked.

"You knew the boy?" His eyebrows rose.

I nodded.

"My sympathies, son. For someone to become a vampire, they must partake or drink its blood right before death."

I thought back to the night when my father had nearly died. Not only had he been bitten, but his mouth had been filled with blood, too. Momma had never told me whose blood it was. But now I knew. The baron's blood. That's why he had come to the cottage. He had wanted to ensure my father died and turned.

"How much blood does a victim need to drink?" I asked.

"No one rightly knows."

"What if they drank the blood but didn't die?"

Father thought for a few moments. "Eventually, it'd work through one's system, I suppose. Why do you ask?"

"The baron bit you," I said.

Momma frowned and shook her head at me.

Out of reflex, he placed his hand to his neck, feeling for the scars. None were found. He looked at Momma. "You used holy water?"

She nodded.

"Your mouth was filled with blood. All she had told me was that it wasn't yours. I had thought you had suffered internal bleeding and it was your blood."

He placed his hands upon his upper thighs. "I suffered a brutal assault. There's no doubt about it. Had I died and been turned, these injuries wouldn't still be healing. They'd have already healed."

"But you've never suffered from pain," I said. "Even now."

Father smiled and glanced toward my mother. "Your mother has strong healing herbs."

Some time later, Jacques informed me that the roots he had given my mother produced a tea capable of blocking severe pain for several weeks, which was good for someone with injuries as bad as my father's. Although it wasn't responsible for his coma, it did prevent constant inadvertent pain spasms, which prolonged recovery. Jacques had also mentioned that for anyone without physical trauma who drank the tea felt no pain. It temporarily deadened a person's pain receptors. Quite possibly the person could endure such damage that mentally he might believe himself invincible and keep fighting long after he should have been incapacitated.

"Do you remember how you suffered all of this?"

"I'll get to that. But back to Bodi."

I nodded. "They hired you to kill their son, a child?"

Father closed his eyes and swallowed hard. Tears formed at the edges of his eyes. "They made a proposal, and I promptly declined. I couldn't do it, Forrest. He was a vampire, yes, but in appearance, he was still a boy."

Seeing tears in my father's eyes was rare. The thought of what they had requested continued to haunt him.

"In desperation, they doubled their offer. I walked outside of the tavern where we had agreed to meet onto the cobblestone street. The boy's mother ran after me, begging, pleading, with tears in her eyes. They couldn't stand the thought of their son living a life of the damned. Since you were the same age as he, I put myself into their position. What if you were the one bitten and transformed? I wondered what I would do."

Tears streamed down my mother's face as the same thought ran through her mind.

Father reached over and clasped my hand under his. He whimpered, something I'd never heard from him. "Son, it was a horrid emotional struggle to consider such a thing happening to you, but even after weighing it for a long time, I still was unable to come to the conclusion they had. I couldn't do it, Forrest. Even if you became a vampire, I couldn't kill you. I just couldn't. I'd let you kill me, or turn me. But I . . . couldn't drive a stake through your heart."

Momma leaned to him and wrapped her arms around his neck, kissing his forehead. He shook, sobbing.

I looked away. When I had confronted the same question of what I'd do if my father turned into a vampire, I hadn't weighed the situation too long before concluding that yes, I would. Perhaps it was different from a parent's perspective, after nurturing a child and watching him grow into a man. Maybe it was totally different. But my conclusion was based upon my understanding that my father wouldn't be the man I had known. And he wouldn't. According to the legends, his soul would have vacated the body. Where it had gone? I haven't any idea, but according to the cathedral, a vampire was cursed, forbidden to whatever lay in store in heaven, provided that was how one believed.

My father was a vampire hunter, perhaps not born under the calling, but he had chosen to become one. For the life of me, I couldn't understand why Bodi's parents clearly saw the truth and why my father had overlooked the obvious, based upon his irrational emotional attachment.

I placed a gentle hand upon my father's shoulder. He gripped it and kissed it. I wasn't certain what to do but I finally said, "According to what you and Jacques have disclosed, I'm a vampire hunter. Untrained, but one all the same. But here's something I must say to you, as it is vitally important for you to understand and never question what I tell you upon this day."

Something in my voice had changed, a maturity that he had never heard leave my lips, and he immediately lost his sorrow, staring at me in a new light. I wasn't the eight year old he had awakened to see. The nature and understanding of a true vampire hunter welled up inside me, slowly consuming me.

"What is it, Forrest?" he asked.

"If I'm bitten, and about to become one of the undead, you must kill me."

He and my mother gasped.

"Kill me," I said sternly. "For I will no longer be your son, no more than Bodi remained the son of his parents afterwards. Absent a soul, what is left but a cursed being? I wouldn't be Forrest, the child you have reared, but something evil and sinister and bloodthirsty. Something that would kill to feed and have no remorse or second thought about its victims. So tell me something, Father. Is Bodi still alive?"

Father looked away. Shame replaced his sorrow.

"John?" Momma said.

"He is. I regret to say that he is."

"So you refused to kill him?"

My father shook his head. "No, actually, after a couple of days, I took their offer."

"What changed your mind?" I asked.

"Bodi started killing his other classmates. The ones that had bullied him before he met you I suppose."

"Those killings had to be during the week I was dismissed."

He nodded.

I closed my eyes, partially angry with myself and angry with the school for not protecting Bodi before I had enrolled. "And why didn't you kill the small vampire?"

My father stared straightforward, remembering. "I had gone into the city, son, after sunset, to the old cemetery. That's where the boy's parents had last seen him. Even they had sharpened sticks into stakes, intent on stopping his needless slaughter. They didn't want any more children killed by their son.

"Apparently there was a gargoyle statue on the edge of the cemetery that Bodi was attracted to. And that's where I saw him. He was standing upon tiptoe, rubbing the outline of its hideous face. When I saw him, he was much smaller than I imagined him to be."

I nodded. "He was tiny."

"So little and fragile. With his back to me, he looked so innocent, like he couldn't harm a gnat. Had I snuck up and staked him through the heart from behind, the task would have been done. But understand, I didn't feel right about that. I've never done that to an adult vampire. Not that they deserve a fighting chance, but at least the person should witness his executioner."

He sighed and wiped tears from beneath his eyes.

"But I was wrong. When that little boy turned around with a face more hideous than the gargoyle, I froze. I never expected such evil on the face of a child. He was a pure image of what being cursed means. He was vicious. More vicious than some of the older vampires I had hunted and killed. The only reason he didn't kill me when he flung himself at me was because of the silver cross I had tucked inside my vest. His cheek pressed against it, burning his face. For some reason, the cross burned me at the same time."

I nodded. "We saw the scar."

"The little terror shrieked and tore off into a sprint down a dark alley. I took off after him, but he was faster than any child I'd ever seen, especially one that small. Midway down the alley was a gas-lit street-lamp. Bodi was too far ahead for me to catch, but I noticed a gentleman step to the curb, and the child was headed in his direction."

"The baron?"

"Baron Randolph, yes. I shouted for him to stop the child. Foolish request, now that I think about it, to put another person in jeopardy by grabbing a vampire, but I was desperate. But it didn't matter. I didn't know he was a vampire, too, not until I got to him.

"Bodi slowed and turned, stopping right behind the baron. I came running, breathing too hard to talk, and noticed the burnt flesh upon the boy's cheek. There was anger in the baron's eyes as he regarded me. The child placed his hand against his blisters, making a pitiful face that made me feel guilty."

"What did you do once you got to the baron?" I asked.

"I explained quickly that the boy was a vampire and I was a hunter, that his parents had hired me to stake the child. While I pointed at the child, almost pleading for the baron's aid, it was then I noticed Randolph's fangs. His rich blue eyes turned crimson. His features darkened. I went for a dagger hidden in my coat pocket, but he gripped me by the throat and peered into my eyes. My body grew flaccid."

My father looked distance. His lips quivered slightly as he recalled that nightmarish night.

"He compelled you?" I asked.

"He must have," Father replied. "For a few moments at least."

"What do you remember next?"

"A dark room within a series of catacombs," he said.

"His lair perhaps?"

"I think so."

"How did you escape?"

He swallowed hard, his eyes darting back and forth as his memory reeled. "Not easily, as you could see by my injuries."

"I realize that. The baron inflicted all of these injuries upon you?" I asked.

He shook his head. "When I had awakened, I was chained to a pillar and my hands were tied above me head. Bodi was the one who slashed the wounds across my chest and stomach. He and several older vampires fed on my blood, for a day or so, at my best estimate. Hard to know for certain as I faded in and out of consciousness. But they didn't seem to want to kill me quickly. The boy enjoyed drawing pain and blood from me, and the baron allowed it, appeasing Bodi."

"You never suspected the baron was a vampire until that night?" I asked.

"No, it was a total shock. I doubt anyone other than the ones inside his lair even suspect what he really is. He's always been a prominent figurehead, even amongst those with higher authority. He must use his intoxicating charisma to make others fawn over him. That's one of the most dangerous aspects powerful vampires have. They charm others into doing whatever they bid."

I nodded. "He tried it with me, but it didn't work."

Father frowned. "How do you know he attempted to charm you?"

"It's difficult to explain, but when he confronted me that night, I sensed his power. It tugged at me, trying to make my yield, but I think the dagger's blessing gave me the power to resist. At least that's what Jacques suggested."

"Neither Jacques nor I would rightly know, son. Once I'm healed and able to walk, I need to find a *real* hunter to train you."

I smiled and squeezed his shoulder. "I'm certain you can train me quite well."

"The basics but nothing more."

I brought our conversation back. "Is Randolph the vampire that turned Bodi?"

"I'm not certain, but he highly favored Bodi."

"In what way?"

My father grinned. "Much in the same way a grandparent spoils a child. He let the little tyrant do whatever he wanted. For a small child, he was overly violent and hostile. He held so much anger."

"He had been picked on and ridiculed a lot by others due to his tiny size."

"Well, he unleashed his anger and directed it toward me. I was his object of aggression."

"Since you were in the baron's lair, *how* did you manage to escape?" I asked.

"By accident, I suppose. You see, during some of the times I faked being unconscious I learned that the baron wanted to kill me, but Bodi pleaded for him not to."

"Why?"

Father shrugged. "I really don't know since I was responsible for the cross shape on his cheek. Maybe I reminded him of a family member. I have no idea. The baron explained in order for me to be spared, Bodi needed to be the one to attend to me, and that meant cleaning my wounds every day. He explained if the injuries weren't attended to, infection would set in, and I'd die anyway. Bodi agreed. At that point, my legs were fine. The major injuries were the cuts on my upper body where they had cut me to feed."

He paused to drink some water. His hand shook. "And here's where Bodi's tiny size worked in my favor. Since I was chained too high for him to reach all of my cuts, the taller vampires held him to collect my blood into a chalice.

"After they had fed from me during another session where Bodi had caused me immense pain, another vampire lowered me, thinking I had fallen unconscious so the boy would clean my wounds. Bodi tended to stop his torture whenever I became lifeless. I suppose he lost the exhilaration if I weren't screaming. Once I had caught onto that, I overly displayed the pain and dropped to silence, drooping my head forward and closing my eyes."

I smiled at his brilliant survival instinct.

Father cleared his throat. His voice was growing hoarse, but he continued anyway. "Usually an older vampire stayed in the chamber with Bodi while he cleaned my lacerations. But, for some reason, no one else was there. Just the child and me. Remember how I had said that I couldn't bring myself to stake him when I was first approached by his parents?"

I nodded.

"After a couple of days of torture, my attitude toward this violent little monster had altered in such a way, that if I'd had a stake, I'd have driven it through his heart and out the other side, but as it were, I had no weapon at all. Bodi took wet linen and began washing away dried blood. I opened my eyes at the tiniest sliver, watching him. He finished with one cut, lifted the cloth, and as he turned to dip the cloth in more water, I wrapped my hand firmly around his throat.

"He attempted to scream but I clutched his throat so tightly he made no sound at all. He bore fangs and his eyes filled with rage. I rose, lifting him with me, and looked around the chamber. His clawed hands flailed at my face, but I kept him out of reach, so he dug his claws into my forearm. He gnashed wildly with inhuman strength, trying to growl. When I noticed the narrow door that led to the stairs, I flung him across the room against a marble casket. His head struck the cold stone, but he scrambled to his feet and tore after me anyway, seemingly unharmed."

Father sipped more water. Sweat formed on his forehead. He seemed paler and his eyes vacant. He was reliving the nightmare. "All I could think was to get out of there as fast as I could. I ran up the stone steps two at a time, reached the next level, and immediately had to turn and head up another set. I did this twice, almost shrouded in darkness, with the little monster rushing after me. His growls weren't human. He was indeed a monster."

Momma took a cloth and wiped his brow. She eased onto the bed beside him and wrapped her arms around him.

"Bodi shrieked from the level below, and an army of other hissing cries were moving directly behind him, all coming for me. I hit the double doors after the final set of stairs, knocking them open with a thunderous crash. Free, or so I had thought. The doors opened into the cemetery. The sun hung in the western sky with enough light to keep the vampires from emerging and pursuing me. I slowed my pace and looked back, puffs of white exited my nose and mouth as the harsh cold settled around me. Their fiery eyes glowed in the shadows where the sun couldn't reach. I read their anger. I felt their bloodlust and sensed how badly they wanted to kill me. The sun was there with what should have been a few more hours for me to get farther away. Then snowflakes drifted around me."

"The blizzard," I said.

He nodded. "The band of gray clouds moved swiftly, sunlight rapidly fading. I ran. It hurt my lungs, but I forced myself to keep going. Heading through the alley, I found a discarded shirt and coat in a pile of garbage. Probably left for the derelicts, but the alley was empty of people. I imagine everyone was hidden anywhere they could find warmth. I grabbed the clothes and put them on while I ran, thankful the vampires had never removed my slacks and boots.

"I paused midway down another alleyway to catch my breath. I was weak from the loss of blood, and the cold brought chills and aches unlike any I'd known before. Daylight had dimmed, but it was still bright enough that I didn't fear encountering my bloodthirsty pursuers. Once I caught my breath, I hurried and took a shortcut across the park to get to our forest path. But heavier wet snow fell, and was piling fast. My boots slipped on the ground and prevented me from keeping enough traction to run. Never had I witnessed a snowstorm like this one."

I nodded. The storm had blanketed the forest within a few minutes and didn't stop during the night.

Father closed his eyes and sighed. I almost expected him to stop talking, but he seemed determined to disclose the events, perhaps to strengthen his resolve by expounding upon his strong will to survive. Being alive signified that he had won his battle with Baron Randolph, for now, at least.

He continued, "At the edge of the park, the land slopes sharply. Without a natural trail, it's difficult to move. I slipped and fell several times because the building snow deceived me. It had buried holes, loose rocks, and jagged tree branches, making it impossible to know where to safely step.

"At one point, I fell into a narrow groove that was a runoff ditch whenever we have heavy rains. I grabbed a tree branch and pulled myself up. The overcast skies had shut out any remnants of the sun. Nightfall was still an hour or so away, but the full sky was dark. I looked back toward the park, and I saw him."

I frowned. "Who? Baron Randolph or Bodi?"

"Randolph." The expression that swept over Father's face was that of pure fear, and even now, safe inside our cottage, the power of the baron gripped him.

"You can tell me the rest later," I said. "Get some rest."

He shook his head. "No, son, you need to know what we're dealing with. The baron has power unlike any vampire I've ever faced."

"You've killed six vampires, right?" I asked.

"Six. And all of them together wouldn't equal the baron's strength."

"The six you killed. Did you kill them individually or all together?"

"Each separately. I don't have the gift like you, so I'd never put myself against more than one of them at a time. That's why I ran out of the lair."

"That's a wise decision for anyone," I replied. "No shame in that."

My father grinned and then laughed.

"What?"

"In time, son," he replied. "You'll see, in time."

"What exactly shall I see?"

"The power that will bless you. All I do is try to help eliminate the vampire population, but I'll never be remembered as one that made a phenomenal difference in thinning their numbers. There's the strong chance that you might. You're young but already formidable."

I never understood how that was a trait anyone coveted. I wanted to present myself as a giant with a tender caring heart. But I was still young. I had no knowledge of how killing vampires weighed upon the mind and soul. Of course, these undead were vile creatures and a plague that deserved to be eradicated, but it still took quite a lot to drive a stake through something's heart. A lifetime of killing them could eventually lead someone to become cold and indifferent to the world. Merriment shouldn't become a correlation for killing the undead. Anyone that took delight in such violent acts probably had psychological problems they had left unchecked. Jacques and my father both had told me that I was going to be renowned for my bestowed duties and feared by the undead. In theory it sounded like a wonderful reputation. But over time, the reality unveiled itself as a solitary life constantly moving from city to city.

I acquiesced with a slight nod toward him. How else did you really reply to such a statement made by your father? He esteemed what I was to become. I still was uncertain about it. By saying more I could enact a hidden jealousy on his part, causing a rift between us.

My silence was an invitation for him to continue.

"The baron stood several hundred yards away," he said. "He stood at the edge of the park beneath a towering tree. An instant later, he was on the slope standing face-to-face with me. No footprints were on the snow behind him. He was . . . just there. A sudden shout escaped me and I toppled backwards, falling into the rough snow-covered gulley. A branch snapped beneath my weight, its sharp jagged end protruding from the snow near my waist. I gripped it in my hand."

"Did he not say *anything*?" I asked.

"No. Not then. Holding the sharp stick, I scooted backwards, hoping to slide down the slope outside of his reach. He smiled, revealing his fangs. His eyes were demon-like and red. Bramble thorns clawed at my coat, and my struggle to get away opened the lacerations on my stomach. A thin line of blood seeped through the thin shirt, drawing his hunger. His eyes flicked toward the blood. He went for my throat before I could stop him.

"There were two sharp pricks, a moment of pain, and then forceful suction. I almost froze, but I remembered the stick. I rammed the stick into his gut. I had no way to strike his heart. How I wished I had. But the stick went deep. He reared back and pulled away. The stick protruded from his side. I rolled over and pulled myself down the gulley with my knees and elbows until harsh pain radiated in my left leg. I roared in pain and rolled. I looked to see him swing his cane above his head and then he thrashed my right leg. I felt the snap and the pain was too much."

Momma closed her eyes and covered her mouth.

"How did you get away from him?" I asked.

He shrugged. "I awakened a short time later. Snow caked over me like a thin blanket. My legs throbbed with pain. I glanced around and couldn't find him. I wished the wood had found his heart. I pulled myself down the sloped gulley. The trees grew thicker, so I knew I was almost home. I expected at any time, the baron would appear and finish me. Like I feared, he stood directly in my path."

My father took a deep breath and caressed Momma's hair with his hand as she laid her head against his chest. "He clutched me by the throat, bit his wrist, and filled my mouth with his blood. I tried to spit it out, but he forced his wrist harder to my mouth. I gagged. It was horrible. With little effort he flung me through the air, down the slope, and I awakened later. Numb from the cold, I hardly remember further pain, and faintly remember knocking on our cottage door."

His face appeared aged, reliving the event. He no longer held the boldness that had always overshadowed him. He was vividly weakened by his fear.

"Since he came to our home looking for you," I said, "it seems that he must have thought you dead after he tossed you down the hillside."

Father nodded. "By all accounts, son, I should have been dead."

I rose to my feet and kissed the top of his head. "The important thing, Father, is that you're not. Get some sleep. I'll tend the fire and gather a few pails of snow to melt."

He smiled and pointed a finger. "You're a good son, Forrest. Don't forget about keeping the stake on you during the night."

"I won't."

"Might be wise to take it whenever you go outdoors."

"It's not nightfall, yet," I replied.

"It's always nightfall somewhere, Forrest, especially when you close your eyes."

CHAPTER 10

nother three weeks passed before Momma and I helped my father to the edge of the bed so he could stand for the first time since Jacques had set the bones and she had bound his legs. He had endured five weeks of being bedridden and had nagged us the entire previous week to let him get out of bed. My mother remained adamant, refusing to allow him to get up.

Needless to say, the cottage was filled with their constant bickering—him wanting to get up and her insistent refusal to let him. I spent a lot of time outdoors cutting wood, hunting, and thinking.

After Father had given us the details of how the baron had nearly killed him, I didn't bother asking for the conclusion of what Jacques had told me about Father becoming a vampire hunter. I could wait. There were other subjects I also wished to discuss, but his aggravation of being stuck inside the cottage didn't put him in the best of moods. Whenever his patience was shortened, one didn't seek conversation with him. Avoidance was best.

While tending to my outdoor chores, I thought about Bodi quite often. I brooded about him actually. It troubled me that a child had been turned into a vampire. Someone my own age. He was trapped inside a child's body, growing in age and wisdom, but robbed of everything a normal person experienced during adolescence and early adulthood. He'd never experience such things. Being turned into a vampire was unfair for anyone, but for a small child that had looked more like a toddler, that was a horrible fate for someone to endure.

Although I had befriended Bodi when I first enrolled in school, his inner turmoil had already blossomed before we met. His inner pain was coiled tightly, awaiting its opportunity to be released. He had felt helpless, defenseless, and ignored and didn't have any way to enact upon it. His imagination must have constantly entertained horrible things to happen to those who had mistreated him and set an unprecedented need inside his mind to gain the gratification of watching his enemies suffer agonizing deaths. Becoming a vampire had given him the power to recompense evil to them for their misdeeds. He needed to be stopped before he killed any more children, which unfortunately meant that he needed to be killed. There wasn't any other choice. Otherwise, his urges to inflict pain steadily increased like an insatiable appetite, and I suspected his brutality would evolve into bloody mutilations that no one had ever witnessed before. I never mentioned my thoughts about Bodi to my father or mother, though. Neither would have been pleased by my conclusions.

I didn't struggle with the decision like my father had. I knew what happened if Bodi continued his undead existence. But my intent wasn't to go after him. Not directly. Not unless it became absolutely necessary, and no other alternative could be found. What I wanted was the master, or at the least, the one who had turned Bodi. Killing the one responsible for turning him should destroy Bodi, too.

At least that was what I had interpreted from my conversation with Jacques. He had implied that the dagger allowed me to control the master, and if I killed the master, his offspring died as well. Did that occur *only* when you killed a genuine master? What if one of his offspring created a new vampire and you killed that vampire's chosen? Did that also kill the new vampire? These were questions for which I needed answers. I needed to understand the hierarchy and its limitations.

By trial and error I eventually learned the truth.

I didn't know who had turned Bodi, and it was my hope that if I killed the vampire responsible, Bodi crumbled to dust as well. That way, I didn't personally need to stake Bodi. But things never worked exactly how one hoped.

Momma and I helped my father to his feet. With his arms draped across our shoulders, he minimized the amount of weight he pressed down with and gradually increased it until all he needed from us was balance.

"How do your legs feel?" I asked.

"Weak. A bit sore. Hold onto me and help me across the room."

He gripped my arm tightly. His first few steps were staggered and slow. He walked better than I had anticipated, especially since he had gained weight. Color had returned to his face. All he needed was to build up the strength in his thin legs, and he had his freedom to get out of the cottage again, which would probably be an even greater blessing for my mother.

Father grinned. "A couple of days hobbling around the cottage, and I'll be ready to head outdoors for fresh air."

I nodded.

"As soon as I'm able, you know what you and I shall do?" he asked.

Giving a slight shrug, I replied, "No, but I'm guessing you'll tell me."

"We'll visit our neighbor Fane and barter with him to give us a ride in his wagon."

I frowned. "To where?"

He pointed and shook his finger toward the ceiling. "Ah, we must have an expert craft you a hunter's box. You'll need holy water as well, which requires us to visit a priest."

"A *priest?*" The word was foreign to me and made me uncomfortable. Why exactly? I wasn't certain.

"Certainly," he replied. "Who else can bless the water?"

"It's a religion that we are not associated with, Father."

"So?"

"Doesn't that make a difference?"

He frowned at me. "How? In what way?"

I shrugged. "It's not important."

A cross. Holy water. Their book. These things and what they represented were foreign to me. How could you properly use them, when your faith abided in different rituals? These relics seemed essential to my father. But yet, other than securing vials of holy water, he had never graced a cathedral door to my knowledge. Seemed to me that you needed to have faith tied to the relics before they properly worked. Our ancestors came from the Old Believers, rebelling against the Orthodox, and essentially, my elders had turned from any type of organized religion due to its strict control and assertiveness. They had reverted back to paganism. At eight years of age, I had not been exposed to anything other than watching my mother gather herbs, ritually read her worn Tarot cards each night, and she often gazed at the stars. We were modest people, and until going through my father's hunter box, I had never suspected we had any cathedral symbols within our home. Had my father converted to this religion without our knowledge? I didn't know. For me to become a vampire hunter, was it expected of me as well? I hoped not.

"Blessed salt," he muttered. "You'll need that too."

I thought about the burnt cross outline on my father's chest, and the one he said Bodi bore on his cheek. Obvious power had caused the heat that burned him and Bodi. How and why?

The blessed conflicted against the eternally damned came to mind. At least that was in the legends. Although we had gone to school to learn, children were given to superstitions about the supernatural. Being in the country where these creatures stalked the night, how could we not whisper our fears to one another? We sought knowledge that could protect us. Strangely, Bodi had become what we feared the most.

My father busied himself sorting through his hunter box. I couldn't help but to think his former suggestion was accurate. I did need outside training. Someone experienced with my particular calling and not self-proclaimed. Only then would my understanding be enlightened, and I'd have the proper guidance.

CHAPTER 11

One week later, my father and I visited Fane. By chance Fane happened to be taking his small wagon into the city and absolutely refused to accept Father's monetary offer.

With a fierce frown, Fane shook his head and waved his hands. "I'll not have it, John! Your money's no good here. I'm heading to the city. You and your son are quite welcome to ride along. For free, mind you!"

My father shook his head, insistent. He held up animal hides. "What about these?"

The hides were mine from all of the game I'd hunted during the winter months while Father was recuperating.

"I'll not have your money or your hides, but instead, you two help me load and unload my wagon, and I'll consider that payment enough."

"Deal!" my father said, shaking hands with Fane. Afterwards, my father set his hat upon the driver's bench while he helped load the wagon.

Fane grinned apologetically toward me. "My back's not what it used to be."

I liked old Fane. Most of the time he wore a gray wool hat atop his head every time I had seen him. His hair had oddly receded and looked like those strange men that wore brown robes and wandered into

Bucharest every now and again. He had a short circle of hair with a bald spot on the top of his crown. Theirs was intentionally cut that way. Fane was cursed with it by nature. Monks—I later learned these men were called—were a party to which Fane didn't reside.

Fane was also quite plump and jolly. Like us, he rented little property, but he was fortunate enough to own an old horse and wagon.

I helped him load his wares into the back of the crude wagon. My father lifted lighter baskets and crates, hobbling slowly and wincing occasionally.

"You okay, John?" Fane asked. "You look to be in pain."

"I'm fine. Just old and stiff." He was walking, at least, but it was doubtful that he'd ever have full mobility he once had before his legs had been shattered. Whether he wished to accept it or not, I didn't see his vampire hunting days lasting too much longer.

I lofted an empty wooden barrel onto my shoulder that Fane had been slowly rolling along its edge.

He smiled at me and then looked to my father. "Your son has grown like an ox and has the strength of a bear. How ever do you feed him?"

My father chuckled. "The boy holds his own. He's become a great hunter and quite accurate with a rifle. He keeps meat in our pot."

Fane made a strange face in jest. "No wonder the wildlife is growing scarce in our neck of the forest. He must keep a hearty appetite."

"Indeed," my father said with a wide grin.

"How old is he now? Twelve, fourteen?"

"Eight," my father replied with a great sense of pride, almost like I was a prized heifer or bull.

Fane's brow rose. "Oh, surely you jest."

Father shook his head and placed his hand over his heart.

"My word," Fane said. "So young and already the size of a man. I imagine he eases your labors. And I dare say that he could probably pull my wagon faster than the old mare, eh?"

I smiled and shook my head. In a weird sort of way, such comments brought a sense of pride to me, and made me work harder and faster.

We finished helping Fane load his wagon. My father rode on the seat beside him while I rode on the tail end of the wagon, sitting on the edge, letting my feet dangle above the compacted dirt trail.

My father hadn't taken his hunter box along, but each of us concealed a wooden stake inside our coats. We had no intention of being outdoors after dark. The sun had barely risen by the time we had reached Fane's cottage.

Fane directed his horse and soon we were passing our cottage on the way to Bucharest. Smoke drifted out of the chimney and snaked a thin path through the trees.

All of the snow had melted. Winter had gone and the cold spring had arrived. Little sprigs of grass protruded in places at the edges of the road. Crocus flowers bloomed, giving color to an otherwise dull brown forest floor. Bits of blue lichens and green moss clung to the sides of the trees and twisted roots. My mind absorbed these delicate colors while I thought about other things.

During the entire time my father had been healing, never once had the baron revisited. No vampires had attempted any attacks on my family at all. Perhaps the baron had given up his pursuit to kill my father or me? I doubted so, but at the time, I still didn't know if the two hunters had been successful in killing him. But they had never returned for further information about Jacques, so I concluded they had either failed miserably or fled into a neighboring country, ashamed of their cowardice.

Jacques had not returned, either. I sorely missed him, even though I didn't really know him. He was one of those people, that upon first meeting, you felt like you had known all of your life and hated to see his departure. So many things I wished to discuss with him, especially the puzzlement of the *holy* relics Father carried and insisted were tools a vampire hunter needed.

My young mind reserved doubts about any intrusive religion being forced upon the civilizations around the world. One either accepted the proposed faith or was butchered as an infidel. More strife and wars were caused by the feuding religions than the eternal peace they offered for succumbing to them. Bucharest had already experienced such hostilities and the oppression indicated another uprising would eventually occur.

After a quarter hour of traveling, the towering buildings became visible above the treetops. Although walking wasn't terribly faster than a horse drawn wagon, it allowed the luxury of taking in the scenery. It also permitted a person extra time to think.

Fane and my father discussed various subjects while we rode, mostly about the harsh blizzard and his rapid depletion of supplies. By the time the horse stepped onto the cobblestone, Fane asked my father something that troubled me.

"You don't keep any animals, do you John?" he asked.

Father shook his head. "No, why?"

"During the severity of the period when we were snowbound, I lost three of my hens, two goats, and one sheep."

"That happens in severe weather."

Fane shook his head. "No, I don't mean that they froze to death. They were bled dry."

I looked over my shoulder toward them.

Father couldn't hide his astonishment. "In what way?"

"Puncture wounds at the throat on the goats and sheep. The hens were decapitated."

"What did the puncture wounds look like?"

"Two holes side by side. I've never seen anything like it before. I've not ever given credence to the old wives' tales, but if I did, I'd think a vampire. Silly notion, eh? But I know of no natural predator that could leave such marks."

My mind raced. That would have happened a little over a month earlier, not too long after the baron had made his appearance and threat known to me. I faithfully watched our cottage door on a nightly basis without ever a vampire rattling at the door.

"Perhaps a mink?" my father suggested.

Fane craned his head to the side, thinking. Slowly he nodded. "Perhaps on the chickens, but not with the goats and the sheep. The height and all."

"I see your point," Father replied. "Was that all in one night or scattered across several days?"

"All at once."

"And since?"

Fane shook his head. "Not lost another. The hens can be replaced quite readily once the temperature warms enough for the remaining ones to set on eggs, but those were my only two goats and the sheep I needed its wool. I'll have to replace them. All in due time, I suppose."

"Should it occur again, don't hesitate to call upon me. I'd like to have a look if you don't mind."

"Of course. But I'm hoping never to see such ever again."

Father nodded. "You and I both. Horrible to think something travels in the darkness of our woods at night, capable of such a thing."

"Since you have no livestock, you have less to fear," Fane said with a grim smile.

"Alas, you're right."

The horse's hooves clapped upon the cobblestone. Other people milled along the street and traders were gathering near the square. Since the weather stood to be warmer and dry, hundreds of people cluttered the city—shopping, trading, and gossiping. Military guards marched in small bands, as a threat to keep peace in the city.

Fane pointed. "I'm going to the marketplace first. Is there anywhere you wish to be taken?"

"Here is fine," my father said. "Thanks for your kindness."

"Oh, no trouble at all. Leave your hides with me. I'll sell them for you."

"Thanks, Fane," I said, pushing myself from the back of the wagon.

He nodded. "How long were you two intending to be in the city?"

"A few hours," my father replied.

"You should find me parked near Dyre's Tavern. Come inside and have a drink with me before we return to our homes."

My father straightened his sheepskin hat. "Look forward to it."

Fane nodded, snapped his whip, and rode toward the market square.

Father smiled at me. "Forrest, we need to find you a hat since you pass for a grown man, so you'll look more proper."

"I doubt they'll have one that fits me." My brown hair spilled down to my shoulders in thick curled locks. In spite of its length, it wasn't ragged or uncomely. My mother kept the ends trimmed on a regular basis, but since she liked my curls, she never cut it short.

"We shall look. Every man of importance wears a hat."

Glancing around, I didn't see a man or a lady *without* a hat. Even the peasants poorer than we, wore hats. Children, too. My father had given me one of his about a year earlier. I could no longer pull it over my crown. I had grown quickly. I knew we couldn't afford to find one my size, so I had never said anything.

"Where to first?" I asked.

He glanced around and whispered, "To get you a hunter's box."

"Is it nearby?"

"It's a place hidden on the outskirts of the city. We must remain inconspicuous because the shop where we're headed is owned by people shunned by a majority of the city."

I didn't say anything. I simply nodded. He seemed more uncomfortable about us being seen entering the shop and associating with the people who suffered ridicule and were deemed outcasts rather than having any sympathy for them. After all, he was seeking these shop owners to construct my box to store vampire-hunting tools. Why be worried about what the outsiders thought about them? His fear was hypocritical. I didn't understand why he felt that way.

Over a period of several decades, I came to discover that I trusted the subjugated and persecuted folks far greater than the people who had oppressed and herded them into settling the wastelands where no one else wanted to reside. Those in higher authorities tended to be deceitful and abusive with their power and position. The baron certainly came to mind as someone who had made his gains from taking advantage of the downtrodden. But other vampires, like the baron, were hidden right out in the open, without being suspected for what they truly were. They had obtained high places of authority in the most unexpected places. If ever unveiled, a panic would ensue.

To get to this shop, we walked through several intersecting alleyways in the city. The architecture became less glamorous. Gradually, we moved into an even more depressing area where the buildings had suffered severe damage during the Great War. The buildings stood in disarray. The interiors of some were burned out with only the brick walls precariously holding the outside structure erect. And yet, poor unfortunate families chose to risk their lives beneath possible collapse than to suffer and die from exposure.

Children with tattered clothes and dirty faces peered from the hollowed buildings. Hunger burned in their eyes. Others coughed pathetically, sick with disease. Mothers held sorrow in their hopeless expressions while desperate men dug and scavenged for bits of food through the piles of garbage the city sanitation had dumped in the street.

While I looked at these poor people, I had never known such destitute places existed. None of the children left the buildings. They skeptically watched us in fear. The men ignored us; too busy searching through the trash.

"Don't stare, Forrest. Just keep walking."

I hadn't realized I was staring, but it was too horrific to look away. For a moment, I glanced over my shoulder to see the cathedral looming a few blocks away. The morning sun gleamed off the stained glass windows. I looked again at the poor people starving to death so close to one of the most ornamental buildings in the city, and I wondered how they viewed the supposed beacon of hope.

I watched the dirty street as I walked, avoiding the temptation to continue looking at the rundown buildings and the hungry people. The rotten stench of death flowed with the morning breeze. The ripe scent was strong, indicating that something big was dead; or quite possibly, a lot of people were. The smell was thick. I pressed closely behind my father.

But then he stopped walking. We heard her wailing cries. The anguish in her voice wasn't something either of us could ignore. We turned.

A woman stumbled outside of a narrow doorway with a young boy in her arms. His body was limp. His arms and legs draped downward like wilted flower petals. He was obviously dead. But he hadn't died from hunger or disease. On his neck were two fresh bleeding holes. A vampire's bite.

"Forrest," Father said, "let's hurry and get out of here."

Panic rose in his voice. It was broad daylight with few shadows and no clouds in the sky. It wasn't even close to noon. I didn't see how it was possible for any vampires to be out until I glanced into the next building. Deeper in the dark shadowed recesses, glowing eyes watched us.

Dozens of sets of eyes set their attention upon us. Their eyes reflected in the light much like a wolf's did in the glow of a bright lantern at night. These people were no longer human, but undead vampires. Their hunger was visible, and their hatred toward us evident. The unfortunate weren't like us. We were strong contenders, their enemies, and a threat to their existence.

This impoverished area was a vast feeding ground for vampires.

The sunlight didn't reach far enough inside the building to affect them. Between them and the open door was a pile of dead bodies. A moving mass crawled on the corpses. Beady red eyes looked at us.

Rats. Dozens of them.

"This isn't the lair where the baron had taken you, is it?" I asked, picking up pace to catch my father who was moving much faster than I thought possible, given his stiffened legs.

"No."

"There are at least a dozen vampires back there."

He nodded. "Probably a lot more than that, son. It's a different lair."

"Is there not anything we can do to help those children?" I asked with anger rising in my voice.

"Just the two of us?"

"Yes."

Father shook his head. "You don't have the experience, and there are far too many for us to fight even if you were a seasoned hunter."

"And none of the city's officials are willing to exterminate these vampires?"

"Why should they?" he asked.

"Because hundreds of these people are potential victims."

"The magistrate knows it. The cathedral priests probably know it, too. They won't do anything because these are people they don't want in Romania anyway. They're fodder. This satiates the vampires and keeps them from moving into the renovated part of the city where the businesses and bank are."

If this was a separate lair from the baron's, I wondered who the master was. The notion that the city officials thought they were safe by allowing these vampires to feast upon the poor discarded vagabonds was preposterous. The vampires didn't have to drain these people completely to feed. Left unchecked, this lair could immensely multiply their numbers to form a vast army and completely annihilate the city. Even as a child I realized the potential danger the city faced while the council did not.

Sadly, in some ways, the ones the vampires chose to kill were better off. They suffered no more from the aches of starvation, but it still wasn't right. There was a greater chance the vampires eventually turned them than destroyed them.

My father panted and groaned, trying to force his legs to run when he no longer possessed such ability. He wasn't moving from fear, as the vampires weren't about to step into the sun to pursue us. I believed he was still trying to protect my innocence. He was being a father, and although I appreciated it, it made no real difference. In passing the building with the peering vampires eyes, the unfortunate child in his mother's arms, Bodi, and the baron, I didn't have any remaining innocence left for him to preserve. It was too late. The mental scarring was inevitable, and I had already been exposed to the madness. I knew what was out there. I understood the dangers. All I needed was training and experience. Turning back wasn't possible.

"Slow down," I said, placing a hand on his shoulder. "You're going to hurt yourself. It's daylight. They're not going to attack us."

"It's not them I'm worried about."

"Then what?"

"The rats. A master has control over certain animals. I just wanted to make certain we got far enough away so the rats didn't swarm after us."

I glanced back. "They're not coming. It's okay to slow down."

Father stopped, leaning forward with his hands on his knees to catch his breath. He gasped and panted and wheezed. I was amazed by how many city blocks he had moved at such a rapid pace. After a couple of minutes he looked at me with hurt in his eyes.

"Forrest," he said, wiping drool from his mouth with the back of his hand. He stood, took a deep breath, and pointed back in the direction we had come. "That's why I didn't want to start your training. It's the disturbing things like that. When you're still just a boy—"

I smiled and nodded. "I know you wish to protect me, but you can't do that forever. In size I'm a man. My mind might be eight years old, but with each passing day it's catching up. In many ways, my mind has probably aged twenty years since the night the baron arrived at our cottage. With everything I've seen during the past month, did you ever consider that perhaps there's every reason for my training to begin? I know it isn't a coincidence for all of these events to occur for my benefit, and by now, I'm certain you agree."

Father stared at me for a few moments. He grinned and nodded. "Come on, there will be no further excuses or delays on my part."

CHAPTER 12

The road ascended from the slums into another section of the city where restoration had hidden most of the war's former scars. At first, it didn't dawn on me, but later I realized my father's underhanded craftiness. He had deliberately led me through the poverty-stricken section of Bucharest. He knew the vampire lair was there, and we could have completely bypassed it, never setting a foot outside of the renovated sections of the city.

I suppose he had been testing me to see exactly how I'd react and whether I'd retreat. My first inclination after seeing the appalling setup was sheer anger. I wanted to find a way to rescue the poor innocent people, but we lacked the numbers to attack and I lacked the experience. I'd never deny that, and it was all the more reason to start my training.

By nature I've never been squeamish, so the dead bodies didn't sicken me. What was occurring in the slums, however, shocked and repulsed me. I never imagined how cruel some city magistrates were, and that they were content doing nothing to rescue these unfortunate people.

We moved not as quickly as before but at a decent pace. My father was limping. Every step he took made him wince and gasp. I didn't know how much longer he could walk without sitting down to rest.

He leaned against the side of a building and nodded toward the street ahead. "The shop is the third building down. A set of steps leads down."

Along this narrow street men and women walked. No horse-drawn carts, but a few men on horseback were spread out amongst the modest pedestrians. I waited until my father regained his strength before heading toward the stairs.

Young men and women with painted clown faces stood close to the shop stairs entertaining children. Not certain why, but these individuals made me uncomfortable. Perhaps because I didn't know what their faces actually looked like. None of them approached me, but it might have been due to the natural frowning glare on my face. It was probably in their best interests to keep their distance.

The young ladies painted animal features on the children's faces and two young men juggled. Several others addressed passersby, offering to read their palms and tell their fortunes. Most declined, while a select few were unable to overcome their curiosity and offered their hands.

It took only a few moments for me to notice quick hands looting billfolds and jewelry from their unsuspecting victims. Slight of hand. The onlookers were losing small fortunes to the cunning performers who were masters of misdirection and not privy to any supernatural knowledge. I'm not certain how I had been given that insight because I had never watched any tricks like these, but I noticed each person that was robbed.

"Keep a watch on any of your valuables," I whispered to my father.

We kept our backs toward the building's edge until we reached the cracked stairs. Father walked down the steps and stopped at the door. I stood behind him, but kept my attention toward the entertainers.

A purple silk curtain hung on the inside of the window, preventing anyone from peeking through the glass. No other windows were along the wall. My father turned the wrought iron doorknob and eased the door inward.

A loud squawk pierced my ears and paused my advance across the threshold. Lit lanterns hung on various posts inside the rectangular room. Candles flickered on draped tables and countertops. In spite of the flames, the overall shop was dim.

The air smelled of jasmine, rose, and other delicate perfumes, which made me think of my mother. She'd have enjoyed coming inside the shop with us. Seldom, though, did she ever venture into the city. Crowds made her uncomfortable. I thought, if I'd had money on me, that I'd have picked her up something fragrant to bring back as a gift. Of course, Fane had promised to sell the hides, but after he gave me the money, I'd have to walk all the way back. He'd never wait long enough for me to return to the shop and back to the tavern, even if I ran the entire way.

Father gripped my forearm and pulled me inside the shop, promptly closing the door behind me. The bird squawked again from inside a large cage several feet away. It was the most magnificent creature I had ever seen. Feathers of deep green, bright red, blue, and yellow decorated this marvelous bird. Its curved black beak clamped down on a metal wire of the cage wall. The harsh sound it had made seemed much louder than possible for an animal of this size. I was enthralled.

"Like the bird, do you?" a young lady asked, sitting in the shadows where I had not noticed her.

She was dressed in a long frilly dress, purple, with a black corset that tied in front beneath modest breasts. She held an extended decorated fan in her right hand, hiding the lower part of her face. Even in the shadows, her eyes were the most beautiful blue, almost glowing and warm, unlike the icy shimmer they displayed. Her long red hair hung in neat spiraling curls. Her pale skin was nearly ivory in color but speckled with countless reddish-brown freckles. To me, her beauty was unlike anyone I had passed along the streets of Bucharest. I stood, stunned, staring at her, admiring everything about her and found myself quite speechless.

"You like the bird?" she repeated.

I blinked and shook my head. Swallowing hard, I glanced away from her, back to the bird, and back to her once more. Her rare beauty drew my continued gaze like a magnet. "Yes, beautiful. Quite beautiful."

Her eyes brightened at my compliment, which she believed was directed at her; and I had intended it for her, although I hadn't meant to say it aloud. It was one of those moments when the mouth spoke before the brain bid it not to, not that a young beautiful lady didn't deserve to be complimented. She did. But I was too young to understand the nature of flirting, and this was purely unintentional on my part.

She fluttered her eyelashes, lowered the fan, and smiled broadly, revealing her delicate nose and cute dimpled chin. Her lips were narrow and painted light pink, revealing the full beauty she bestowed.

Flustered, I sought to find something else to turn my attention toward since fleeing out the door or turning invisible were options unavailable. So, I turned and reached toward the birdcage.

"I wouldn't put a finger any closer to him," she said. "Beak's like a barber's razor."

I lowered my hand and slipped it into my pocket. I had no idea why I was so nervous. My hands were sweaty. I felt heat rising around my neck and was certain my face had flushed red. Looking around, I noticed my father had stepped into the adjoining room of the shop, occasionally watching me out of the corner of his eye and grinning while he looked at some long candles.

"Where does a bird like this come from?" I asked, afraid to gaze back into her eyes. Looking into them had made me uneasy, not in a bad way, but I didn't understand the reason behind my discomfort or why I felt strange being near her. It was almost as if she'd bewitched me with a spell.

"My father traded for it from a man that had done an expedition in South America. It's a parrot."

Her voice was soft and throaty. Her accent was much different than others I'd spoken with, even different from the two Britain hunters. I liked her accent though and the odd way that she pronounced some of her words. It was something I could listen to for days on end, in spite of my nervousness.

Not certain what else to do, as I was mentally too young and naïve to understand infatuation and the power it holds when struck by imme-diate attraction to another person, I started to back away.

She stood and walked closer to me.

I quaked inside. I had stood my ground against a master vampire, and yet, I wanted to bolt from this beautiful young lady. I didn't understand, and my father was getting farther away in the neighboring room.

"Seems a bit odd, a husky man like yourself coming into a candle shop with all sorts of potpourri and perfumes. You sure you're in the right place?"

I nodded. For the first time I felt like being a child inside of a man's body was a curse. I didn't know how to act and wasn't certain what to say. I nodded but didn't dare gaze into her eyes.

"That old man? Is he your father?"

"Yes," I said softly, like the small child I was inside.

"What's your name?" she asked.

"Forrest."

"My name's Roisin, but I prefer Rose," she said with a smile before covering her mouth with the edge of the fan.

"It's nice meeting you," I stammered.

"You're awfully quiet and shy to be so big. But it's not a bad thing. Most lugs your size act like brutes and are all about toughness and intimidation."

I shrugged.

"We also do fortune telling here, but not like those peddlers out on the streets. We're not into robbing people, and I'm actually quite good at reading fortunes. I'd be happy to tell yours while you wait on your father."

I looked down. "I don't have any money with me."

"I'll do it for free," she said, taking my hand and leading me back to the little table where she had been sitting. "You sit in that chair."

I sat down. Plopped down, actually. She took a lit lantern from its hanging nail on a post and set it on the table. She took my hand again.

"You have huge mitts, you have."

I gave her a confused expression, not understanding the translation.

"Hands. You hands are *huge*."

I nodded. "Where are you from?"

"Ireland."

"What brought you here?"

"According to my father, opportunity," she said, gently holding my hand inside both of hers. "Between you and I, I've never seen it. Nothing has captured my interest in this city, until today."

She ran her index finger down the center of my palm, which made a strange tickling sensation through my hand and partway up my arm. I liked her holding my hand but didn't understand *why* I did. The more she talked, the more I began to believe that she was in her late teenage years. She rambled somewhat urgently, like she was trying to keep my attention.

For a few moments, she traced the lines on my palm, lines I never really thought about until she placed emphasis upon them. She frowned and chewed her lower lip. I could see the confusion in her eyes.

"Something wrong?" I asked.

She frowned, tightening her brow even more.

I tugged to pull my hand free of hers.

She held tightly and shook her head. "No, I'm not finished looking at it."

"You looked confused."

"That's because I am," she replied, cocking a skeptical brow at me and quickly looking at the lines on my hand again.

"Why? Is something wrong?"

"Not *wrong*, but quite . . . *different*. First set of lines I've ever seen like this, which is why I'd like to study them a bit longer. That is, unless you *mind* me holding your hand?"

I shook my head and blushed. "No, not at all."

A broad smile spread across her cute lips. Her eyes peered into mine. "Your lifeline is incredibly long, but there are other things about you that don't seem right."

I fed upon her every word. The flow of her accent and the way she said the words, held me spellbound, without any magic. "Like what?"

"Well, I understand why you're so quiet. You're a deep thinker, using your logic. That's what this line details. And . . . you'll be a man who will serve your life doing great services for others. Are you a religious man?" she asked.

"No." I bit the word with a quick breath. My brow formed a brief tight frown.

"Hmm. Not a priest."

I shook my head.

"That's *not* a bad thing," she said, teasing. She adjusted herself in her seat while holding fast to my hand. "Priests don't marry."

She seemed relieved for a moment.

Rose shook her head a few seconds later. "You sure you're not a priest?"

"No, why?" If she only understood my thoughts and feelings about the cathedral . . . I could explain that, but I was certain she'd not like my assumptions.

"Your marriage line and heart line are almost invisible," she said. "Sort of like a priest's. At least that's how I'd imagine a priest's lines to be. A priest would never oblige me to do a reading. They consider mediums as hands of the devil."

"What does it mean for those lines to be short?"

"You probably won't seek any long-term relationships, or any that you do have will be abruptly cut short." She sounded disappointed and released my hand. Her face saddened. "And the remaining things I sense and see, I . . . I don't think I should share them."

"Why not?"

Rose said, "Like I said, I've never encountered lines like yours on another person's hand. And it's best I don't disclose anything more because there's a good chance I might be wrong."

Perhaps since I was feeling more comfortable around her, and her holding my hand had definitely helped, some of my boldness was returning. I wanted to know what she believed she had seen. I needed to know. I had already determined I'd never have a significant other or ever experience what my parents had.

"What else?" I asked, braving a look into her eyes, wishing she'd take my hand into hers again.

"Forrest," she said softly. "I fear what I've read may be wrong. When I look into your eyes, I see purity and innocence, like a child. Your mannerisms are humble, shy, and gentle in spite of your massive size.

But I read a ruthless coldness etched into your palm. I perceive a violent life ahead for you with lots of loss and heartache. It conflicts with what I see sitting across the table from me. It troubles me greatly."

I gave a gentle smile. I wanted to tell her that she was correct and these things she had seen would soon become a constant reality in my life. I had already sensed some of these based upon my own logical reasoning. After all, how could you stake vampires through the heart and not become cold inside. That was a service for others, to protect the innocent, but it created vile enemies, too. Remaining vampires would seek vengeance, and that didn't necessarily mean coming after the hunter. Instead, they'd want to cause mental anguish by slaughtering the ones dear to the hunter's heart.

Rose stood and walked to a shelf. She took an object off of the shelf that was covered with a black square silken cloth. She set it on the table. "Would you mind if I looked further?"

I shrugged.

She frowned. "You don't seem upset about the things I've told you thus far."

"Should I be?"

"I've always been quite accurate."

"Who's to say that you're not now?"

A worried expression came to her face. "And the details don't bother you?"

"It does me no good to worry about the future, does it? There's nothing I could change, but I can be prepared to face it."

"If you knew the certain future, yes, you could do things to avoid the pain. There are always choices and decisions to make. Choosing the correct path in life often takes planning."

I gazed into her eyes. "Sometimes destiny allows no other choices."

"You think such is true for you?"

I sighed and held my hand onto the table palm up. "Did I have any say in how these lines on my hands were formed?"

Rose took my hand, as I hoped she would. "I never looked at it like that."

"You believe in what you read?"

She nodded and squeezed my hand.

"Then I thank you for giving me some insight into what lies ahead of me."

"The things I've mentioned . . . you'd be content living such a life?" she asked with sadness returning in her eyes.

"I cannot change what I've been chosen to do."

She studied my eyes keenly. "You already know something, don't you? There's something you're not telling me."

I shook my head, but I could tell she didn't believe me.

"And what is that exactly? What have you been destined for?" Her eyes beamed with interest at the mystery of my statement.

I looked away. "Probably it's best I don't reveal that."

"You've captured my curiosity, so don't withhold this from me."

I smiled. "We've only met. My secret has no bearing on you."

"All the same, Forrest, I'd like to know. To remove my doubts that I'm right or wrong. Could you not oblige me that much?"

"Perhaps another time?" I said, rising.

"Oh no, sit down!" She squeezed my hand tighter, shaking her head. Her blue eyes were frigid.

Surprised by her abrupt change in attitude, I sat. Besides, she was holding my hand, and I didn't want to pull away. Her hands were tiny compared to mine and quite warm.

"If you're not going to tell me, let me read it for myself." She lifted the black cloth. A clear ball of polished glass rested on a dark cushion.

"Forrest?" my father said, sticking his head through the door from the adjoining room.

I turned and pulled my hand free of Rose's. "Yes, Father?"

"He will see us now."

I smiled at Rose. "Sorry, but this is why I'm here."

"You're here to see my father?" Her eyes grew fearful.

"I suppose so."

She frowned. "For what, exactly?"

I stood.

"Wait," she said, reaching for my hand but I was out of her reach. Looking into the glass ball, she said, "I see something."

"Forrest, come along," Father said, sternly, in a voice I didn't dare ignore.

"Sorry. It's nice meeting you. I do hope we can talk more later."

Her eyes were spellbound upon the ball, like she was seeing something inside the glass. Her interest bore into the shadows; mesmerizing her so intently it was as if I no longer existed.

In a way I was thankful the glass ball had kept her attention when my father had called me away. Had she been looking at me during those few seconds, she'd have seen further evidence about my actual age. My childlike innocence, as she had referred to it, was probably due to my age. But that was fading, and perhaps, it would be gone entirely by the next time I visited this shop.

I hurried to the next room where my father stood waiting. He gave a smile. "Pretty young lady, eh?"

"She is," I agreed with a blush and a slight smile.

"She seems interested in you."

"I'm too young, Father."

"Perhaps, right now," he said. "But there's always the future."

I thought it an odd statement, given that she had been divining my fortune and future. Both seemed bleak, and if the glass ball gave her any further insight, she'd know exactly what I presumed to be true.

"Don't worry, son. Your mind will mature to a better understanding about ladies. There's time ahead in your favor."

I liked his optimism. However, I didn't hold the same hope. I never would.

He gave me a reassuring smile. "There's someone meant for everyone in the world. You simply have to find them. That's the most difficult part."

I doubted his statement. Even before some of the things Rose had revealed to me, I expected to live a lonely life. Tragedy sought me. I didn't intend to ever pull someone else into the agony of my personal life. Perhaps my mind was being overly dramatic about the dismal future I walked toward, but I didn't envision a cheery domestic lifestyle. If I was doomed to live a long life, it wasn't filled with many good things. I'd be alone.

CHAPTER 13

Father led me through the adjoining room and into a narrow hallway. At the end of the hallway, which was eerily dark, a rickety staircase led downward to where there was no light at all. From the top of the stairs there wasn't any way of knowing how far they descended or what they led to.

I looked at my father with uncertainty.

He shrugged with raised eyebrows and extended his hand for me to lead.

Was this some kind of initiation? I wondered.

I took a slightly uneasy breath and headed down. Once enveloped by the shadows, my hand rested upon the hilt of my dagger. I didn't know what lie before us, but if anyone thought it was in good jest to suddenly shout and lunge toward me from down below, the person would be severely injured or dead because I'd take any advance as an attack, regardless. In this darkness, I wasn't about to risk my life or my father's, especially after seeing the brood of vampires in the slums. My father had brought me here for a serious purpose, and it dealt with my fate. I wasn't here to play any games.

The stairs must have led downward two stories. It seemed an unnecessarily long walk. I walked directly into the closed door. My hands slid along the cold metal door for several moments as I searched for a knob or handle. All my hands eventually found was a keyhole.

"You have to knock," my father said in a whisper. "There's no doorknob."

I pounded three times on the door. On the other side of the door, metal scraped sharply, loudly.

At the top of the stairs, Rose said, "Forrest! Wait! Don't go in there. I have some urgent news for you!"

Engulfed inside the darkness, I looked back, trying to see her. The door swung open in an instant, a stern hand grabbed my arm, and yanked me through. My father was pulled through as well.

Before the door slammed closed, Rose made one more frantic shout, "Forrest, no!"

CHAPTER 14

"Rose is an animated one," the man said with a deep voice. He wore a hooded robe and held a lantern in his hand. Other than his lantern, the room was cloaked in darkness, preventing me from seeing his face.

He lowered a long iron slat into its bracket to further secure the door. Then he lowered two more flat iron bars into place. Not only was the door locked, it was braced by three iron slats. It seemed to be quite a lot of reinforcement. My father and I had no quick retreat from this room.

My hand returned to my dagger. Although I didn't feel threatened, I wanted to be prepared, just in case.

I didn't look at the lantern, but I watched the cloaked man in its glow. I had learned by watching the flames in our hearth during the dead of night that once I glanced away, my vision became shadowed by the outline of the bright flame, distorting my view. It was best to watch the target and *not* the light.

"I know what you seek," he said softly. "And I've been expecting you since around two weeks ago."

"Why?"

"Come," he said. "Let's sit for a while."

He turned. My father and I followed the lantern's glow. As he walked, the light revealed shelves filled with old dusty tomes. My interest immediately was drawn to these books full of wisdom. Even though the man had not properly introduced himself, I found myself wishing to spend time with him and delve into his shelved world of knowledge. Few things I ever coveted in life, but books were my foremost desire, far greater than their weight in gold.

He led us to a small table near the center of the room. After we sat down, he lit a long match and walked around, lighting candles set in all four corners of the room. Two of the walls were floor to ceiling bookcases. Another wall had various woodcarving tools on a thick wooden table with saws and chisels hanging on the wall behind the table. An unlit lantern set there as well.

There were no windows, and the room seemed to be at least a couple stories beneath the city, which I thought quite odd. After the sulfur smell of the match faded, another scent dominated. A musty smell permeated the room; a smell that came only from aged tomes.

Once the candlewick flames grew higher, my eyes scanned up and down the rows of books. I must have smiled because after our robed host sat down, he said, "You have a hunger for knowledge, do you?"

"I do."

My eyes continued to roam the shelves. Most of the books didn't have engraved titles on the spines, but those that did indicated the books told of the occult, the dark arts, and the creatures that ruled the night.

"That's good. The greater a man's knowledge, the better equipped he is, inside and out. Such holds true for women as well. My daughter has probably read every volume contained inside this room. Some of them twice. She might fancy your company, should she discover your love for these tomes."

My father said, "I think she already does."

"Does she now?" the man asked. His voice rose with amusement.

My father nodded and opened his mouth to speak.

"Why did you say that you've been expecting me?" I interrupted, before I found myself betrothed.

He waved a hand in the air. "Spirits have spoken to me and told me that a novice vampire hunter has been issued forward. For the past few days, I thought perhaps I had misheard. Has something delayed your arrival?"

I shrugged. "I had no forewarning to come."

"It is I," my father said. He briefly explained the baron's attack and how much time it had taken for my father to heal from his critical injuries.

"Ah," he said. "It seems we have a common foe. Thus, the prompting of your issuance, young man. No matter, I heeded the voice and have already prepared a hunter's box for you."

"May I ask your name," I said. "Or is that a mystery I am forbidden?"

"My apologies," he said. He lowered his hood. His hair was dark, possibly brown or brownish-red, but in the dim lighting, I couldn't be certain. His skin was pale, paler than his daughter's, and there were dark spots on his face. Not freckles. Scars perhaps? His eyes were dark, unlike Rose's, and his face had no facial hair. "I am Roy. We moved here from Ireland after the reconstruction began due to the great famine in our homeland. My wife, Rose's mother, passed away two years ago."

Sadness hollowed his eyes. He rose from his chair and walked to his woodworking table. He grabbed the handle of a wooden box, much like my father's, and heaved it off of the table, returning to us and setting it before us.

The hinges reflected polished silver in the lantern's glow. Two crosses were engraved in little silver squares at the outer edge of the case. Unlike my father's box, this one was constructed out of a dark, rich mahogany. My initials were engraved at the bottom of the case between the hinges. FW.

I glanced at my father. "Did you already give my name to him?"

He shook his head.

"I told you," Roy said. "The spirits informed me. I was given precise instructions on how and what exactly I needed to build for you. Open it."

I stared at the dark box for a few moments, intimidated by what I might discover once I looked inside.

"Go on, son," my father said with a proud smile.

I stood and looked down at the chest. Unlatching the two well-oiled clasps, I rested my fingers at the outer sides of the top half of the box. Warmth welcomed me. Slowly, I lifted the lid. My heartbeat thumped harder inside my chest. Excitement rose inside me, much like the first night when I opened my father's box, but this time the sensation was stronger. The box and its contents were bestowed unto me and whatever Roy had blessed his handiwork with, the power leapt toward me.

The hairs on the back of my neck and my hands stiffened. Chill bumps prickled up my arms and down my back.

"Don't be uneasy about taking anything out," Roy said. "From this day forward the box is yours should you choose to take it."

"I'd rather not disturb the contents just yet, if you don't mind," I replied. I shut the lid and refastened the clasps. I remembered the sensations that had run through me when I held the tools of my father's box. These feelings I didn't wish to undergo until I was alone. I didn't understand why, but I felt like that should be a private moment for me because energy pulsed from the items, almost pleading for me to use them.

"Is there a problem, son?"

"No, sir." I glanced from him to Roy. "What is the price for this?"

My father withdrew his billfold from his vest pocket.

"It is a gift," Roy said. "One that you cannot buy with gold or money."

"This was expensive to fashion," I replied. "As were the stakes inside. You must have spent weeks carving the stakes and properly fitting the box compartments together."

"The time crafting these wasn't a sacrifice, Forrest; not when we're fighting the undead." There was hardness in his gaze and coldness in his voice. "You've been predestined to kill the vampires, and I am a handworker crafting the proper tools as I have been instructed. Consider this a gift, a token, for what I pray will protect your life while you eradicate the cursed undead."

"I cannot take these for free."

"My daughter," he said, clasping his spotted hands together while resting his elbows on the table. "She's exceptional at reading the cards and telling fortunes. There is a strict tradition for those who master reading the cards. Someone gifts a deck of cards to you, usually handed down by a parent, aunt, or a close relative. You don't buy a set. Rose received her mother's cards when her mother died. We believe that a bit of the person's former power remains with the cards, even after death, and unseen guidance provides additional aid in telling a new generation's fortune."

"Are you also a hunter?" I asked.

Roy shook his head.

"Then I do not understand how your comparison relates."

"Quite simply, I have been given an ability to fashion killing tools. Since you didn't handle or examine any of the box's contents, there's no way that you noticed the carved symbols I've delicately engraved in the stakes, nor did you see the other magical rune markers from a long dead culture that the cathedral priests have tried to eradicate. Our battle isn't simply against the undead, but against those tearing down our heritage and traditions as well, simply because ours doesn't coincide with theirs. So, while I am not of the chosen lineage as a hunter, I do possess the necessary talents to aid hunters in their pursuits. Because of this, I refuse your money. You cannot purchase what I was blessed to offer as a gift. It was indeed a honor to craft this for you."

He smiled.

I nodded. "Thank you for this special gift. I am humbled to receive such and promise to use it for the duty to which I am called."

"You see, Forrest," he said softly. "*That* is my payment. That is my reward. A part of me travels with you to kill the vile beasts of the night when physically, I am unable."

I sat down. "May I ask you something?"

"Certainly."

"Why have you chosen to lock yourself down here in complete darkness?"

He stared into my eyes for a few moments, still clasping his hands together. "There are different kinds of darkness. Some evil ones choose to live in darkness, while others like me, are cursed from ever walking in the daylight."

I frowned. "What kind of curse?"

Roy lowered his hands near the lantern's light and offered a slight shrug. Dark scabs covered the back of his hands and his fingers, much like the spots on his face. "I cannot go into the sunlight without severe consequences. I have no idea why, and the few doctors I've seen haven't a clue as to what's wrong with me. I blister easily in the sun. Severely at times, so this is the best alternative I know. To hide in a place where the sunlight cannot penetrate."

"And your door?" I asked, pointing over my shoulder with my thumb. "You have it secured tighter than a prisoner's cell."

"With these boxes I craft, I have my enemies. I have no luxury here, other than my books, and this place is indeed my prison."

"You leave Rose to fend for herself?"

Roy shook his head. "She's well capable of defending herself. In ways you and I cannot."

"How many of these boxes have you made?" I asked, primarily because I'd like to know how many of my hunting brethren were out there.

"Four? Five maybe."

"That's not many."

"Your kind are *few*. Besides, I'll be seeing you again. Over time, you'll need to have new stakes and other supplies. Of course, you can make stakes yourself in times of need, but mine do have a quality that lasts much longer. As your prowess increases, you will also seek me for better, more unique weapons. I've not met a vampire hunter yet that hasn't innovated a weapon for me to fashion."

Father was quiet during my conversation with Roy, and I appreciated it. He didn't try to undermine me because of my youth. He never really did at any other time either. Often he regarded me based upon my size and not how long I'd been alive.

"When were you last visited by a hunter?" I asked.

Roy looked toward the ceiling as his mind thought. "About a day before I felt the need to build your hunter's box."

"Name?"

"Dominus."

My eyes narrowed. "That's his real name?"

Roy smiled. "Probably not. But it's what he goes by."

"He lives in Bucharest?"

"I don't know exactly where he resides," he replied. "Why?"

"I seek the counsel of a vampire hunter."

Roy looked toward my father and then back to me. "Can your father not help you?"

Father cleared his throat. "It was my suggestion to him."

"I see," Roy said. "And why would you persuade your son to do so?"

"He is chosen. I was not." Father took a deep breath. "I'm certain Forrest has questions about impulses he senses that I have never felt."

I nodded. "I do."

Roy eased back in his chair, resting his hands upon his lap. "Vampire hunters are often solitary. Although, they do occasionally hunt in pairs. I've heard of trios every now and again, especially when they seek to kill a powerful master. Bucharest could stand a good cleansing. The vampire population is almost as bad as vermin."

"I took Forrest through the slums this morning."

"Then he has seen the growing infestation," Roy said.

"I have," I replied.

My father leaned forward on the table. "You mentioned that the baron is our common enemy? In what way?"

"He killed my wife," Roy said evenly.

We all remained silent for several minutes. Finally, I said, "I'm sorry for your loss."

"Yes," Father said. "My condolences as well."

Roy looked at me sternly. "Whatever you do, *never* tell Rose."

"She doesn't know?"

He shook his head and looked away. "I'm sure if she wanted the knowledge about how her mother had actually died, she could seek the guidance of her powers. Perhaps she knows and wishes to spare me, thinking I don't know."

I placed my hand upon the hunter's box. "Baron Randolph will die from one of these stakes you've carved."

Roy's eyes widened. "Forrest, no. I appreciate the sentiment. I do. But a master vampire is well outside your league currently. You've never killed a vampire, have you?"

"No, I haven't. But I didn't say *when* I'd seek to kill the baron, but I will be the one to deliver his death. He attacked my father, nearly killed him, and had Father died, he'd have turned into one of the undead. If you know where I can find Dominus, please tell me."

Roy ached with pain inside. It was evident on his face. Perhaps it stemmed from his wife's death, and some remorse possibly came by revealing the vampire responsible for killing her, which now was a common thread between us. He might have even feared that I'd die prematurely based upon my sudden zeal, and if so, he'd be partly to blame for my death.

"Dominus, from what I've been told, frequents the eastern graveyard at midnight on Saturdays, killing stray vampires on the day of the risen."

I nodded. "Thanks."

"Do note that he's a brazen and hardened individual. He has killed a great number of vampires. His eyes are dark like coal and his face has many scars. He's quiet most of the time, so I don't know how much he will tell you. Can't get him to carry on a conversation with me. He leaves a list with me and comes back days later to fetch it. I wish you peace and safety."

I smiled and reached for the hunter's box.

Before my hand could take the handle, Roy stood and placed a hand atop the box. "Although I've fashioned this as instructed, understand that by accepting it, you are bound to the life of a vampire hunter. There's no turning back from the calling. Ever. Only death separates you from your burden. You still have a choice without consequence if you don't wish to accept the box."

This had been another test, as a true hunter could never deny his calling. There were great consequences for not accepting. I felt it in my soul and even in the dim lighting, I read it in his eyes. A sly smile tugged at his lips.

I grabbed the handle and slid the heavy box off of the table. "It is my duty. It is my calling. I know I'll never have rest if I don't accept it. I've known for some time, and destiny has yielded its light for me to behold what I truly am. You're right. There's no turning back. I accept."

CHAPTER 15

When Roy unlatched the iron door to his dark library, my father and I ascended the stairs. Rose stood on the top step with her hands clasped at her waist. Sadness furrowed her brow, and tears moistened her eyes as she gazed at the hunter's box in my hand and then stared into my eyes.

"You had a choice, Forrest," she said softly.

I nodded. "And I chose the correct path."

"Indeed," she whispered.

She stepped aside for my father and I to leave the stairs.

My father glanced at me and smiled. "I'll be in here. I saw some candles your mother might like."

The moment he turned away, Rose gripped my left hand. Her desperate eyes searched mine. All I could do was smile at her.

"Forrest," she said in a near whisper. "I saw something in the crystal ball right after you left. Something horrible. I tried to get to you before my father took you inside his chambers."

"Why? Is something wrong?"

Tears streamed down her cheeks. "I'm afraid I cannot bear to tell you the news."

"Why not?"

"I cannot hurt you in such a way. Besides, it's too late."

"What is?"

All the beauty she beheld on her face was twisted and oddly shaped as her sorrow took control. She sobbed and suddenly wrapped her arms around me, squeezing me in a fierce embrace. I was surprised but also overjoyed at being so close to her.

"Be vigilant as you return home," she said. "That's all I can say. I'm so sorry."

She bolted down the narrow hallway. Her fancy shoes kicked off as she ran. Her tight, long curls bounced down her back.

I hurried down the hall in long strides. I entered the room where my father was looking at the candles. He gazed at me with strange curiosity.

"What did you do?" he asked.

I shook my head. "Nothing, I swear."

"Clearly, boy, she is quite upset."

"Not my doing, Father. I think we should find Fane quickly and get home."

"Why?"

"She saw something in her magic ball. I fear we may have had problems at home during our absence."

Father's eyes widened. He set down the candles and followed me into the next room. I looked at the table where I had met Rose. She wasn't there. Her cards and the glass ball were where she had left them.

"Rose?" I called, looking around, hoping for a response but received no reply.

Grabbing the doorknob, I pulled open the door. Father walked out before me. The strangely decorated people were still trying to call the passersby toward them to pickpocket. I glanced around.

"What is the quickest route to return to the market?" I asked.

"We were to meet Fane at Dyre's Tavern."

"Where is that?"

He pointed past the entire extravaganza, in the direction we had not come. At least the streets and walkways were smoother than the slum shortcut had been. But the amount of people milling around in the streets was far greater, presenting an obstacle of its own.

I pushed my way through the colorful painted, creepy faces, never pausing whenever they attempted to stop my stride. Only once did I have to forcefully push a man out of my way. He crashed to the ground as his hand slipped from my empty coat pocket. I held no wallet, so his attempted theft did him no good. My father limped to my side and became ever mindful of what few valuables he carried.

About a block later we were past the would-be thieves and blended into the crowd as they sought different wares. With winter past, and the cold spring upon us, it didn't really matter to most of these folks if they bought anything. The expressions on their faces revealed their happiness of finally get outdoors after being stuck indoors during the brutally harsh blizzard and the frigid winds that had followed.

"So, Father," I said while walking and not looking toward him. "Tell me how you knew about Roy and his workshop? The detail on the box I'm carrying is far different than yours. I take it that he didn't make yours?"

"No, son, he didn't."

"Who told you how to find him?"

"Before the baron had tried to kill me, I asked around at the pubs."

I laughed. "Asked around? Father, certainly that placed immediate attention upon you."

Father frowned and his face reddened. "I wasn't asking for a box maker. I wanted to find another vampire hunter to kill Bodi because I didn't want to have that kill on my conscience for the rest of my life. A man told me about Roy, that he occasionally spoke with hunters. At the time, I had no knowledge he crafted tools for vampire hunters."

"Did you speak with Roy then?"

"I sought him out. He said that he couldn't help me."

I looked into his eyes, not pausing in step. "Did you mention me to him?"

"I did not!"

"But you and mother knew. Why not solicit his advice?"

"I still hoped that it never became necessary for you to become one."

I shook my head. "I don't understand how at times you wish for what I am to remain a secret, and yet, back there, you were overly proud of what I am chosen to do."

Father gasped and limped harder, trying to keep pace with me. I slowed slightly. "Until you have children—"

"I *doubt* that's in my future."

He pointed a stern finger at me. "Should you *ever* have such a blessing in life, then you will understand why your mother and I have had mixed feelings about your destiny. We love you, as parents rightly do, so in our eyes even though you've grown so fast, we feel partially robbed. Eight years and you're already a man. At times, seldom anymore, I see the child that you are. Just that brief glimmer in your eyes, and then it fades. We want you safe, above all else. That's why I held back, but we couldn't suppress the truth from you forever. Fate made certain of that. I hope that you understand."

I placed my hand on his shoulder and smiled. "I believe I do. It's not been easy for me, growing at such a rapid pace. I've felt as an outsider to the others my age, and without doing a single thing wrong, I was forced out of the school, even though I'd have rather stayed. But, it's not only the school where I didn't fit in, it's life overall. I don't think I'm not meant to find a stable home. I'm different so I have to keep traveling and hunting to places where my services are needed. I don't have any other choice."

"I know. I don't begrudge your gift, none in the least. I only wish I could do more."

We walked in silence for a few city blocks. I walked. He hobbled. There were things he wished to say to me. I could tell by the look in his eyes. Why he held back, I didn't know. He was stubborn sometimes, like my mother had often accused him. In spite of his evident pain, he didn't complain. He continued trying to keep pace with me.

Ahead, the large wooden sign hung over the walkway. The carved letters were burnt and black, to make the words standout from the surrounding wood.

Dyre's Tavern.

I held open the door for my father to enter first. A few men sat at various tables with tall tankards of dark ale. Since it was still early, the place looked nearly empty.

"Do you see him anywhere?" Father asked me.

"No, sir."

"Probably still in the marketplace."

"Then we should head there."

My father looked longingly toward the bar. I'd never known him to drink in taverns, but I never ventured into town with him.

"Father, we need to hurry."

He nodded. "I'll be quick."

He hobbled to the bar, pulled his billfold from his inner vest pocket, and said, "Double shot of plum brandy."

The barkeep turned and poured his brandy into a thick glass. My father set some money on the bar and quickly down his drink. He nodded at the keep. "Excellent!"

I opened the door and let him pass through first.

After a few minutes, he immediately appeared more jovial. He smiled and greeted people in passing. I noticed he walked a bit easier, too.

"Is all well, Father?"

"It's better now. That numbs my pain somewhat. I'd have bought another but you'd have had to carry me."

I grinned because I knew I was capable.

My mind reverted back to Rose as we pressed our way through the crowds, heading toward the marketplace. Seeing the future, as she had said she was capable, had to be a curse of its own at times, too. After all, terrible things occurred in life and seeing them beforehand wasn't necessarily a great thing when it wasn't something she wasn't capable of preventing in someone else's life. What had she seen that disturbed her so badly about my life? Whatever it was had disturbed her so much that she could not face me.

I held up my left hand and studied the lines on my palm. I thought of her holding my hand and the strange warmth that had come to my chest. I shook away the feeling and looked hard at the lines. They were different than others she had read, but even more disturbing was whatever had surfaced in the clear glass ball. I didn't understand her mysticism, but there was no mistaking her fear.

I wanted to run, but I knew my father wasn't capable of doing so. The vampire box I carried was quite heavy. I was able to tote it, but even at my size, the weight seemed to increase the longer I carried it. Burning pain tugged at my right triceps and shoulder, but I forced myself to continue. I understood why my father had never packed his with him when he had gone hunting. One needed to travel light so he didn't wear himself out before he encountered a vampire. No need giving your adversary a keen advantage before the fight ever ensued.

Finding Fane and persuading him to head home would save us some valuable time, and I looked forward to resting my arm before it completely went numb. Besides that, Father needed to sit and rest. This was the most exercise he had endured since he was able to walk again. He was pale and covered with sweat. Ahead, a wooden arrow with 'Market' painted on it directed us properly, so we headed in that direction.

CHAPTER 16

We found Fane with his wagon fully loaded. He gave us what money he had received for selling our animal hides, but he refused to head back until after he had drunk several rounds at the tavern. No amount of pleading or money from my father convinced old Fane any differently.

"I'm sorry," he said. "I told you my plans when we arrived, and I'll be happy to let you ride back once I'm done."

For a moment I entertained the idea of telling Fane that we had a possible tragedy at home, but I cast aside the thought. His first question would have been, "What makes you believe that?"

I didn't know Fane too well, but I was certain he'd not change his mind because a palm-reading fortuneteller had told me to be vigilant when I returned home. What exactly did she mean by the statement? He wouldn't know, and I was still partially trying to figure it out.

If I were simply to be on the lookout for a problem, Rose wouldn't have been overly upset. At least I didn't think she should have been. Ever since the night of my father's attack, I had been vigilant and waiting, ready to act. Nothing had ever happened.

The sky was a brilliant blue with no clouds at all. The brightness of the sun made colors snap in full vividness all around us. Even walking on foot, we'd get to our cottage well before sundown, so we didn't need to worry about the vampires. And yet, pressing at the back of my mind was urgency unlike ever before. We needed to get home.

"I happened to hear your problem," a man said. "Where do you two wish to travel?"

He was dressed in light brown farmer's attire and his dark eyes studied my hunter's box with keen interest. He wasn't a big man. In fact, he was thinner than my father and perhaps an inch shorter. Tiny in comparison to me. He fashioned a goatee on his chin, and his skin was tanner than most of the other people around us. He wore an odd hat on his head. I wasn't certain what nationality he claimed.

Bucharest was in an economic transition. Immigrants flooded the city in droves, bringing with them their skills and added money. Businesses and factories were being assembled. I suppose as the city had attracted outsiders, it had also invited undead vampires within their numbers. But in the beginning of industrialization, so came opportunists in the line of thieves.

The man smiled, trying to be friendly, but the shape of his goatee and the contrast of his smile didn't work in his favor. Instead, he acted like a person with something to hide. The shiftiness of his eyes bothered me the most.

My father gave him the directions to our cottage, before I had a chance to persuade him otherwise.

"My horse and cart are near the water gardens," he said, pointing. "I live on the other side of the forest and use the narrow road to travel. Be happy to offer you a ride."

I was at the point of simply declining, but my father readily accepted. The way he shifted his weight from foot to foot indicated his legs were bothering him and the temptation not to have to walk any farther was too great to resist. He had placed a lot of strain upon his legs, and he looked relieved to be able to sit down for a while. I understood, so I followed behind him and this man.

"What is in the box?" the man asked as we left the bustle of the marketplace.

"I'd rather not say."

His eyebrows rose with greater curiosity. "No?"

"No," I replied with an even frown.

"It is an odd box," he said. "Quite unusual."

"I agree."

"Is it for traveling?"

"You might say that."

"Ah," he said, smiling. "You travel often?"

The water gardens were coming into sight. I didn't see a horse and cart parked anywhere near the gardens as the man had told us.

Without replying, I took my father's wrist and slowed our pace. Father looked at me, surprised.

The man also turned with a perplexed expression. "Is there a problem?"

"There's not a horse and cart near the gardens," I replied. "What is your reason for lying to us?"

My father looked ahead, stepping on tiptoe. He frowned, realizing the same thing. He looked at the man. "What scheme are you playing?"

"No scheme."

"You offered us a ride," my father replied. He grew angrier because his mind had already accepted that we had a ride where he could rest and maybe take a nap along the way. I also thought that maybe he was hungry, too, because his temper often got the best of him when he had not eaten in a while.

"I offer you a stern warning instead," he said, his eyes growing fierce and darker.

"And what would that be?" I asked, moving the briefcase to my left hand and placing my right hand upon the hilt of my dagger.

His eyes shifted to my hunter box and then to my dagger, before finally resting on my harsh glare. His Adam's apple bobbed. The first crack in his attempt to intimidate me had appeared, making him hesitant. "The baron . . . demands your blood."

"Does he now? And *who* are you?" I asked, pulling my dagger from its sheath and stepping closer.

"His servant," the man replied, shaking.

I sensed a faint wave of the baron's power, weaker than the afternoon when we had stood face to face, and I knew this man wasn't lying about *this*. The baron controlled him but from a great distance.

My eyes narrowed and my hand tightened upon the blade. "In the daylight? How can that be?"

He shook his head. "I'm not a vampire like he. Just his servant."

I scowled intensely. He backed away. "Where is the baron? I wish to pay him a visit."

"Forrest," Father said, in a near whisper. "Don't make a challenge. The time isn't right."

"He has forbidden me to give his whereabouts," the man said.

"Even if I cut you?" I made the threat only because this man had confessed to having a direct tie to the baron, and I knew it was true, which made this man my immediate enemy. Although I had never drawn blood from another person, if it became necessary to protect my family, I didn't have a problem doing so.

His eyes nervously regarded the knife and then gazed into my eyes. He read the seriousness of my intent and nodded. "I cannot disobey. None of his servants can abandon his command. You could torture me until death and the information will still not be given unto you."

"What does he mean, he demands my blood?" I asked.

"He issues you a final warning."

"I'm listening."

"After he butchered the two vampire hunters you sent to kill him, he has countered. His warning is for you to never threaten him again."

"Or?"

"He will drain your father's life and then yours."

I read the fear in this man's eyes as he spoke. He didn't want me to hurt him. As a servant, he was here delivering the baron's message when he really wished he were elsewhere. He didn't appear to have any weapons, but I kept my knife out anyway. I don't know why, but I wondered if this encounter was what Rose had warned me about. Had I not noticed he was lying about the horse and cart, would this man have killed us?

"The baron attacked my family first," I replied. "He has made an enemy out of me. I retaliated for what he did."

"And after today, he considers both parties are even."

"Meaning he and I? A truce is what he's proposing?"

The man gave a solemn nod but couldn't suppress his fear.

I gave a nod in return, but I didn't indicate that the battle between the baron and I was over. After all, Bodi was still alive . . . well, undead. I wouldn't be satisfied with any truce as long as the child remained cursed as a vampire.

"May I leave?" he asked.

I stared at him for several minutes, contemplating whether I should allow him to leave or not. Finally, I nodded. "Go."

He closed his eyes with relief. "Thank you."

He tore into a sprint, running back toward the marketplace. Sliding my dagger into its sheath, I grabbed my father's hand. "Come, Father. Let's get home to Momma. I imagine she has a fine meal prepared."

"What did he mean by the two vampire hunters that you sent after the baron?"

"It's a long story," I replied.

"We have time. It's still a good walk until we reach the cottage."

"True."

So as we walked I told him what had transpired on that day when the two hunters at the frozen brook confronted me. It was enough to pass the time.

CHAPTER 17

*A*rriving at the cottage about three quarters of an hour later, I noticed no smoke rising from the chimney, which was odd, given that it was chilly outside and my mother was often cold natured.

After I had told Father about the events with the two vampire hunters, my mind went back to thinking and sorting through various bits of information. Perhaps I should have been a sleuth since I spent the majority of my time analyzing every different angle of each situation, near to the point of madness at times, even as a child. If this was a trait the vampire hunters were gifted, it wasn't a bad one and was something to use to my advantage during my hunts.

The baron's nameless servant had made mention that the servants weren't actual vampires but were controlled by the master vampire. They were still human. They were able to move about and do whatever their master bid during the daylight when a vampire wasn't able to. Why would a human yield himself as a servant for the undead? What did he stand to benefit?

I didn't know.

I wondered why the baron considered us even. Father would have been the first strike against us. I considered sending the two hunters after the baron as my strike back. In my mind that's what made us even.

However, the baron had considered something else as my first strike that I had not. Nor did I later. But this miscalculation on my part forever changed my life. *This* was what Rose had seen and what she had refused to tell me. The information, as she had said, would have come too late, and because she knew, she was heartbroken.

Father and I left the main road and walked down the narrow path that led to our front door. The door was closed, but I sensed something amiss. An uneasiness rose inside me. My hand reached for the hilt of my dagger.

Father must have sensed something was wrong, too, as he slowed his pace and swallowed hard, glancing toward me. His face paled. He eased closer to the door and from the edge of the woodpile, someone moved.

Father grabbed the doorknob and turned.

In a blur, the man was beside me, shaking his head. "Forrest," he said. "Don't go inside."

Jacques?

Father pushed the door wide and entered. A second later he wailed with a sound I'd never heard before and certainly never expected to come from him.

I took a step, but Jacques grabbed my arm firmly and pulled me aside. "Don't go inside, Forrest. You mustn't."

Tears crested in his eyes, and I felt them burning at the edges of mine. My throat tightened. I felt numb even before I knew for certain, but I kept walking. I had to know. I needed to see. He pulled harder, trying to dissuade me, but I was stronger, kept walking, pulling him with me.

"Please, Forrest," he said, pulling backwards, digging his boots into the ground, but he wasn't able to stop me.

The world seemed far away, in so many ways. I heard and saw my environment, but the sensation was different, like I wasn't inside my body. I felt light, floating.

Jacques had told me the night we had talked that we would meet again, and that sorrow would bring us together. He hadn't lied.

Father knelt on the floor, shaking, wailing. At my age, I had never seen so much blood. I didn't know a body contained so much blood.

Momma's body lay on the floor, lifeless. Her dead eyes were wide open, frozen in horror.

My knees buckled as I set my down my hunter box. Jacques wrapped his arms up beneath my underarms as he caught me from behind. He eased me to the ground, outside the door, and allowed me to sit. He pulled the door closed, leaving my father on the floor beside my mother's body.

Anguish creased his face. He was speaking to me while placing a hand upon my shoulder, but my shock prevented me from hearing anything he had said. Silence swallowed me. Coldness crept inside me. Chill bumps covered me. I shook from all of the cold. My stomach felt hollow. I stared blankly at him.

I'm not sure how much time had transpired before I finally became aware of my surroundings, but Jacques sat in front of me. Father's wailing had ceased, replaced by heaving sobs.

My eyes met Jacques'. "Who did this?"

"His body is behind the woodpile."

"That doesn't answer the question."

"I don't know who he was. But he's dead. I ripped his throat out."

"He was human?"

Jacques nodded.

"The baron sent him."

"Baron Randolph?"

"Yes."

"What makes you so certain?" he asked.

I explained the human servant we had encountered in Bucharest.

"He considers *this* even?" Jacques asked, pointing toward the door.

I frowned, reaching for my hunter box. "That's what his other servant told me."

"He's a fool."

"He has guaranteed that I will kill him," I replied, forcing myself back to my feet.

Jacques stood and offered his hand to help me up. I accepted.

"No offense, Forrest, but you're not seasoned enough to face him.

He's baiting you, hoping to draw you into his lair so he can use his minions to kill you. Apparently, he fears you."

"He should've left well enough alone," I replied.

"I see you have your hunter's box?"

"Father took me to get it today."

Jacques studied it for a few moments and then he grinned. "I'd ask to see it, but the crafter must have something against my kind."

"The silver?"

He nodded.

"He never indicated such," I said.

"I admire the man's skill. Nice box. I'm sure its contents are well-crafted as well?"

I shrugged. "I've not inspected them yet."

"Why not?"

"That's something I wish to do in private."

"Ah."

I stared at him for a few moments and then I gazed past him toward the woodpile. I walked past Jacques. I needed to see who had killed Momma. As I got nearer, I wondered how it was that the servant happened to arrive at the cottage on the exact day when Father was taking me into the city. It was almost as though the baron had expected my father and I to leave my mother alone.

An undead vampire or creature might have been stalking the cottage for a long period of time without the need to feed, but a human servant could not. Could he?

"Do you not find it odd," I asked Jacques, "that this man knew the precise moment when we had left our cottage?"

"It is peculiar," he replied.

Anger welled inside me, fueled by my intensifying rage. My even voice became deep, different, when I spoke. I can't explain it, but I was no longer a child. "I've waited each night for the baron to attack since my father had nearly died. Watched and waited. Nothing. No attempts to break into our cottage during the night. No trace of a single footprint outside our home the following mornings. And today, the first day that we ventured outside of the forest, he sends this servant to kill my mother."

Jacques eyes grew fierce. For a few moments, I saw the beast inside him desiring to break free. "I know."

"Tell me something, cousin," I said. My jaw tightened.

"Anything," he replied.

"Is it also coincidence that you arrived today as well?"

The question didn't anger him, but his expression indicated that it hurt him, cutting him deep inside. "What are you insinuating? That I had *anything* to do with this?"

"How did you know to come here? Today, of all days?"

Jacques sighed and turned.

"Don't dare turn away from me!" My hand was on my dagger without a thought of even doing so. "Look into my eyes and reply. How did you know?"

Now, my cousin was angry. His gaze into my eyes looked more animal than human. His features hardened. In a split second, he could have turned and attacked me, only I didn't know that. He fought against his inner beast not to do so. His eyes darkened like a wolf and long canine teeth formed in his mouth.

"Forrest," he hissed, forming tight fists. Drool formed at the sides of his mouth. Thicker hair appeared on his hands and his cheeks. "I would never attack my family. You are still a boy. The circumstances behind what I am and what you're becoming, they are new to you. Do not expect to understand everything in only a few days. It will take the better part of a lifetime for you to learn. You will need allies. You will find few. I am your family and your ally."

I removed my hand from the dagger with remorse. "My apologies, Jacques. I reacted from—"

"I understand your reaction, Forrest, and your anger. You have every reason to lash out from hostility and hatred, but not at me. To answer your question, I came to your cottage because I sensed in my spirit that your mother was hurt. I got here too late."

"She was already dead?"

He nodded. Slowly, his features were returning to normal. "Yes. She was dead, and I followed his scent into the forest. When I found him, I killed him and brought him back."

I stared down at the dead man. The gaping bloody hole in his throat was dark. The blood was drying. My rage didn't lessen because he was dead. In many ways, I wished that Jacques had allowed me to kill this man, but justice was done.

Like the man who had deceived us on the street, this dead man's eyes held fear and hopelessness. But in appearance, he looked nothing like the other servant. This man was fair skinned with light hair and blue eyes, which meant the baron didn't favor strictly one particular stereotype. So his servants could be any nationality, male or female, and not easy to distinguish. The baron was resourceful and he hated me. I was guessing that his hatred toward me paled in comparison to mine for him.

"But how would the baron have known we were gone?"

"He probably had spies."

"These servants."

Jacques shook his head. "No. A master vampire can control certain animals. Rats, bats, and owls."

"Wolves?" I said, looking at him.

He gave a half smile. "*Not* this wolf."

"I need to check on Father."

He clasped my shoulder in passing. Once I was past, he followed me. I pushed open the door. My father held Momma's hand in between his, pressing it to his cheek. He sobbed. I don't think he even knew we had come inside. Seeing the agony on his face was another reason I didn't want to seek a wife. Not that I didn't want to ever know love and companionship, but I didn't wish to put another into harm's way.

For a moment, although I don't know why, I saw myself in my father's place with Rose being the one dead. That was how grim my outlook on life was. I turned away.

Father needed to deal with his grief. I did, too, but not until the baron was dead. I wanted anger to rule me as I sought to find him. I headed back outside. Jacques followed.

Once outside, he shut the door.

"Have you ever heard of Dominus?" I asked.

He shook his head. "No, who is he?"

"Another vampire hunter. One I need to talk to and see if he will train me."

"How did you learn of him?"

"From the man who built my box."

"Where does this hunter reside?"

"Not sure. But I was told that he hunts at midnights on Saturdays in the east cemetery. He shouldn't be hard to find."

"That's tomorrow night. I will accompany you," Jacques said.

"No. You don't have to."

"I need to, Forrest. The baron might have said that you and he were even, but he knows killing your mother will send you after him. He's counting on it. He'll have spies in the forest, Bucharest, and quite possibly near the cemeteries. For all you know, he might have watched all of your activity while you were in the city. He's not going to ease up his pursuit, even though he has said he will. He will try to kill you before you gain any experience at killing vampires."

"I appreciate your offer, but—"

"Without me, you won't go."

"Is that a threat?"

"No, of course not. It simply means that I offer you my assistance and an extra set of eyes. Don't forget that I am seasoned as a fighter. I have experience. I can get the best of you in a grappling match, regardless of how much you outsize and outweigh me."

I nodded. I knew he was telling the truth, at least right now.

"Besides," he said, "I can sense his presence if he's close-by. He might even try to control me, which would give me his exact location."

"I can sense him, too. And what prevents him from taking control of you?"

He pulled his medallion from beneath his shirt. "This. It is blessed by a priest, preventing vampires from taking control of my wolf."

"You used that to produce the explosive silver light."

Jacques smiled. "Your father told you my secret?"

"Part of it. Where is your cane?"

"Against the tree."

"What should I do about my father?"

"What do you mean?"

"With Momma dead, what becomes of him? He's not physically able to fight vampires anymore. I know his rage will insist otherwise."

"You'd deny him the opportunity to seek his revenge? He'd hate you for doing so."

I thought about it for a few moments. "You're right. He would."

"Understand something, Forrest. He and your mother loved one another greatly. His legs might be stiff and slower since he has healed, but mentally, he's sharp. He's killed a few vampires. He will be needed in the fight. As badly as he'll want to see Randolph dead, you'll have no chance of stopping him from trying."

"I don't want to lose him, too. I lack the expertise to watch out for him and myself."

"Don't insult him, Forrest. He won't want you to even consider trying to protect him. Stubborn men don't die easily. Just think about what he's already survived."

My mind revisited finding him barely alive at the foot of our cottage door. His will power to survive was remarkable. If his need for revenge was a tenth of that, I doubted the baron had ever seen that level of rage. The baron had created a foe that would never relent in his seeking vengeance.

I thought about what Jacques said. The baron might have watched our entire visit to the city through his servants' eyes. I immediately worried about Rose's safety. Her father kept himself locked behind an iron door, deep underground, but she resided on the upper floor. Even though he had said that she had power capable of keeping herself safe, I held my doubts. I could only hope that the baron was ignorant of our visit to the shop. Otherwise, their safety and anonymity had been exposed.

When my father and I had crossed through the slums, no one had followed us. We could have easily seen them on the street behind us. So there was a good chance that they didn't know. However, the servant who had spoken to me kept his attention on my hunter box. He seemed overly interested in its contents. I held no doubt that he'd inform the baron that I now had it in my possession, but I didn't know whether the baron would recognize the woodworking or not. Were there any others in the city who built boxes for hunters? I didn't know.

The cottage door creaked open. My father staggered to the threshold and leaned upon the doorframe to hold himself up. His eyes were red. His face was drawn in. I had never seen this man in shambles. Everything about him was different. He seemed to have aged several decades.

"First the sorrow," Jacques whispered to me. "Then comes the rage."

$\mathcal{R}$age left unchecked wasn't a bad thing when it was used to hunt down a murderer. Such fury buried the ache of loss for a period of time. However, if the vengeance wasn't fulfilled within a short amount of time, the mind lingered closer to insanity as the relentless pursuit to find the target obsessed the soul.

Jacques and I had done our best to scrub the cottage floor clean where Momma had been slaughtered. But blood cannot be fully removed from hardwood floorboards as the stain goes deep, so we placed a tan deerskin over the spot.

We had buried my mother near the patch of wild crocuses. They were her favorite flower, and she had often sat near the large tree admiring their beauty on the warmer early spring days. I cherished the thought that she'd rest peacefully in her one place of serenity she had treasured when she was still alive.

Nightfall had long passed as we approached the east cemetery to find Dominus. The gas-lit streetlamps ended short of the cemetery, adding a more sinister display to the gravestones, especially when the near full moon shone overhead, creating odd shadows that occasionally moved. Spindly leafless trees formed strange silhouettes. The night air was crisp, forming frosty clouds from our mouths and noses as we walked.

For me to say that I held no fear or nervousness would have been an outright lie. Apprehension tapped at my mind, tightened my chest, and turned my stomach, as I wasn't certain what I'd run into first—Dominus or a vampire. Upon such a first meeting, I didn't know which of the two might be worse.

Roy had given few details about this hunter, other than Dominus was sullen with dark eyes and a scarred face. Although he was a fellow hunter, there was no guarantee he'd even speak with me alone, and much less the chance since I was accompanied by my father and a were-wolf. No success came without first deploying the proper action though. By arriving, it showed great initiative on my part, or at least I thought so.

Father had seldom spoken a word since Momma's death, but this night he had let me know that he was coming to the cemetery with us. The dead set determination in his eyes meant there wasn't any reason to argue the point with him. He wasn't accepting debate on the matter, and I never offered to say otherwise. I simply looked into his cold gaze and nodded. I understood, and I didn't blame him. He had lost his one true love in life, something I didn't expect to find for myself, and he'd never rest until his vengeance was satisfied.

I continually thought about Rose; worried about her actually. I couldn't help it. I liked her immensely and couldn't shake my feelings for her. Momma had always mentioned that love comes from the heart. I supposed so, since that's where the stirring ache came from whenever I thought about Rose. And there had been something about the endearing way she had looked into my eyes upon our first meeting that led me to believe she liked me. She hadn't been shy about it, but not overly energetic, either. While she had predicted that I was a loner, and I kept insisting to myself that I was as well, she lingered in my mind and made my heart ache, but in a good way.

But seeing how my mother was murdered to incite my father and I, I needed to sweep all of my thoughts about Rose from my mind. I never wanted her to die in such a way. As long as she or any other person remained close to me, they were never safe.

Baron Randolph had not only killed my mother, but he had killed Rose's mother as well. As I reflected about that, I realized I must dismiss Rose from my thoughts. A master vampire possessed the power to read the minds of his servants, and I wondered if he might be capable of doing that with me as well. I didn't know, but I refused to risk it.

"You okay?" Jacques whispered.

I nodded.

"You seem deep in thought."

"Wouldn't you be in my situation?"

"I suppose so."

I pointed toward a massive flat gravestone that looked more like a table than a marker. "Let's wait there."

"Out in the open?"

"I'm not trying to hide from him."

"It's not him I'm worried about."

"The baron?"

Jacques nodded. "Yes. Exposing yourself so readily isn't a good strategy."

"I doubt he'll be here."

"A cemetery is his territory. It's where he obtains fresh recruits."

"They have to be buried in a graveyard first?" I asked.

"No, but the majority of them are."

"Why do you think that's the case? Why not take the body to the lair and wait?"

"Not sure. Could be that there's a fine line between the killing and turning point."

I frowned. "I don't follow."

"A vampire feasts on a victim's blood, but sometimes they take too much and drain the victim, killing him or her before the person can ingest the vampire's blood. When that occurs the victim won't rise as a vampire and remains a corpse."

"I see. Let's position ourselves at the stone anyway. It puts us nearly dead center of the cemetery where we can watch in all directions. We certainly cannot be cornered. Honestly I'd rather be exposed than cornered."

"I agree."

"Besides," I said, "I can set my hunter box at waist level to access its contents without having to stoop or squat. I never thought this box would be so damned heavy."

Jacques grinned.

We walked to the large stone and I set my hunter box upon it. I had only brought the box for one purpose. Well, two reasons actually. One, I figured since Roy had crafted Dominus' box and mine that there'd be no doubt we were on the same side. And two, easy access to the tools should we encounter any vampires.

After my mother's burial, I took my hunter box outside of our cottage and found a private place where I could inspect all of its contents. Like my father's box, mine contained holy water, blessed salt, a bible, a cross, and several stakes. Mine also had rosary beads, dried herbs of some sort, and a wooden mallet. There were some cloves of garlic and two dark glassed bottles containing liquid, but I didn't know their actual contents. One other tool that I rather liked was a small iron ax. On the back part of the ax blade was a metal claw like some hammers had, which was excellent for prying open wooden coffins should the task ever become necessary.

Several compartments inside the box were empty, but looked to be places to add weapons later. Roy had mentioned that I'd eventually have need of other weapons after I had matured as a hunter.

The cold night air was silent, other than the occasional whispering breeze. My father remained quiet and stationary. He held a stake tightly in his right hand. From a distance it was unnoticeable. Jacques sniffed the air in long deep breaths as his eyes studied the shadows and his ears altered slightly, listening for sounds undetectable by my father or me. I wondered if Dominus had chosen not to come to the cemetery on this particular night. It was feasible that a vampire hunter might be needed elsewhere or perhaps someone had hired him.

Jacques' eyebrows rose. "We have company."

"Where?"

He nodded toward a massive evergreen cedar at the edge of the cemetery. If someone was hidden within its massive shadow, I couldn't see the person.

Father turned in the direction we were facing. He squinted.

"I don't see anyone," I replied.

"He sees us."

"Is it the hunter or a vampire? Or can you discern from here?"

"It's not a vampire. I sense power, so it's possible he might be the hunter you seek."

The man stepped outside of the tree's shadow, forming a unique shadow of his own. From the distance between us, I didn't know his height, but he wore a tall hat and a ragged overcoat that hung to his knees. In his right hand he held what appeared to be a crossbow, but it could have been a large handgun. The shadow of a long cross was in his left.

Apparently Jacques noticed the cross when I had. He whispered, "Hunter."

While I quietly questioned whether or not I should make my approach, the man headed directly toward us. Not quickly, but at a steady, slow gait with both hands at his sides. His boots clicked softly upon the cobblestone walkway.

I slid my hand into my coat pocket and wrapped my fingers around a stake. Realizing my foolishness, I left the stake in favor of my dagger strapped to my belt. But neither weapon I possessed quick access to was good against a man who held a ranged weapon.

When he came to within ten yards of our proximity, he stopped coming toward us. My eyes had adjusted to the pale moonlight enough for me to partially make out his face. His face was scarred with a scraggly thin beard. One thin line ran down his left cheek. Another near his right eye. An inch over, and he'd probably have lost the eye. Two parallel scars ran at a diagonal angle on his brow. His left jaw was bulged with something he held in his mouth.

"Who's the wolf?" he asked with a tight stare on Jacques.

"Are you Dominus?" I asked, stepping in front of Jacques. I wasn't certain if this hunter only killed vampires, and since Jacques seemed his first interest, I wasn't taking any chance that he killed werewolves as well.

"Depends," he replied, noticing how I had become a body shield for Jacques.

"On what exactly?" I asked.

"Your reason for bringing a werewolf to a cemetery hunt."

"I came as his ally," Jacques said.

"And the old man?" the hunter asked.

"My father."

He remained silent, his eyes studying us. The longer he did, the more uncomfortable I became. I never realized how intimidating silence could be. Loud boisterous people tended to try to frighten and bully others into fear or submission, but their success was nothing compared to a man who spoke little and kept a solemn uncertain stare. It was impossible to detect his intentions, and whether or not he sought peace or was bent on killing us without ever muttering another word.

"Why are you three here?" he finally asked in his hoarse voice. His accent held a long drawn out drawl, unlike anything I'd heard before. He chewed on the lump in his mouth a couple of times.

"I wished to speak to you."

"About what exactly?" The coldness never eased in his eyes or expression. I imagined his soul was frigid.

"Training. That is, if you're Dominus."

He chuckled. His voice rolled deeply. "And if I'm not?"

"Then we're wasting one another's time, aren't we?" I stated with a tinge of anger looming in my voice. My impatience was getting the best of me. Standing in the center of a cemetery where possible vampires lurked, discussing whom he might or might not be *was* a complete waste of my time.

"I am Dominus, but who told you I'd be here?"

"A mutual friend."

"I have no friends," he replied, coldly. "And neither will you, if you're a true hunter."

"Roy, the woodcrafter, told me I could find you here."

His jaw tightened and his eyes narrowed. He seemed angered about where I'd gotten my information. "I'm a hunter, not a trainer."

"Did you not have a trainer at one time?" Jacques asked. Aggravation rose in his tone as well.

"Who yanked the wolf's leash?" Dominus asked with a tightened brow. "It wasn't I."

Jacques hands formed into fists, and he started to walk around me. I placed a firm hand against his chest and shook my head. "Ignore him."

Dominus seemed determined to draw Jacques into a fight. His dislike toward werewolves was obvious. I wondered why and what his motive was. The silver tips of his arrow gleamed in the moonlight.

Jacques eyes narrowed. His teeth ground audibly. At least I hoped that was what I had heard. It might have been his jawbones starting to widen.

"Easy," I whispered. "He has silver on the arrow."

"He has to actually hit me for it to be effective," Jacques replied.

Dominus took two steps closer. His hand tightened on the loaded crossbow and his finger edged toward the trigger. He spit brown juice onto the cobblestone. "You have odd company, boy. I've never encountered another hunter who brings his Poppa along, and certainly never one who has partied himself to a werewolf. I think it best that you find yourself another hunter who doesn't mind training a young'un who won't step outside of his father's shadow."

I kept trying to ignore his crass insults, and each time that he spoke, it was getting harder. I tried to suppress my festering anger, as I was the least experienced fighter in the cemetery, but I found myself about ready to charge at this man. "I know of no other hunters. There might not be another for hundreds of miles."

"Dozens of 'em here in Romania and Transylvania, boy, which isn't many given the number of vampires we have. But the vampire hunters are around, if you know where to look."

"I don't have the time to search."

Dominus laughed. He extended both of his arms out at shoulder height. His crossbow was still in his right hand and the cross in the other. "Take a long hard look at me, boy. Is this what you want to be twenty years from now? Cause this is what you'll become. A body riddled with scars, a heart colder than ice, and a life without friends or family. You won't know love, as that will only be a myth. A hunter leads a solitary life."

Roy had said Dominus seldom spoke, but maybe the hunter simply didn't like Roy. Dominus certainly had said far more than I expected and seemed quite theatrical while doing so.

"I have no choice in what I am," I replied. "But, without the proper training, I probably *won't* be here twenty years from now."

"Harsh as it may sound, but I'm going to send you on your way. I hope you can find another hunter. I don't have the time."

"My time is greatly limited for even considering a search for another hunter."

"What's your rush, boy?" he asked. "You can't learn the mastery to kill vampires in a few days' time. Nothing I know will simply rub off on you. It takes years of fighting these undead bloodthirsty *mongrels* before you get the proper knack for it. No offense intended to your werewolf companion."

Jacques jaw flexed. "A lot taken actually, since I'm not the same thing."

Dominus grinned. "It's too easy to rile up a werewolf, and this one's no exception. I figure it's because werewolves tend to suffer from emotional insecurities."

"I have no insecurities," Jacques replied.

"Starting to get a bit antsy? About ready to sprout fur and fangs?"

"Again, I'm *not* a vampire. I don't have fangs."

Dominus chuckled and then his narrowed eyes peered toward me.

"I appreciate you at least listening to my request," I said, trying to remain cordial, in spite of Dominus trying to antagonize Jacques. I wasn't certain Dominus really wished for Jacques to attack. Even though his arrow tip was silver, I had seen how fast Jacques moved. I doubted Dominus could hit Jacques before the werewolf ripped his throat out. But still, I didn't want to see such an event unfold, especially since I had been the one that brought us all together. "Since it seems I cannot persuade you to train me, may I ask you a question?"

"You may ask, but it won't guarantee I have an answer."

Through gritted teeth, I asked, "Have you seen a child vampire in this cemetery?"

His eyes widened momentarily with surprise, and then he nodded. "Once. Why? How do you know of him?"

"His name is Bodi. He was a schoolmate of mine."

Dominus gazed at me with solemn eyes. He put his crossbow into its holster on his back. "The little scamp caught me off guard. I never suspected he was a vampire."

"Do you know the vampire who turned him?"

"No. I'm not inclined to keep track of vampire pedigrees," he replied.

"Would it not be beneficial to know?" Jacques asked. "Considering that if you kill a master, you kill everything he or she has sired as well."

Dominus gave Jacques a long intense stare and finally acquiesced a nod while he chewed what I assumed was tobacco. "You're right, wolf. I tend to await the stragglers when they first rise from the grave. I kill them before they have a chance to find their lair. That was why the child had caught me unaware. I thought he was lost because that's how he appeared to be . . . *lost*. But the little boy was a vampire. Hell, who'd turn a child? When I approached, his disorientation vanished, and the vicious little fiend attempted to bite me. Had it not been for my cross, he'd have probably been successful. But, I've never followed a new vampire into its master's lair. So no, I know not who has sired this child into the world of darkness. Vampires are already damned in the eyes of our Lord, but I'd think an even greater damnation should befall any vampire that chose to defile a child in such a way."

"Agreed. What are the chances that he might have been turned by Baron Randolph?" I asked. "The master vampire."

He cocked a brow as he studied me. "You know of the baron?"

I nodded, as did Jacques and my father.

"Few even know he is a master vampire. And you, a new member of the hunters' regime, how is it that *you* know already?"

"It's personal," I replied.

"How so?" he asked. His eyes held keen interest.

"He nearly killed my father over a month ago, and he had one of his human servants kill my mother yesterday, which is the reason I sought to have you train me."

"You wish to go after a master?" he asked, shaking his head. For a few moments he eyes held genuine concern.

"Not immediately," I replied. "But I will kill him for his transgressions against my family."

"That's a bold statement, young hunter."

"I intend to fulfill it without fail."

Dominus studied my eyes for a long minute. A smile curled his lips. "I sense the courage within you. Perhaps I acted in haste in discarding your request."

"The four of us share a common enemy," I said.

He nodded. "We do. But I don't know that what I can teach you is much different than what anyone else could teach you."

"Perhaps not. But what about the premonitions I have?"

Dominus gave me an odd stare. "Premonitions? You have those?"

"On occasion, but I suppose sudden impulses are much stronger."

"What kind of impulses?"

I walked to the massive stone where my hunter box set. "Before Roy constructed this box and the tools for me, I studied my father's tools while he lay near death. Each thing I touched beckoned me."

Dominus frowned. "In what way?"

"For me to take the stakes and rush out into the night to find the vampires and turn them into dust, even though I had never been trained."

"How long have you known you were a hunter?" he asked.

"Less than two months," I replied.

"Damn." He rubbed his chin. "How old are you?"

"Eight."

Dominus grinned. "So you're one of *those* kind of hunters?"

"What kind?"

"One of the Chosen. In other words, you were born to be a hunter with the wisdom of a former hunter."

I nodded. "And you're not?"

He released a harsh grunt of a laugh. "I suppose I am, but I was born in the wrong part of the world."

"And where was that?"

"America."

"Gentlemen," Father said. "We have company."

All three of us looked in the direction my father nodded. Two dirt-covered corpses were dragging themselves out of the ground from two fresh graves.

Dominus laughed and looked at me. "I thought those two would've risen by now. You want training?"

I nodded.

"You're about to have your first lesson."

CHAPTER 19

Jacques turned and pointed. "Two more to the south of us."

"It's about to get messy," Dominus said. "Now, wolf, don't be cutting in . . . what's your name anyhow, boy?"

"Forrest."

"Wolf, don't intercept Forrest's vampire. A hunter can't have hand-holding or coddling."

Jacques shook his head.

"Forrest," Dominus said in the utmost seriousness. "The most important thing about killing a vampire is not getting bit."

I rolled my eyes. "I think that's a given, even for me."

Dominus released a throaty laugh and gave a menacing grin at Jacques. "Yeah, well, it kind of goes the same about werewolves, too, but some folks don't get it and end up werewolves anyway. Ain't that right, wolfie?"

"Look here," Jacques said, taking a step toward Dominus. "I've had enough of your pompous, belligerent—"

"Jacques!" I said, glaring at him. "There are four of us, and four vampires. You two can settle whatever differences you have afterwards."

"You see, boy, *that's* why you don't bring a wolf to a vampire hunt. You never know *who* they'll turn on."

Jacques jaw tightened. His inner wolf gleamed in his eyes, begging to be released.

"Dominus," I said. "You're not only angering him, but me as well."

"Good," he replied with a grunt and twisted smile. "Now how about the two of you take that anger and start killing vampires."

Perhaps I had been wrong in pursuing Dominus as the one to train me. I had no prior knowledge of who he was, nor did I know what to expect upon meeting him. But I had been desperate and thought that finding any hunter was in my best interest. His name, Dominus, had seemed like a strong title, someone capable of ripping his way through a cemetery full of vampires without blinking an eye or flinching. That's the naivety of an eight-year-old mind, and something I needed to shake myself free from as soon as possible. But the name he carried was one that he had apparently chosen for himself. Not one from his parents or one predestined for him.

"All kidding aside, Forrest," he said in a low serious tone. "And I'm sure your werewolf friend can attest to this, vampires can move fast, sometimes as quick as the blink of the eye."

I nodded. *And so can werewolves.*

"You ever scuffle when you were in school?" Dominus asked.

"Scuffle?"

"Fight."

"No. I was four times the size of most of my classmates. I'd have crushed them."

"You ever fight *ever*?"

I shook my head and pulled my stake from my coat pocket.

He glanced back to Jacques. "On second thought, wolf, you might want to stand ready. Don't want the boy killed on his first hunt."

"The name's Jacques," he said.

Dominus pretended not to hear, and looked toward me. "Vampires are extremely strong. You look capable of doing a lot of physical damage to ordinary humans, but be prepared when fighting one of these blood-suckers. Young ones are disoriented when they first emerge, so use that to your advantage. While you might knock one off balance with a good punch, they recover quickly. And no matter how hard you hit one, it only pisses them off."

I nodded, taking in the information.

"The stake must penetrate the heart, all the way through. I know, before you get all defensive and say that you already know that, you must realize that *near* the heart isn't good enough. Okay?"

"Okay."

Dominus stood at my side as the two vampires approached. One was a fair skinned blonde male and the other a female with dark hair and brooding eyes. For whatever reason, I never had taken into consideration that women were amongst the undead vampire legion. I don't know why I had thought that, but the sudden realization also made it harder for me. I didn't like the idea of killing a female vampire, but I supposed it was better than she killing me.

The female stood on the right dressed in a modest white burial gown, showing modest cleavage; and the male to the left wore a cheap suit, one I wouldn't *want* to be caught dead or *undead* in.

"Which one do you want?" Dominus asked.

"The male," I said quickly. I didn't want my first kill to be a woman, and I wasn't certain I could drive the stake through her heart.

He raised his crossbow toward the young woman. She bore her fangs and hissed. Her contorted face absorbed her beauty, making her a hideous monster. Dominus fired and the wooden arrow pierced through her heart. She collapsed with a sharp shriek, dissolving into dust before her hands could even reach for the shaft.

"He's all yours," he said, nodding toward the remaining vampire.

I liked the thought of a crossbow. It killed from a distance and was less personal. Using a stake was much different, being an intimate slaying, and also more dangerous for the hunter.

The male vampire's eyes shifted back and forth between Dominus and myself. After watching the female crumble into dust, he was more cautious in his approach.

I must admit that I was hesitant in my advance, even with the stake in my hand. I thought about what Dominus had said and realized that accuracy was most crucial. I'd never really given that much thought. To think that all I needed to do was stake the heart was one thing, but approaching a moving vampire was everything different than what my imagination had pictured the situation to be. He wasn't simply going to stand there and expose his heart. He was going to fight and do his best to kill me before I could kill him. A moving target made accuracy a lot harder.

There was nervousness in the new vampire's expressions, as his mind struggled to adapt to his surroundings. He was in a new reality, the world of the undead, and I was in a new world, the life of a hunter. Everything shrank around me. Nothing else existed except this vampire and myself. The gravestones around us vanished. Sounds minimized to the point that I heard the slow, almost absent, heartbeat of my undead enemy before me. My peripheral vision prevented me from seeing what was to either side of me.

He looked confused and betrayed, plus the slightest bit angry. Perhaps the eternal undead life wasn't something he had bargained for or even wanted. Perhaps it was the horrid suit someone had buried him in? Nevertheless, he was pacing opposite me in a circle as we studied one another before attacking.

His eyes watched the stake in my hand. He held no knowledge of the power he possessed as a vampire and seeing me with the sharpened piece of wood, it must have dawned upon him that I was his enemy. Regardless of whether he had sought to live forever or not, as I later learned some foolish humans actually *requested* to be turned, he suddenly took a more offensive stance toward me.

I imagined the majority of creatures on earth wanted to live, no matter what their state of being was. True, some people chose to end their lives, thinking they have nothing else to live for, but this wasn't an attitude one found in nature. I've never happened upon any beast of the wild standing at the edge of a cliff contemplating a leap to end it all. And this vampire was no different than those beasts. He did a quick soul-*less* searching and determined he wanted to kill me in order to spare his own life. However, even inexperienced, I held selfish counterplans of my own.

Where Dominus, my father, and Jacques were during this confrontation, I didn't know. I was shielded inside an invisible dome. My mind had thrust away all other outside distractions.

My thin undead enemy hissed. Fangs protruded in an instant. He flexed his hands and sharper nails lengthened. Amazingly, I needed to be properly trained to battle against these undead, and yet, they possessed immediate access to their defensive mechanisms. By height I was at least six inches taller, and my weight was probably three times his. Staring into his nervous eyes, I knew if either of us moved first, it'd have to be me.

I placed my right foot forward, and he backed away, his eyes watching the stake. I moved the stake out to my side, only to see his attention following it. I rotated it in a circular motion and nothing on his part changed. The stake held him spellbound. I wondered if Roy had enchanted the wood or blessed it after carving it into shape. He had mentioned carved runes . . .

I rushed toward the vampire, and his eyes averted and focused upon me, widening like a wild animal. He shrieked, and then growled like a threatened dog. He reared back his head, exposing his fangs even more. I didn't realize how long vampire fangs actually were. While it should have been intimidating to me, I felt a mental prodding to aim for his heart.

Since I was taller, I approached with a rapidly descending swing and aimed at his chest where I estimated his heart to be. He retreated slightly but arched forward, trying to bite my wrist. I countered with a sharp left hand swing with my fist, catching his jaw. The impact sent him reeling, and he flipped over a rugged gravestone, crashing to the ground on the other side.

I rushed to the other side of the stone, but he was gone.

I looked around, trying to find him, and an odd sensation pricked the back of my neck, like an insect crawling. I turned to see him approaching swiftly. His eyes were red, crazed, and angry. He struck me with such force that my back hammered against the massive stone where I had set my hunter box. The air was knocked from my lungs and the pain dazed me. Breathing in, *hurt*.

By instinct or another hunter's foreknowledge, my left hand

clutched the vampire's throat before he had a chance to bite me. He clawed at me, trying to lean his head to my neck to bite my throat. Dominus was right. The vampire was incredibly strong, but my determination to survive unbitten was stronger.

I clenched my fingers tighter around his throat, watching his eyeballs bulge. His sharp nails tore at my coat, but its thickness prevented him from cutting into my flesh. He attempted to growl, but with my hand choking him, only a pathetic noise emitted.

Pain radiated down my spine and the back of my head ached. In spite of the vampire's strength, he was extremely light, and I could have easily flung him backwards, but I didn't want him to come charging back at me. I figured he'd be on me before I was able to stand. As long as I held him by the throat, I controlled this fight.

I drove the stake into his gut. I knew it wasn't going to kill him, but being so close, I didn't have an easy aim for his heart. His eyes widened in pain. I smiled, only because I didn't know for certain he'd experience pain. Now, he was tugging back and pushing with his hands to get away from me, but he couldn't pry my tight grip off of his throat.

I yanked out the stake and plunged it into him again. Warm blood coated my hand as I twisted the stake even deeper.

He muffled a groan and winced. Blood leaked from the sides of his mouth, crimson contrasting with his pale complexion.

I left the stake in his side and pushed myself to my feet, careful not to release my chokehold as I rose. Once I was standing, I gripped the end of the stake and yanked it out. With my hand on his throat, I lifted him off the ground and slammed him on his back. His ribs cracked and his neck snapped from the violent impact. His eyes widened and his weakened hands clawed desperately into the earth.

I placed a knee to each side of his waist and straddled him. Veins swelled on his purpling face from how hard I was choking him. I thought it was odd that you couldn't kill a vampire by strangling him, even if you kept him from breathing for such a long period of time. Slowly and carefully, I positioned the sharp tip of the stake directly over his heart, looking into his eyes. I applied slight pressure, feeling the tip dent into his skin.

The fear in his eyes did nothing for me. No remorse, no regret. He knew I was going to end his undead life. Perhaps his fear was his uncertainty for what transpired next. I wondered about that myself. According to the cathedral, vampires were cursed beings without a soul. No chance of a heaven, and every certainty of hell.

"To hell with you," I whispered, plunging the stake through his ribs and into his heart.

There was the slightest moment of relief reflected in his gaze. Once that passed, his body crumbled beneath me and his burial clothes were gone. After several gusts of wind, his ash remains would be gone.

I remained in that position for a few moments. My hands shook. My heartbeat pulsed in my ears. It wasn't from fear, but a strange rush that empowered me.

"Not exactly the orthodox way of slaying a vampire," Dominus said with a wild grin. "But it'll do. Not bad work for a first kill."

White dust clung to the drying crimson blood on my hand. I stood and dusted off the powdered remnants from my pants and the ends of my overcoat.

"Why does their clothing vanish?" I asked.

Dominus chuckled. "My guess is the heat from their disintegrating bodies as hell swallows them also turns their clothes to ash as well. I don't rightly know."

Shaking myself from the mental fog and trying to calm from the euphoric energy welling inside of me, I remembered my father and looked for him. I didn't see him, and immediately I worried about his welfare.

CHAPTER 20

"Where'd my father go?" I asked.

Dominus pointed. "Over there."

Across the cemetery my father stood over a vampire that clung to a granite gravestone. This vampire was young, maybe in his early twenties before his transformation. Father held his silver cross inches away from the side of its face. It screamed as smoke billowed off of its flesh.

"Your Poppa likes to torture 'em, eh?" Dominus asked. "He's been kicking and punching it from the time you started fighting yourn. I like his style."

The vampire flung itself over on its back, trying to get away from the cross. The anger chiseled in my father's face was frightening to behold. I'd seldom ever seen him mad, and I'd certainly never witnessed the man with pure vindictiveness possessing him. His burning rage wasn't with this particular vampire, and I doubted in his previous slayings that he had ever been so brutal. He was torturing the vampire, but I assumed that in his mind he was picturing the baron as he unleashed his violent anger.

I took my stake off the ground and started toward my father.

"Ah, let him be, Forrest. It's good for him to get his aggression out."

Even though he was right, I ignored him and didn't bother giving him a response. Prolonged blind rage left one open for unexpected vulnerabilities, especially when dealing with a desperate vampire.

Jacques had already disposed of his vampire and turned his attention toward my father, too. We met halfway across the cemetery.

"You survived your first kill," he said.

I shrugged. "He didn't give much of a fight. I expect that the older ones are much harder though."

"They are."

My father kicked the vampire and struck him in the back of the head with the silver cross. As much as it had hurt my father to walk great distances after his injuries, he fought with the vigor of a much younger man. Sweat covered Father's reddened face. He took in gulps of air.

"Father, don't you think you've tortured him enough?"

"I'm drawing him out," he replied.

"Who?"

"The baron."

"And how are you doing that?"

"This spawn of the devil is his making. Randolph feels his anguish." He kicked the vampire in the gut and then he pressed the cross to its face. "A true master will come to protect his sired."

Jacques shook his head. "We don't know who turned this one."

"I do," he replied.

"Did he confess that to you?" Jacques asked.

My father's face was dark red. "He didn't have to."

"There's no way for us to know, John."

Tears formed in my father's eyes. The swollen knuckles on his right hand were split and bleeding from battering the vampire. The assault would have killed a normal human but seemed to have hurt my father more than the undead vampire that was hiding his face from the cross.

Jacques gave an even smile to my father. "The baron's not coming. If he were, he'd have already appeared."

Jacques reached for the vampire.

"Don't you touch him," my father said in a harsh tone. "Jacques, don't."

My cousin grabbed the vampire by the neck and dragged his body thirty feet away.

"Jacques!" Father hobbled, trying to get to his cousin.

Jacques grabbed the vampire's head, jerked it back and twisted in one swift motion. Then he yanked hard, pulling its head off of its shoulders. The vampire burst into dust.

"How dare you," my father said in a shaky voice. "How dare you rob me of my revenge!"

I ached inside for my father. I grieved for the loss of my mother, too, and it hurt seeing him torn up inside.

Father kept coming toward Jacques. I stepped between them.

"Know your place, son!"

The fury in his eyes was unyielding. He was near to striking me, and even if he did, I wasn't moving, nor would I exchange blows with him, despite my size. He was my father, and I sensed his anguish. No one acts properly when weighed beneath such pain, but I'd guarantee he wouldn't lay a finger upon Jacques. And yes, Jacques was more capable of defending himself than I could, but the last thing I wanted was for the two of them fighting one another. I hoped that could be avoided.

"It *is* my place, Father. He's family, what little of family we have left. You turn your anger against your own blood, and you're handing Baron Randolph a victory. Is that what you want?" I braced myself, expecting him to strike.

He looked at me for a long time, breathing hard and grinding his teeth.

"We all grieve about Momma," I said, fighting burning tears.

Jacques nodded.

Father closed his eyes, took a deep breath, and held it. His hands shook, and the shaking radiated up his arms and through his entire body. After he finally calmed, his voice crackled and whined at a high painful pitch. "It's just that I miss her so much, son. I'd rather the baron had robbed me of my life than to have taken hers."

"I know, Father."

Big tears spilled down his cheeks. "Besides you, she's all I ever had in this world. The only good fortune I truly had. She blessed me with you.

You're a gift unlike any other. I can still see her in your eyes, son. Yours are identical to hers. And soon . . . you're leaving to pursue the destiny given to you. I'll be alone then."

"I'm not leaving Bucharest until after the baron is dead, and even then, you're welcome to travel with me."

A relieved smile came to his face. Embracing me, he patted my back. "You're a good son."

"Have Jacques escort you home. I need to stay with Dominus throughout the night. I don't know if he'll train me further than tonight or not, but at least he can answer some questions for me."

Father pulled back and patted both of my shoulders. "Always know, son, that I am proud of you."

He stepped to the side of me and looked at Jacques. "My apologies, cousin."

Jacques smiled. "It's late, John. Let's get back to your cottage. There might be vampires along the way, so keep a watchful eye."

"If there are, please allow me the first chance to stake them."

"Sure," he replied, and then he smiled back at me. "But be quicker this next time, okay?"

I watched them walk along the cobblestone path until they reached the street where the gas-lamps lit the way. The thought suddenly dawned upon me that I'd never asked my father to finish telling me the story Jacques hadn't completed. The insight of knowing exactly what had prompted my father to become a vampire hunter when the odds had been set against him was information I coveted.

Dominus walked slowly toward me with his hands resting on his belt. "Well, I speculate that I'll never come across a trio such as yours during the rest of my life. You are definitely an odd bunch, but you get the job done. Too much scuffling amongst yourselves, though, but with the death of your Momma, I suppose that's expected. A good mother is the foundation of a sturdy home. Kind of unravels a family for quite some time after she's gone."

I frowned at him. His accent made it difficult to understand some of his phrases, and some of his words simply didn't register in my mind, as they were lost in translation. I hated to ask what certain words meant because I didn't wish to offend him, and I didn't want to make myself seem unknowing.

"You said that you're from America?" I asked.

"Yep."

"What brought you to Romania?"

Dominus grinned. "Now that's a long story, but the night's early. I suppose there's time to tell ya."

CHAPTER 21

ominus and I sat upon the large stone at the center of the graveyard. He took a leather pouch out of his inner coat pocket, reached in with his forefinger and thumb to grab a wad of moist brown leaves, and then he tucked them in between his left cheek and gums.

"What part of America are you from?" I asked.

He scratched his aged forehead for a moment. "After I entered the Civil War, I didn't stay long in any given place. You'd asked earlier if I was a hunter like yourself, *chosen*, and I suppose I am. But hell, it took a damned long time for me to figure it out."

"How did you learn that you were?"

"Lots of people think that the vampires are predominant in this country, but Forrest, they are scattered around the world. War torn countries are places where vampires slink through villages and cities during the night, feasting on the weak and dying. War battlefields are the main places you'll find these beasts, after the sun has set. Vampires comb the death fields and infirmaries because blood is everywhere. They thrive the most during bloody wars. Sometimes I have to wonder if vampires are some of the government officials that promptly declare war against other countries just to get the blood."

"I wouldn't think they'd need something so drastic."

Dominus glanced across the cemetery, as I had been doing periodically since I didn't want a vampire to approach without us knowing it was there. "They hide themselves better during a war."

"How's that?"

"With injured people near death, it wouldn't be unusual for a vampire to drain and kill a human without anyone thinking the death suspicious. No one would question the death. They'd toss the body out on the heap to be buried in a field the next morning. And that was another frightening work detail."

"What?"

"Finding empty graves in the cemeteries on certain mornings without no evidence that anything had dug up the body. Seeing barefoot prints walking away from the grave. I sensed something sinister at play that no one else did. I never told anyone because I didn't know how to actually explain the feeling."

"Did you see vampires during the war?"

Dominus nodded. "Yep. The first one I encountered frightened me severely. I had peered outside my tent during the night and watched it attack one of the watchmen. The vampire had compelled the man and then bit into his throat. There wasn't any struggle, and the next day our search found the watchman in the heap of dead soldiers. He was pale, drained of his blood, and the bite wasn't like an ordinary vampire bite. The vampire made certain to shred the throat to look like a savage animal had tore into him."

"So what made you decide to come to Bucharest?" I asked.

"The war ended and these vampires vanished. Right before it was over, though, I had met another soldier who confided in me about his fears. Well, let me rephrase that. He was drunk out of his mind. Once a man drinks that much, he spills his guts about things he'd rather keep secret. Anyways, he'd seen several of these bloodsucking beasts lurking in the foggy night searching through the infirmary tents. And then I told him about what I had seen. Another man listening to our conversation knew what they were. How? Not really sure. But he knew how to kill them. We carved stakes from crude dead pine limbs and cornered two vampires in a tent. He died after he killed the one. The other one had snapped his neck before either of us could react. I got lucky and killed it as it turned on me. It was dumb luck, really, because it staked itself when it flung itself at me. It doesn't matter who you are or what walk of life you come from, once you see such hideous undead creatures, you're never the same."

Dominus paused and his eyes searched the gravestones again. He scratched at the scruff of hair on his chin before he continued. "Anyways, I hated the war. I hated killing my own countrymen. Hell, it was a *senseless* war! Relatives on opposite sides of the battle line were shooting at one another. But what troubled me the most was discovering the vampires during the war. I traveled to New Orleans in hopes of working on a clipper ship, anything really, to get away from the reconstruction of the south. I met a black man in the French Quarter of New Orleans outside of a shop that associated with some dark magic; voodoo, they called it."

"Like Roy's shop?" I asked.

Dominus spit onto the cobblestone and shook his head. "Nothing like that. Roy's place pales in comparison. I'm talking some gut-wrenching, frightening stuff. Forrest, you're young. You're going to encounter a lot of dark things as you mature in your life as a hunter. Vampires aren't the only enemies you will encounter. Ghouls and zombies are undead creatures that rise from graves in the dead of night, although they are often rarer to find. This man showed me these creatures, and he knew about vampires and informed me of the infestation in Romania."

"Did you have a trainer?"

"The man in New Orleans gave me some pointers, but once I got here, I acted out of sheer instinct. You said that you get premonitions. I get impulses from time to time, too. When I do, and it's seldom, I act on them. But overall, I want to rid the world of as many vampires as possible. It's my contribution and penance for killing men during the war."

"Do you only kill the young vampires?" I asked.

"Not always. I have killed some older ones, which isn't nowhere nearly as easy as the ones we killed tonight. I could've taken all four of these in a matter of minutes by myself. The older vampires are wiser, more cautious, and seldom are they caught out in the open. Killing the new ones is a matter of keeping the population in check. I only hunt predawn patrol at this cemetery each Saturday. During the rest of the week, I'm at different cemeteries or out in the countryside, hunting the older ones."

"How many have you killed?" I asked.

"Hell, I stopped counting after a hundred. It's no longer a number's game to me. It's a survival tactic. Once you build up a reputation after that many kills, it's the other way around. They start hunting for you."

A light fog formed along the south side of the cemetery.

He stood and stretched. "I reckon that's all of 'em for tonight."

"You sure?"

"Yep." He took a glass flask from his inner coat pocket, yanked out the cork, and turned it up. It looked like an elixir bottle but I doubted that's what it contained.

I slid off the stone and stood. "I like your crossbow."

Dominus nodded. "It's quite an accurate weapon for hunting the freshly risen, but not so good when fighting an older one. You've never witnessed speed until you try to kill one of those."

"Did Roy make the bow?"

His eyes narrowed and he chewed the wad in his mouth. Finally, he shook his head. "No. Any crossbow will do as long as you use wooden arrows."

"You don't seem fond of him."

He shrugged.

"He told me that you didn't talk much, and he never could get you to talk to him."

"Forrest, I don't like talking to others, period. I prefer my privacy. And why should I give him information about me and what I do? He knows little about me, and yet, he sent you to the only place where he knows I hunt. He only knew that because I had let it slip. Imagine had I given him a lot more information? It'd put me to greater risk."

"From whom?"

"Other hunters."

I frowned. "Why would other hunters try to hurt you?"

"Let me clarify that," he said. "Hunters that have been turned into vampires."

Chills rushed through me. My eyes widened at the thought. Jacques had indirectly warned me about those on the evening when we first met.

He grinned and winked. "Yeah. You catch on quick. You understand. A master vampire who turns a hunter has a powerful tool at his disposal. They become much stronger than we are, faster, and ruthlessly coldhearted. And because they were hunters, they can anticipate our moves. I've never fought one, and hope to the heavens above that I never have to, but I've spoken with villagers in neighboring areas that have seen good hunters like you and I killed by one."

"And why would you suspect Roy to give information to one of those?"

Dominus sighed. "I don't think he'd intentionally do so, but he lives in that underground dark room of his, which is the best haven for an undead hunter to be. For a while, I truly wondered if he wasn't a vampire. He never comes out into the sunlight. Ever."

"He has a disease."

"Yep. I realize that now, but for a long time he had never told me his reasons. I never sensed him to be a vampire though. He didn't make me uneasy in that sense, but it was everything else: The dark room, wearing a hood to hide his face, and his constant secrecy. He finally confided in me after the baron killed his wife."

I nodded. "He told me about that, too, on the day my mother was killed by the baron."

Dominus frowned. "Before or after?"

"Before."

He frowned and his jaw tightened. "Interesting."

"Why?"

He shrugged and changed the subject. "How'd you befriend a werewolf?"

"He's my father's cousin."

Dominus cocked a brow. "Is that a fact?"

I nodded.

"Why didn't you get your father to train you?"

"He told me some useful things, but he's not a hunter like us. I was hoping to find someone who understood the inner connections to whatever guides us."

Dominus smiled. "That voice doesn't resonate too loudly for me, at least not if you drink enough."

He turned up the flask again and then he corked it.

"What do you plan to do until sunrise?" I asked.

"Walk the streets and alleyways since nothing else should appear here tonight."

"Think you'll encounter more vampires?"

Dominus chuckled. "The area's highly populated with them."

"Is Dominus your given name?"

"You may be the size of a man, but you're ever as inquisitive as the child you are."

How could I argue with that? I *was* still a child, mentally. To the best of my knowledge no potion or concoction was available to age my mind. I suppose the hurt showed faintly on my face.

He sighed. "I chose the name for myself when I arrived."

"Why?"

"I never liked the name Frank, which my folks had named me. Besides, Dominus sounded, well, *dominant*. Works good for me so far."

I extended my hand toward him. "It's time I head back to my home. Thanks for giving me a bit of your time."

"Now, it's not that I think you're incapable of handling yourself, but I think you should stick with me until dawn. I'll follow you back to your cottage in the morning, if you don't mind the company."

"That's fine. My father won't mind if you need a place to sleep."

Dominus said, "Besides I need to apologize to your cousin. I was a bit hard on him."

"I thought you had something against werewolves."

"Let's just say that I've had some bad experiences with them. Not all are defenders of humans. Some are controlled by vampires."

"He was a prisoner of one of Dracula's grandsons for a time."

"I suppose it's good fortune that he escaped."

I nodded.

"With his hatred toward vampires, he will prove to be a strong ally for you."

"He's already become one."

"Tomorrow night, well after dark, I'll take you to a little village where a small clan of vampires hide. Between the two of us, I think we can exterminate them."

"How many?"

"Six."

Upon first meeting Dominus and being exposed to his crass nature, I didn't expect I'd want to associate with him at all. But once it became only the two of us, he opened up more readily. The vampire hunter's life might be one of the loneliest occupations in the world, but even the most reclusive eventually desired the company of someone else, if only to exchange stories. Once Dominus decided to give me details of his past, he had lowered his emotional shield, but it wasn't something I had expected him to do for any extended period of time. Quite possibly he could decide after the morning sun broke the sky, to revoke my invitation for tomorrow night's journey. I decided to take it an hour at a time. No need getting my hopes up for an entire day.

CHAPTER 22

$\mathcal{D}$ominus and I had taken a small alleyway where the thin veil of fog hung like a curtain of smoke. I thought about my father as we walked and stopped walking.

Dominus turned to face me. "Is something wrong?"

"My father was in the baron's lair, and he said that the doors he fled through opened into a cemetery."

"What doors?"

"From some type of crypt with stairs that led to the baron's chambers?"

Dominus thought for a moment. "This cemetery doesn't have anything like that."

"Do you know one that does?"

He nodded.

"Can you take me to it?"

Shaking his head, Dominus looked into my eyes. "Not tonight. I wouldn't face a master vampire alone, and right now, with your lack of experience, that's what I'd be doing. No offense."

I didn't take any.

He gave a slight grin. "Hunt with me for a few nights and prove to me you're capable of defending yourself. Then, if you have enough gumption, I can take you."

I frowned, staring back at the cemetery. His offer was the best I'd get, and given the circumstances, I didn't blame him. I had one vampire kill to my credit, which was essentially nothing since the vampire had not been raised for even an hour.

"What caused this contention between the baron and your family?"

"Bodi, the child vampire."

Dominus chewed the tobacco and then spit. "How come?"

"My father was hired to kill Bodi by the child's parents. The baron interfered and tried to kill my father."

"So the baron turned the child?" Dominus asked with narrowed eyes. His gaze darkened.

"I hope not," I replied. I explained what else my father had said about being imprisoned inside the lair.

Dominus gave a sharp whistle and shook his head. "My guess is that the baron must have then. He took an immense affection to the child. A master does that to his own children, those he turned himself. If one of his children sired a new vampire, he'd not be as given to protect it. For the baron not to kill your father based upon the child's request tells me the child is his direct sire."

That assumption, which I believed was probably the case as well, left me with only two choices to remove Bodi from remaining one of the undead. I had to kill Baron Randolph, which destroyed all of his offspring, or I had to stake Bodi. The second choice I'd rather not be responsible for doing.

We continued walking. The fog grew thicker, the air colder.

"Grab onto a stake," Dominus said. "We are surrounded."

In the next moment, sets of red eyes peered from the shroud of fog all around us. I set my hunter's box next to a tall gravestone with an angel atop it, reached into my pockets and withdrew a stake in each hand. No time like the present to learn whether or not I was *destined* to be a vampire hunter.

"I guess, Forrest, that we're not gonna have to wait until tomorrow night for more training. Now's the time for you to keep your wits. I have to tell ya that I've never seen this much activity in one night, which only leaves one explanation."

"What's that?"

"Randolph truly hates you, and he's sent these vampires to kill you tonight."

I gave him a narrowed side-glance.

"Ah, now, don't let it get to you," he said with a wink. "We ain't in this business to make any friends; just to put the undead back in the ground where they belong. Watch yourself."

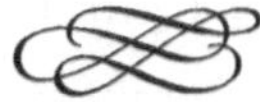

CHAPTER 23

The vampires standing around us weren't fresh from the grave like the other four we had killed as a group. I didn't have any idea what age these were, but there were at least a dozen of them standing in the perimeter around us.

Dominus said, "Should we survive this, you're going to have to tell me exactly what you've done that pissed off the baron so sorely. Cause it certainly isn't your total number of kills."

Glancing around, I noticed the undead vampires gazing at us. I had attended one funeral outside of my mother's, and I remembered how uncomfortable I had been seeing the dead body at the wake. The pallid skin tone. These standing around us held the same flesh tone except they breathed. Their eyes moved, watching, and some with reddish glows like a demon. Seeing a living corpse was unnerving, and had I already not been exposed to their existence, I'd have probably frozen.

Dominus looked serious, but his eyes held a bit of excitement like someone who hadn't eaten for days being seated at a king's table. His crossbow was loaded, but he really only had one shot to use effectively. With the number surrounding us, they weren't going to allow him to reload the bow.

Two vampires were watching me from the shadows. Perhaps it was my massive size that made them hesitate, or they simply were sizing me up on how to attack since I held a stake in each hand and towered like an imposing wall.

Dominus' crossbow twanged as the bowstring released and fired the arrow. Everything was happening so fast and unexpectedly since he had told me that we weren't going to encounter any more vampires. He probably had one opportunity for a clear shot. I was nervous, but not as much as I probably should have been. I couldn't waste my time determining how to defend myself. I simply needed to rely upon instinct.

Of course, Jacques' words often hung in my mind about never allowing myself to be turned by a vampire. Dominus reinforced that by telling me about vampires that were former vampire hunters, and the dangers they imposed upon our survival.

Even though I didn't have much hand-to-hand fighting experience, I reasoned that with my size and strength all I needed was to deliver accurate strong strikes. That didn't mean I held any advantage over these vampires because I obviously didn't. They were incredibly fast and the least of their physical force equaled my maximum, which is why hunters like us relied upon stakes and other tools to equalize the playing field.

I worried about my father and Jacques. They had left the cemetery to return to the cottage. Now we were divided, and we were weaker. As a group of four we could defend ourselves against this group of undead that surrounded Dominus and I.

Father was perhaps the weakest of us. And his battered hand had probably stiffened and was bruised, making any defensive fight more difficult, if not impossible, should the baron have sent vampires after them as well. But I wondered if my father had been correct in his logic. He had said that he was beating the young vampire to stir a rise of anger in the baron. The torture would make the master of the victim vampire step in to protect his offspring. The baron hadn't appeared, but instead he had sent his lesser vampires to do the dirty work for him.

I was beginning to believe that the baron, although a master vampire, was more spineless than what a lesser vampire should be. He feared me a great deal; or rather he feared my possession of having a dagger, which could make him submissive to me. Needless to say, I didn't feel his presence within the vicinity of where we stood surrounded by his underlings. He was too frightened to even make an appearance to see if his minions were successful in killing us or not.

This confrontation was a test for me, not Dominus. Dominus had already established himself as a hunter with well over a hundred kills, if I believed his boast, and I did. He was proficient, seasoned, and had scars that proved his combatant encounters weren't all so gracefully quick and easy with the firing of a crossbow. With the crucial scars on his face, it wasn't difficult to imagine that he probably had much worse disfigurements elsewhere on his body. There wasn't any possible way to have his experience without having acquired battle scars as well.

The baron wasn't one to offer a fair fight, but I never expected the undead to abide by any sets of rules or standards. He was given to finding his pleasures in torture, as he had with my father. The baron held no mercy. He thrived on prolonging agony for as long as possible. He fed on it, but apparently from a great distance. His thirst for blood, torture, and agony should have been no surprise because all vampires descended from the true vampire master who knew no limits to the devices of inflicting the most inhumane disfiguration in Romania's history. The dragon himself: Vlad.

By all rights, my father should have died long before he crawled to our cottage door and knocked for help. But determination like his didn't die easily. Though capable of walking now, my father would never be at one hundred percent like he had been before. His legs carried him, but slower and with great pain.

The baron had insisted through his human servant that he and I were now even, meaning *after* he had killed my mother. I regarded my sending the two hunters after him as the attack that made us even, but her murder was an instigation on nothing less than the brink of war between he and I.

Here was where I had miscalculated, the one violation on my part that I had not considered, and it occurred to me only moments before this impending fight outside of the cemetery ensued. When I had stood outside our cottage and defied his mind control, he viewed my lack of submission to him as a threat, and rightly so because I intended to kill him for what he had done to my father. In actuality, my defiance wasn't an attack, but he viewed it as such. I'll admit that it was an insult to him that I hadn't yielded, but he had attacked my family first. And after my mother's death, I'd never relent in my pursuit to turn the baron into dust.

Three vampires rushed through the fog directly at Dominus. They were blurs of movement, and I don't understand how Dominus managed such an accurate shot within a mere second, but he shot one of the vampires through the heart. Its body crumbled less than a few yards from where Dominus stood.

Dominus dropped the bow and spun, which brought the long end of his coat upward like a windblown cape. He pulled something from his coat pocket and threw it at another vampire. The glass orb shattered against its face. The vampire shrieked, smoke and steam rose off its blistering face as the liquid ate its pale flesh like acid.

Holy water?

His left hand was balled like a fist. He flung it open at the scalded vampire's face. A cloud of white powder clung to the vampire's already melting skin. The powder intensified the pain, sending the vampire to its knees. It ripped and pulled away its flesh, trying to rid itself of the maddening pain. The third vampire watched in horror and slowed his pace toward Dominus.

I marveled at how Dominus moved in such a fluid-like motion, channeling an unseen force as he defied and challenged the powers of the undead. He had tapped into a surge that allowed him to be one with all of his weapons. His mind, soul, and spirit reacted to his attackers without any hesitation. He calculated their approach and reacted in kind.

Dominus rushed toward the third vampire and drove a stake through its heart. Once it dropped to the street as a small pile of ash, he took the stake and killed the suffering vampire.

Two vampires came straight for me. My first instinctive reaction was a quick hammering punch, even though my fist was still enclosed around the stake. My thick fist struck the vampire in the center of its chest with enough force to knock it backwards. It stumbled back into the fog and fell over a tombstone, clutching its chest. Nice to know they could feel pain from such a punch.

Trying to mimic Dominus, I spun, but not elegantly or accurately like he had. The movement was foreign and clumsy to me. I suppose it never hurt to try something new, but it became obvious that I lacked his experience in fighting tactics. This was a spur of the moment motion on my part and not fully thought through. I suppose it took practice—a lot of practice—to perfect. And because I stumbled with the awkward movement, basically due to my massive size and overly large feet, I made myself dangerously vulnerable to my attackers.

As I pivoted full circle, the stake in my right hand caught the vampire in the side, a few inches beneath his ribs, but not in his chest as I had imagined. The sharp point went deep, a good six inches, but nowhere near his heart. The vampire replied with a harsh growl, hissed like a terrified cat, and gnashed his teeth but abandoned any thought of continuing his attack toward me. Instead, he yanked at my hand with his clawed fingers, trying to pull out the stake.

What I liked the most about the constructed stakes was the blunt ends were encased inside a pure silver grooved layer. Although the silver wasn't deadly to a vampire in the way that it was to a werewolf, it was toxic in the sense that it prevented quick healing.

Since the baron enjoyed making others suffer, I thought why not return the favor? While he might not actually experience the pain that his spawns were suffering, he'd at least hear their anguished cries and hopefully recoil from his agony of losing more of his children.

I released the embedded stake in the vampire and tossed the one in my left hand over into my right. While the angered vampire was preoccupied and desperately tugging at the stake lodged in his side, I took both hands on the blunt end of my other stake and drove it through his heart. After he disintegrated, I plucked the other stake from off the ground and turned, ready to remain on the offensive.

A female screeched in agony. The strong smell of garlic lofted in the air. She raked her fingernails across her pale flesh above her cleavage. Bleeding ulcers foamed. Madness widened her dark eyes. No white was visible in her gaze, just the darkness of a frenzied soulless creature. Her fangs appeared, but her attention fixated on the growing holes on her chest.

Dominus tossed another handful of darts toward her. The metal tips embedded in her arms, her chest, and her face. Again, the strong garlic odor permeated the air. Some of the vampires near her, including the one I had hurled over a tombstone, darted and disappeared through the veil of fog while a few more braved an attempt to rescue her by intervening.

In a sense this was a familial reaction, to protect their own. They were a family, or as Dominus had described, a clan. They were more powerful in number, so they needed to prevent us from slaying them.

Dominus laughed, expelling a few obscenities that I supposed folks in America found offensive, but I didn't have any understanding of what he meant by the words. Within a moment's time, he drew two silver-plated swords and decapitated two of the male vampires before I ever saw him move. More surprisingly to me was from where had he drawn the swords? I didn't even know he possessed them.

The female covered in garlic sobbed with her head in her hands. When she finally glanced up, the flesh of her face had peeled away, revealing only bone. The pale white bone of her skull gleamed in the faint moonlight. Her eyes were full black, and her beauty was gone.

She bore her fangs, shoved herself to her feet, and flung herself toward him. He stepped aside and extended a sharp sword in her path, nearly splitting her body in half. Before she uttered any further sounds, he spun and with the other sword, he decapitated her, ending her suffering.

I thought it odd that we were more merciful in eradicating the vampires than the master had been toward my father.

We were silent for several seconds. Both of us searched the rest of the foggy area, looking for movement. Nothing stirred, at least nothing within our line of vision.

Dominus looked at me with a wide grin on his face. "Well, Forrest, that was invigorating. Fighting alongside with you makes me regret that I stopped keeping my kill count."

Invigorating seemed the appropriate word, even for me. A strange renewed energy rushed through me with each of the two vampires I had slain. It was difficult to explain the sensation. I felt like every muscle in my body had increased in size and strength. I supposed it was euphoria.

"Dominus," I said, "I'd feel better if we headed toward my cottage."

"Thinking that your father's in trouble?"

"It has crossed my mind."

"Seems possible, I suppose, since they waited to attack after we were separated. My guess is that the baron's attention is more preoccupied on you than your father. But let's go make certain."

I nodded and turned to get my hunter box.

"Now," Dominus said. "I need to point something else out to you."

"Sure."

"There's a reason why a hunter doesn't keep his box on him whenever we go searching for the undead. How much does that box weigh?"

"Not sure."

"If it's like mine, it probably weighs a good thirty pounds or more. That's a lot to lug around. It's an anchor you don't need. You have a pretty nice coat, but you need to find yourself a better one that's lined with numerous pockets. Every tool you have stored in your box, you should have the exact same thing tucked away on you, too. That way, you don't have to dig through the box. Hell, make certain you don't take it out during your hunts. Use the box to store your supplies or when you travel to other cities or countries."

We walked down the narrow street, heading out of the city.

"The baron didn't show up," I said.

"Did you really think that he would?"

"As much as he hates me, eventually he's going to."

Dominus laughed, "Boy, he fears you for some reason. Vampire progeny tend to have an undying loyalty to protect their masters, even when that isn't reciprocated."

"I sensed the baron's presence."

Dominus stopped walking. He cocked a brow as he looked at me. "You're sure?"

I nodded.

"How close?"

"He wasn't close at all."

"Your father was in his lair, correct?" Dominus asked.

"As best he understands."

"I'm going to let you in on a secret. One of Dracula's original fortresses rests underneath this city, buried long ago."

Chills rushed up my arms.

Dominus nodded. "There are tunnels, rooms, and prison cells beneath some of the streets. Some of the tunnels are connected to others that will lead to the baron's lair. You noticed how quickly the rest of the vampires vanished?"

"Yes."

"They know the quickest access to those underground tunnels. Now, I told you that I wanted to ask you something after this little skirmish ended."

"Okay?"

"So here it is. Do you have any idea why the baron fears you?"

"He fears what I can do to him," I replied.

"And what can you do?"

I pulled open the right side of my jacket, revealing the dagger sheathed on my belt.

He frowned. "A dagger?"

"It has been blessed by a gypsy witch."

"Blessed to do what exactly?"

I explained to him what Jacques had told me.

"That's a powerfully strong weapon, boy."

I nodded. "I know."

"With that in your possession, killing the baron won't be nearly as impossible as I had imagined. But it still won't be easy. I doubt the four of us could successfully fight our way through the baron's lair to get near him."

"You think there's that many vampires?"

Dominus released a deep laugh. "There's armies of them. Not necessarily in his lair, but the city has no shortage of vampires. You could spend your life here hunting nightly and not make a dent in their population. Your father is fortunate that he managed to escape the lair. I doubt any others ever have."

"But if you kill the master—"

"*If* is a mighty large word for only two letters, son."

Frustrated, I sighed and started walking. "There has to be a way."

"Oh, there's a way, but it will take far more than the four of us. There's something you need to know about Baron Randolph."

"What's that?"

"He holds a seat with the city council, so he has a bit of authority in Bucharest. Most likely it's compulsion that allows him such power and control. But you cannot convince the council of what he is. His allure is stronger than reason. Not only has he spilled blood to obtain his stature, he will never be challenged by them or removed from his seat. He's like a devil reigning over the cathedral. He blinds others into thinking him holy."

"So no public challenge will benefit us?"

Dominus shook his head. "No. And because he's a vampire, he's never seen in public during the day, which makes him more mysterious to the city residents. That's why we hunters are predestined. We see through such guises, and we can detect the presence of vampires."

"Does that develop over time?" I asked.

"What?"

"Detecting vampires?"

"You don't now?"

I shook my head. "Not strongly. No."

"Give it time. The more you fight them, the better you'll adjust to their smell and actions. You said that you felt the baron's presence."

"But only after the vampires attacked. I had no forewarning of them. You knew they were around us before they revealed themselves."

"I think you'll learn to sense their presence more readily."

As we walked upon the forest road, clouds hid the moon and darkened the sky. The trouble about traveling on foot during the darkness, especially after fighting vampires was every sound became suspect. Wind shaking a rattling leaf, a night bird flittering through the trees, or an animal scratching the ground in search of food, all of these things made me wonder if lingering vampires followed us. If these sounds alarmed Dominus, it never showed in his expressions. I had a lot to experience before I could ignore all of the odd forest noises during the darkest hours.

Only fools or hunters chose to walk during the dead of night. Perhaps we fit both categories. There were reasons why mothers told their children horrifying tales before bedtime. I wondered if Bodi's mother had done that for him.

The dead of night phrase made sense to me now. That was the time when the undead were able to make their appearance, and certainly why the living needed to be secured inside their homes. We hunters proved to be the only exceptions because someone needed to protect the innocent from the monsters.

CHAPTER 24

I awoke the following afternoon in the cottage still dressed in my hunting coat and clothes from the night before. I hadn't even taken off my boots. I had been too exhausted. I barely remembered lying down. The cottage was quiet, and I was alone, which alarmed me. I quickly rolled out of the bed and stumbled my way toward the door.

I remembered that Dominus had said that he wished to apologize to Jacques, but had he? With the previous contention between them, I worried that things might have gotten worse instead of better.

I swung open the door and the setting sun caused me to squint. Slowly my vision adjusted, and I was able to look around.

My father sat on wide stump near the woodpile. Jacques stood and leaned against a massive tree with his arms crossed. Both were listening to Dominus tell stories about the vampires he had slain. Neither my father nor Jacques were upset. They were amused. Apparently Dominus had smoothed the differences between them.

"Ah, the boy has risen," Dominus said. Smoke puffed from his pipe.

I rubbed my eyes. Everything seemed fuzzy and blurred. Even when I had guarded the cottage door throughout the night while my father recovered, I never slept past noon. In spite of my long deep sleep I was drained.

Jacques shot a quick glance toward me.

"Were you and Father attacked after you left the city last night?" I asked.

"No," Jacques replied.

I looked toward my father. His right hand was swollen and purple. It had to be causing him some added pain. Despite his obvious injury, he held a triumphant smile on his face.

"I believe Father was right," I said to Jacques.

"About?"

"Torturing the vampire to get the master to appear."

Father shook his head. "Dominus insists that Baron Randolph wants you dead more than he wants me. I'm inclined to believe that as well."

Jacques nodded. "I saw the hatred in his eyes the day he stood at the edge of the road facing you, Forrest. He's not going to abandon his pursuit."

"Neither shall I," I replied.

"I doubt he's going to attack you directly."

"No, he's a coward. His actions prove that he is. Otherwise, why does he kill women?"

Jacques frowned.

"The baron killed my mother, but he also killed the wife of the crafter, the man who had built my box."

"He might be a coward," Dominus said, "but his actions are to make his enemies submissive to their fear and in turn, abandon any future thoughts of exacting revenge. It has been the same with every master since Dracula, although it's doubtful any other will be as ruthless as he."

"I'm too angry to be afraid."

"He recognizes that, too, especially after last night," Dominus said.

"I want to go after him," I replied.

Jacques shook his head. "No, not yet."

"He fears me."

"I understand that, but folks controlled by their fear, even vampires, can act crazy and resort to desperate actions. Besides, even if your father's hands were healed, we only have four people. We need more," Jacques said.

Dominus gave me a grim smile. "His next attack will be greater than last night's. He will use older vampires."

"Against which Forrest has no experience," Jacques said.

"He will after tonight."

"Why?" my father asked. "Where are you taking him?"

"Glodrim, which is a small village at the base of the mountain near the bend of the river."

"I know the place," Jacques said. "The vampires hide in the caves during the day."

Dominus nodded. "At my last count, I saw only six."

"And you spared them?" Jacques asked.

"No, I didn't spare them. They're the most troublesome left of their original clan. I'm not agile enough to climb the steep side of the cliff. I assure you, though, with Forrest's help, we'll get them."

Jacques sighed. "I'd like to help you, but I need to return to the tavern near Ploiesti, where your father met the werewolf that gave him the advice that probably saved my life. Did your father ever finish telling the story behind why he chose to become a vampire hunter after encountering Dracula's grandson?"

"I've not asked him yet."

"No time like the present," Jacques said. He glanced at the sun's position. "Besides, I'd best be leaving before it get any later. Even a werewolf has enemies other than vampires."

"Ah, the boy doesn't want to hear about my excursions," my father said.

Jacques flashed a quick smile. "I'm certain he'd like to know how you met his mother. It occurred on the same day, did it not?"

My father's lower lip trembled. I opened my mouth to tell him he didn't need to say anything, it could wait until later, but he held a single finger toward me, indicating that he didn't wish me to speak. I obliged.

Jacques tipped his hat to me and then to Dominus before he sprinted through the trees until he reached the road.

"Our cousin is correct. I met your mother the night I had to kill the vampire to free her and him."

Dominus frowned and turned toward my father. "Wait. You mean that *you* killed one of Dracula's grandsons?"

"Let's not give away the ending," Father replied. "After all, I never interrupted you during any of your tales."

Dominus relit his pipe. "Fair enough. You have my complete attention."

Father had mine as well. For those weeks he was recovering, I desperately wanted to ask him, but with his aggravation of being bedfast, he wasn't mentally capable of telling the tale in the way that allowed him to boast. After last night's challenge and his release of anger, his level of pride and accomplishment had resurfaced. He had never tried to hide his busted knuckles and swollen hand. He did quite the opposite, setting it atop the other hand where it was constantly visible.

Father cleared his throat. "At a rustic tavern in Ploiesti, I had spoken with a man who warned me that killing a wolf might actually kill a werewolf, who could really be Jacques. With that knowledge I decided to return to the place where I had last saw Jacques. I figured he should recognize me, regardless of him being a werewolf or a wolf. At least that much was true."

"And what wasn't true?" I asked.

Father laughed softly. "The other mammoth wolves *didn't* recognize me. Several of them charged at me, but Jacques tore into all three of them. He got between those massive wolves and I, and held them back by snapping and growling. Quite vicious our cousin was on that night. I suppose he was capable of communicating with them, as they sat back like obedient dogs with their pink tongues hanging out and clearly they had lost their interest in me.

"I called his name, and he eased to my side and sat down. One of the most beautiful wolves I had ever seen, but huge. He stood higher than my waist on all fours. Looking into his eyes, I recognized it to be him."

"How did he turn into human form?" I asked. "He never told me."

Father smiled and pointed his index finger as he made his point. "Ah, the man in the tavern had given me a talisman blessed by a gypsy that could release only one wolf from their shape-shifted form. He wore an identical one on a silver chain around his neck."

"The one Jacques wears now?"

"Yes, the very one. After he had been freed from his bondage, he wanted to return and free the others, but his fear toward the vampire was too great. Since I was going, he insisted that I have it. At no charge."

"Hell, I'd have asked for at least a tankard of ale," Dominus said.

"He didn't even have to ask," my father replied. "I bought him several, and during the night while we drank, he gave me details of the best ways to get into the stables and out again with the least chance of being noticed. But he warned me that Dracula's grandson was one of the most powerful vampires left in the area. If he detected me, I had no hope left, especially if he discovered the talisman.

"I was too drunk that evening to head toward the castle, so I arrived the following evening right before dusk, and that's when Jacques had protected me from the other wolves. I used some twine to make a necklace with the talisman and wrapped it around Jacques' neck."

"What happened?" Dominus asked, leaning forward.

"Well, let's just say if ever the opportunity arises where you can watch such a transformation? Don't. It's one of the most disgusting things I've ever witnessed. Actually, I couldn't even stomach watching the entire ordeal. I leaned against a tree and vomited."

Dominus shook his head with slight disappointment in his eyes, trying to suppress his grin.

"Jacques lay nude on the ground. The man who had given me the talisman, I think his name was Rusk, never told me that the transformation back into human form would render Jacques unconscious."

"It did?" I asked.

Father nodded. "I shook him hard and never got a response from him. He snored, but that was it. He was in a deep sleep."

"So how'd you get him out of there?" I asked.

"How else? I carried him."

Jacques probably outweighed my father by a good fifty pounds then. More than that now since my father's legs had withered considerably since his injuries.

"I hefted him over my shoulder and started down the hillside toward the river, the same place where we'd been separated nearly a year before. And that's when I saw your mother for the first time. Olivia was thinner then, and her complexion an unhealthy pale. Her radiant beauty was diminished only by the haunted look in her eyes. Dressed all in white, she was filling two wooden pails with river water and was about to start back toward the estate. The brightness of her clothes glowed, even though the sun had already set."

"Wait," I said. "She wasn't a vampire. She couldn't have been because—"

"No, son, she wasn't. She had been at the river before the sun vanished behind the mountains. But she had been forced against her will to be a human servant for the vampire. He had never killed her."

"And what prevented him from turning her?" I asked.

"I'm getting to that."

I sat on the edge of the stump beside my father.

He said, "I saw a vampire approaching her on horseback. Of course, then I only *suspected* that he was a vampire because I didn't actually know. My suspicion turned out to be correct though. I crouched behind a row of thorny berry shrubs and set Jacques down. Amongst the things Rusk and I had discussed, he told me that a wooden stake through the heart was the best way to kill a vampire, and the safest way to do that was by entering the crypt during the day while the vampire was fast asleep."

Dominus laughed. "Yeah, good luck attempting that. It sounds really good when you're talking about it, but I've never encountered a vampire that didn't have a servant standing guard."

"I don't doubt that," my father replied. "I wasn't fond of the idea of wandering into a lightless crypt, even with a lantern, and still to this day, I'd rather fight a vampire out in the open like we did last night."

"It's safer in a lot of ways," Dominus said.

Father nodded and continued. "This vampire was off the horse in an instant. I never saw him dismount. He stood only a few inches from Olivia, staring down into her eyes. Then," My father's voice crackled. "He fed from her and she from he."

I felt anger and nausea rise simultaneously inside me.

"I shook Jacques, trying to awaken him, but there was no waking him. The vampire stood about twenty yards away, which was too much distance for me to run without being noticed."

Dominus held up his crossbow where I could see but my father couldn't due to how we were seated. Dominus winked. I got his hint. The crossbow held obvious advantages.

"After the damned monster drank Olivia's blood, he turned and whistled. Immediately all of the mammoth wolves galloped down the hillside toward him. All of them except Jacques.

"I peered through the shrubs, careful not to shake the leaves or branches. The vampire looked concerned, realizing that Jacques was not amongst his pack. Jacques later told me that the vampire did have a mental link of control through hypnosis, but the talisman and Jacques deep sleep apparently prevented him from locating us."

"Now, this vampire was the grandson of Vlad?" Dominus asked.

Father nodded.

"I figured him to be more powerful."

"He is," Father replied.

"Is?" Dominus asked. "So he's still alive?"

Father frowned with frustration. He was a great storyteller, and it had been a long time since he had been given the opportunity to do so.

"Sorry," Dominus said, "but I cannot continue with this suspense. It gets me all riled up inside. Besides, the sun will set soon. Forrest and I need to be on our way."

"Very well," my father said with a slight sigh and a droop in his shoulders. "I didn't know exactly what else to do. I assumed that the vampire was going to send the wolves in search of Jacques, but they already knew where we both were. I was so infatuated with Olivia that I couldn't bear to leave her behind bound to the vampire. I couldn't leave her. I had one advantage though."

"What's that?" I asked.

"The flowing river was loud, but it gave me an idea. Before the wolves were sent to track us, I dragged Jacques down the embankment beside the shrubs and lowered us into the cold water. I hoped the chill of the water would awaken him but it didn't. At the edge of the bank, I dislodged a log and positioned Jacques arms over it, then pushed him into the strong current while I held the end of the log.

"We floated toward Olivia and the vampire, unnoticed and unheard. I did perhaps the most daringness thing ever. As we floated behind where they stood, I reached out and grabbed the hem of her dress and tugged hard. She fell backwards with a loud splash. I caught her and she shrieked. Dracula's grandson turned with fury set in his eyes. For a moment I thought I was dead, but there wasn't anything he could do."

"Why?" I asked.

Father smiled. "A vampire cannot cross moving water."

I glanced at Dominus. "Is this true?"

"Yep. Don't ask me how, but it's the truth. The only way a vampire can cross a moving body of water is for another to carry him."

"So that's how you got away?" I asked.

My father nodded.

"And what about her being compelled as a human servant? How did you break that?"

"The strength of such a bond wanes over time. Once his blood got out of her system, she came around. But I took her to a priest. He anointed her with oil and holy water and blessed her. Otherwise, she'd have fallen into a quick transfixion if her eyes ever looked into his."

"Did you ever meet him again?" I asked.

"No," he said, shaking his head.

"Why hadn't he turned her?"

"According to your mother, he was waiting for her to mature a few more years. She resented him for what he had done and for what he had planned."

Dominus stood and looked at me. "Now you understand why you were destined to become a vampire hunter?"

"It's why I did," my father said. "Last night made my seventh kill, but I never got brave enough to go back to where I first saw Olivia."

"Because of your father and mother, Forrest, you were a gift given to them to wipe out the vampire population. It stirred that deeply inside of your mother."

Father nodded. "There were few things she ever spoke harshly against. The undead was the main one."

"Forrest," Dominus said, "say your goodbyes, get your box, and let's travel to Glodrim. It's still a good walk. Doubtful we'll get there before sunset, but we might."

I faced my father. "Don't you want to go?"

He shook his head. "I'm exhausted, Forrest. My hand aches. I can't possibly use a stake properly."

"I hate to leave you behind, all alone."

"I've been around for a long time," he replied. He pulled me close and embraced me, unable to get his arms all the way around me. "You listen to what Dominus tells you. I didn't care much for him when we first met, but he's experienced. He knows what he's talking about, and I'm certain he'll do everything possible to keep you alive. So listen to him and don't get overeager, okay?"

I nodded. "Okay."

"Now get your belongings and get on your way."

I did as he instructed. As Dominus and I headed down the road, I looked back. My father stood at the door and waved. The smile on his face indicated how proud he was of me. For some odd reason, I couldn't shake the feeling that this was the last time I'd see him alive.

CHAPTER 25

Glodrim set down at the bottom of a deep ravine. The road was almost too steep to walk down without running. A narrow river curved around the edge of the village and cut a channel through the massive mountainside.

Dominus had helped line my pockets with the proper necessities, even though he still wanted me to take the hunter box, just in case I needed to restock. In each of my coat pockets I had an ash stake that Roy had given me.

Dominus had made sheaths for each of my forearms so I could conceal two more daggers for quick access. He had given me two round glass bottles filled with squeezed garlic juice. From my box he had taken my holy water vials and had me tuck them inside my vest pockets. Two more stakes that he had crafted while I slept were tucked behind my belt. Each of my boots held an additional stake.

He never showed me how he had made them, but he wrapped little balls of paper around metal barbs coated with garlic. These were in my side pockets as well. All of this for *six* vampires?

Dominus looked at me with a solemn expression on his face. "Forrest, I don't expect you to remember exactly where each item is stowed upon you, but when you're dealing with older vampires, you need to have immediate access to anything that might slow them down. Garlic is a painful poison. It won't necessarily kill them, but the pain it inflicts temporarily disables them. Some flee just from the smell because they know what it can do to them. But above all else, the stake is what you should value the most."

We weren't even halfway down the steep road that intersected the village. The streets were vacant. No lanterns glowed from windows. The town appeared dead and abandoned.

A sign was posted by the side of the road. It stated: Enter after dusk at your own peril.

I set my hunter box beside a large rock near the sign. No need toting it all the way down the hill and back up again. I was heavily loaded with plenty of weapons. It was doubtful I'd need more.

"I wish we had arrived before sunset," he said. "As it is, everyone has barricaded their windows with heavy shutters and sealed every door. Whatever befalls us tonight, we're on our own. No matter how much anyone beats upon a door or cries out in pain, the townsfolk will not offer shelter after the sun goes down."

The three-quarter moon shone brightly, but was setting behind the mountainside. Heavy clouds were moving overhead, making flickering stars vanish. Once the moon was gone and the storm clouds claimed the night sky, darkness claimed everything. Shrieks echoed in the sky. A cloud of bats swarmed from the tiny crevices in the mountain, reminding me of Baron Randolph's first appearance outside the cottage. I didn't know if these were regular bats or the six vampires in their altered state.

"When did they hire you before?" I asked.

"Several years ago."

"Why didn't you return before now?"

Dominus shrugged. "They only paid for the one night."

We reached the center of the town. The ground was level, and the shadows faded one by one as the mountain eclipsed the moon's glow. I reached into my coat pockets, took a stake in each hand, but didn't withdraw them.

Each house door and window was boarded up. We were the only

living beings on the street, waiting for the undead. The sound of our breathing was like a faint breeze.

"So they won't open a door even if they know you?" I asked.

"Not after darkness settles."

"Why not?"

"They won't risk it. They are very skeptical and believe that the vampires can disguise themselves as family members, hoping to gain access to get inside a home."

I frowned and pointed toward the shutters of the closest house. "Vampires have brute strength. None of these boards could keep them out."

"Vampires cannot enter a home without permission."

"They can't?"

He shook his head.

"Why is that?"

"Vampires cannot enter most sanctuaries. Homes are considered sacred by the owners and retain some sort of power that bars a vampire from entering," Dominus said. "But once permission is granted, they can come and go at will. These folks won't risk the chance of seeing through a window after dark because they don't want to be tempted. Would you deny a family member access to your home if you believed they were in danger?"

"I have few left."

He gave me a scornful look.

"Probably so."

"And in doing so, if your relative had become a vampire, that would be your death."

"Why don't the townspeople simply move on?" I asked.

"They are stubborn and besides, it's their homes and land. Why should they be forced out?"

To survive? I thought.

I didn't like leaving my father at our home by himself. I was ready to find a new place for us to live because Baron Randolph knew where we lived. I tried not to worry about Father since I had arrived, simply because I needed to apply all of my focus here. But there was the uncertainty of seeing him alive again that nagged at the back of my mind.

A sliver of light remained in the sky. A cold breeze flowed off of the river and slipped through the houses, swirling around us. With the cool air came a dank smell of death and decay unlike anything I had smelled before.

My eyes searched the shadows, trying to imprint my surroundings like a map in my mind I could use once the final beam of light vanished. Darkness had never bothered me. I was quite comfortable without a light source, which I suppose is odd for a young person. My worry was more toward Dominus than myself. While I was thankful that he was training me, the last thing I wanted was something horrible happening to him. Should he die teaching or looking out for me, his death was on me. His blood was on my hands.

Dominus spat on the ground. "You know that inner voice you said that you hear? Those impulses?"

I nodded.

"I'd listen mighty hard to them tonight 'cause you're going to need to rely totally upon them. Try to stay close to me. But once we're shrouded in complete darkness, we might lose track of one another. Don't panic if that happens. Keep fighting them and don't worry about locating me."

I continued looking around the houses and buildings. The strange thing when light was fleeting and darkness started to dominate was how each moving shadow deceived me into believing it was a moving creature.

The rotten stench grew stronger.

Dominus frowned and looked around. "Something ain't right."

"Do you mind explaining?"

"I think more than vampires are lurking in the village tonight. It might not have been wise to bring you here yet."

"Different types of undead?"

He nodded. "Other things as well. Things that I had hoped I'd have more time to explain to you."

The final ray of moonlight dimmed. The abyss of darkness swallowed the village and us.

"Like what, exactly?"

Dominus chuckled deep laughter. "You probably wouldn't believe me if I described them to you. They're something you'd have to see first-hand. Something like—"

A rush of wind brushed past with the heavy beating of wings. Dominus groaned and his crossbow dropped to the ground. I reached toward the spot where he had been standing. He was gone. I could hear him cursing and his voice was getting farther away.

I stooped and grabbed his crossbow. Gently I traced my fingers along the string. It was still loaded. Although I could fire one shot, I doubted succeeding with any luck of accuracy since I hadn't been trained to shoot it and the darkness worked against me.

I didn't have any idea what had taken Dominus, but we had stood in the crossroads of the buildings and houses, which had greatly exposed us to them. I held no doubt that they had been watching us as we descended the road into the center of town. So the undead had the greater advantage, and for me to remain in the center of the street was foolish.

With the crossbow in hand, I ran toward the front wooden walkway at one of the shops. The wooden awning provided me at least shelter from being swooped away by another of those giant winged creatures, whatever the hell they were. A garland of garlic hung upon the shop door. Several more hung from the awning beams.

'*Six vampires*,' he had said. *Six*.

Scratch that.

My boots clunked on the wooden walkway. I pressed my back against the storefront wall and held my breath. I was surrounded by complete darkness, but I wasn't hidden. Not to them. They knew exactly where I was, and I didn't have a clue where to find them.

I had enough sense to know that by waiting, I'd draw them toward me instead of foolishly wandering through the buildings, exposing myself to their attacks. At least I hoped they'd come to me. It was a waiting game, and trust me, I had a great deal of patience. Sitting at our cottage door, night after night, waiting for the baron, I had learned undying patience.

If I had wanted a better training lesson, I doubt I could have requested it. Dominus was gone, whether he was dead or still alive, it made no difference. I was alive, isolated, and couldn't rely upon him to protect me. I stood alone against whatever undead monsters and flying beasts were out there.

With the total absence of light, eyes couldn't adjust quickly. One needed some fragment of light to absorb in order to see. Undead beasts were like animals and demons so darkness didn't affect them. In a sense I was blind, temporarily, and needed to rely upon my hunter's impulses as Dominus had suggested.

For several moments I closed my eyes, listening for the slightest sounds and movements. Vampires moved quickly, almost silently, compared to normal humans. But for me, I could detect the quick wisp as a vampire zipped from his hiding place behind a water barrel and crossed the street to attack. He came in a forward rush, probably thinking I was unaware of his presence. Before he left the road to step upon the wooden walkway, I fired the crossbow without ever opening my eyes.

The arrow pierced his heart. Surprise widened his eyes. A slight gasp echoed a second before his remains fell to the ground.

To be truthful, I'd have probably missed him with my eyes open, as I'd have delayed firing because my eyes would have struggled to locate him. Instead, in my mind, I visualized his approach perfectly. Without any doubt or second thoughts, I knew where to fire. I saw a clear image of the approaching vampire as if he stood in total daylight with a target marked over his heart. I was following a former hunter's guidance.

I propped Dominus' crossbow against the wall. He had the arrows with him. I hoped that he was alive; fighting with whatever beast had taken him. Reaching into my coat pockets, I brought out a stake in each hand.

Before I turned, another vampire—a female—struck me, sending me into the air. I landed upon my back with a heavy thud. The two stakes tucked behind my belt cracked beneath my weight. I groaned with pain. My stakes fell from my hands and rolled across the walkway. She rushed toward me, landing upon my waist, grinding the hidden stakes into my bruised lower back. She growled, pressing her hands against my chest and leaned down to bite me.

I swung a hard right, striking her jaw with enough force to knock her backwards. Glass shattered in my pocket as she readjusted her knees to pin me again. The smell of garlic lofted in the air. An instant later, she retreated.

Coughing, and rolling to one side, I tried to recuperate from my fall. The impact against the walkway had knocked the breath out of me. My chest ached. I felt around until I found one stake, and then pushed myself to my feet. Leaning against the wall, I yanked the cracked stakes from behind my belt and tossed them to the walkway. They were useless to me now.

If Dominus' count was correct, five vampires were still hiding in the darkness, watching and waiting for their opportunity to kill me. Of course, there could be more. A lot more. It was the other creatures that he had hinted of that troubled me, as I didn't know what I might be dealing with, and he had never told me the proper ways to deal with anything other than vampires.

Whatever the winged creature was, I was uncomfortable stepping back out onto the street. All I could hope was that he knew how to combat and kill it.

Soft pellets of rain fell in a sparse pattern until a steady light mist of a shower whispered its modest impact on the compacted roads, alleys, and wood shingles of the rooftops.

I slid my feet along the walkway until one foot sent the other stake rolling. Following the sound, I picked it up and returned to my place against the wall. I didn't like the thought of having my back exposed. Standing here, I could be attacked from only three sides.

I reeked of garlic. Well, my right pocket did. The smell repulsed vampires, and after several minutes, I wasn't too fond of it, either. There were skunks that smelled better. However, the scent proved to benefit me more than offend. I doubted any vampire would chance getting too close since, according to Dominus, garlic was poisonous to them.

A half hour passed with me standing against the storefront wall without anything approaching me. No sign of Dominus, either. I didn't want to stand in this spot the entire night. The rain was no heavier and played a soothing rhythm as it fell. At the corners of the buildings, small streams of water poured to the ground, drilling small holes into the earth and forming puddles.

Even with the overcast sky and the absent moon, my eyes had somewhat adjusted to the dark. Across the street beneath the awning of another shop, stood a male vampire dressed in elegant clothing with a top hat. Perhaps he had been a wealthy aristocrat before he had been turned? That'd be my guess though I had no proof. He regarded me with a slight, curious smile. His pale skin stood out in sharp contrast to his darker clothes and long curled black hair. Like the baron, this man held a cane, which I was keenly cautious of now.

He studied me for several more moments with his obsidian eyes before turning to face me.

"You are new to this, are you not?" he stated in a proper tone with a delicate accent.

"It's that obvious?"

He laughed softly with sheer mockery. "Aren't you?"

"I am." An answer I should never have given. *Never* reveal your weaknesses.

"Pity that you must die tonight without ever knowing your full potential."

I smiled. My hands tightened around the stakes. "You seem rather confident in yourself."

"Just stating the obvious, *friend,*" he replied. Sarcasm rolled on that final word.

"Like your family member who is now dust and the female that skirted away into the darkness ever fearful?"

He flashed fangs and his dark eyes narrowed. His voice bellowed. "What do you expect from my young and inexperienced offspring? The servants are never better than their master."

I sensed power rolling off of this man, not quite as powerful as the baron, but he was strong. "By what name are you known?"

"You wish to know the name of the one who shall take your life?" he asked, slightly amused.

I shook my head. "No, I plan to add it to my list of kills."

His dark eyes glowed red. "Fool."

"I thought your name would be more stately," I replied with a smug expression and a narrowed brow. Instigation and prodding through insults often baited even the noblest people into imprudent actions. Duels were common throughout the world and even the highest class was not immune from stupidity.

"Undiplomatic fool." His power leapt harshly toward me but curled backwards once it brushed against me.

"So you're not going to offer your name?"

"Aron Rau."

I shrugged. The name held no semblance for me. He might have been known several decades ago, but now he hid in the dark.

From my left a blur caught my attention. I didn't immediately turn because something rushed from my right side, too. Aron didn't move. Not that I had expected him to do anything until it became a last resort. Sending his minions first spared his own life for a while longer. Besides if I killed him first, and he was their master, they'd all die anyway. So, I could understand how, from his perspective, that he wasn't necessarily sacrificing his own children.

The vampire approaching from the right was the female the garlic had repulsed. Leery of being slammed to the ground by her again, I took a long step forward and turned sharply to my right with both stakes aimed for her arrival. I didn't anticipate actually hitting her in heart, and I didn't. The stakes drove deeply, one in her stomach and the other right beneath her throat. Her rapid rate of speed knocked me off balance, caused me to release the stakes, and propelled me around as the male vampire lunged for me.

Knowing I had no way to avoid being struck by his weight, I flung the side of my coat toward his face as I followed my three-sixty spiral. The wet inner lining of my coat slapped his face hard. Garlic juice smeared across his skin and into his eyes. He flailed his arms upward, screaming, and when he fell, he wiped at his face and eyes.

Quickly I reached to the dagger sheath hidden inside my left coat sleeve, yanked out the dagger, and shoved the male vampire to the ground. He was preoccupied, frantically screaming, and still trying to wipe off the garlic. I plunged the dagger through his heart, silencing him.

I glanced toward Aron. He had not moved. He pursed his lips and stood boldly with his chest puffed outward.

The female vampire worked at the two stakes that were driven almost through her body. The silver ends were slick from her leaking dark blood, which prevented her from grasping them. She kept grabbing at them, trying to grip the ends, but couldn't. Her breathing rasped hoarsely where the stake had stabbed through her windpipe. Although it wouldn't kill her, she was more interested in getting them out than attacking me again.

With the other devices in my pockets, I could have added to her suffering, but I didn't feel right about that. When I had seen the first female vampire the night before, I had thought it impossible for me to stake her or any female for that matter. I realized how foolish I had been to entertain such a thought. She was no less a monster than the noble vampire standing across the street. After all, she had attacked me first, without provocation, and she had every intention of killing me. With her, or any vampire, there was no hesitation in their killing or turning other human beings. They were vicious predators without remorse, sorrow, or compassion.

I knelt before her and drove a stake through her heart. Seconds later, the two stakes that had been stuck inside her dropped to the wooden walkway. I snatched them and turned to face Aron once more.

The rain slacked.

"That's three," I said.

He grinned. "And what is the name of my aspiring hunter?"

"Forrest Wollinsky," I replied with a mocking bow.

"You might think me impressed. You're sorely mistaken."

"I welcome your challenge since your offspring are almost as bad as the neophytes I slayed last night."

Two more female vampires appeared, one to each side of Aron. They were beautiful, dressed in fancy gowns. They hugged his arms, smiling at him for a moment, and then they glared sternly at me with hunger in their eyes. These were different than the three I had killed. These were personal, like wives.

"You are *no* challenge for me," Aron said coldly.

He had definitely been an aristocrat with that smug attitude.

"I suppose not since you hide behind your minions."

His jaw tightened. "There is the smell of death on the air tonight. I'm sure you noticed it on your way into the village?"

I had. But the rain seemed to have washed the scent from the air. I shrugged.

"Tonight's a night of sacrifices," he said, his eyes peering toward mine.

Like with the baron, I also kept eye contact with this master. It didn't anger Aron as much as it drew his immediate curiosity.

"Sacrifices?"

Aron nodded. "Three of mine have been offered. What is it that you offer, besides your friend?"

I didn't oblige him with any shocked response since that was what he had aimed to achieve. Instead, my brow tightened, and I peered coldly at him.

He smiled and lifted his left hand palm up toward me. "Perhaps it is a pound of your flesh? Perhaps more?"

The strong decaying smell returned, but harsher and closer. I took side-glances, trying to look around without taking my eyes off of him and his female companions, just in case it was a trap.

Strange imp-like creatures hobbled from one of the side roads. Swallowing hard, I studied these strange creatures. Their pallid skin was covered with bits of moss and lichens. Their faces were hideous with elongated jaws, jagged black teeth, sunken black eyes, and long serpentine tongues that appeared too long to fit inside their mouths. Their arms hung low as they ambled. Long fingernails protruded from their fingertips.

I counted six of them without realizing that I had completely turned in their direction, ignoring the vampire master and his two companions. I had no idea what these creatures were. I definitely didn't know how to combat them. Another half dozen came from the other side of the main road, but farther away.

I glanced toward Aron. He still hadn't moved. A look of triumph beamed on his face. He tilted his head to the side, awaiting my response. He didn't seem to have any intention of attacking the creatures or me. In fact, when he did regard them, there was a bit of apprehension in his eyes, which indicated that they weren't under his power. They were as much a danger to him as they were to me.

He reveled toward me as though I had already died. I hated to disappoint him, but I had no intentions of dying this night. The biggest problem I had was figuring out how to stay alive. I doubted Dominus would make an appearance again.

"Have you killed any of these before?" he asked.

I shook my head. "What are they?"

"Ghouls. They like to eat out your insides while you watch."

Not a pleasing thought for me, but he found it exciting. At least he had beamed a smile while explaining it.

Dominus had mentioned ghouls and zombies; *rare* creatures he had said, but the most valuable information—how to kill them—he had never disclosed.

Before these creatures came in my direction and noticed me, I left the storefront and crossed the road.

Aron's brow rose.

For a moment, I pretended that I was heading toward the shop directly across the road from where I had been standing. Midway across, I tore into a sprint and changed direction. Instead of running away from him, I came straight for him. He seemed confused by my approach. His two female companions flashed fangs and hissed like startled cats.

As I came closer to the walkway where he stood I realized I was taking a great gamble, using the only faith I held. I slipped the stakes into my pockets, and slid my hand to my dagger, pulling it from the sheath, not knowing if the magic placed upon it would even work.

The dagger gleamed with a bluish tint when I neared him. I didn't know if I needed to chant a mantra, say a prayer, or recite a spell. Nothing else was given to me. No directions.

Aron's eyes fixated on the glowing dagger. A slight moment of worry furrowed his brow, but once I crossed the invisible threshold and was close enough to initiate the dagger's blessing, the magic leashed around him, and his worry disappeared. He bowed to one knee and lowered his head. His two companions did the same thing.

"What is your bidding, my Lord?" he asked.

"Stop their approach," I replied, "even if it requires sacrificing your life. Never yield or flee from them."

Aron didn't question the command, nor did he attempt to argue. There was no hesitation. He promptly rushed toward the six closest ghouls. The two females remained bowed before me.

The ghouls charged, gobs of drool dripping off their tongues, and leapt upon Aron. He grabbed one and ripped off its head. The others grabbed his legs and began sinking their teeth into his leg, tearing and ripping away flesh and meat. Aron wailed. Reaching down, he twisted and pulled the head off another ghoul.

I looked at the two female vampires and pointed. "Stop those ghouls."

I knew I didn't have much time to flee if I expected to get far enough away from these ghouls. Sending the vampires to attack the ghouls was merely an opportunistic distraction. I didn't know if the vampires could actually kill the ghouls or the exact opposite. Could ghouls kill vampires?

The other six ghouls approaching from the farthest part of the village noticed Aron and rushed in his direction. By the time the two females reached them, both groups of ghouls had combined. Should they decapitate Aron, the other two vampires died as well. The ghouls would pursue me then.

From what I understood, vampires could be staked, beheaded, or burned to death. I believed if his body was ripped to shreds and eaten by these ungodly creatures, there wasn't any way for him to resurrect. At least, I hoped not.

I sheathed the dagger and ran across the road. After I grabbed Dominus' crossbow, I turned to run back to the mountain road where he and I had descended. As I neared the road, it dawned on me that I was now fully exposed with nothing to hide beneath. No trees, buildings, or mountain ledges protected me from an overhead attack. I had placed myself back out into the open. The winged creature that had taken Dominus had done so before either of us knew the beast approached. There had been no forewarning due to the darkness, so I could only hope that no more of them flew overhead.

My choices were few, however. Ghouls or winged beasts. More a coin toss of fate I supposed, but I needed to keep moving, put some distance between the carnivorous ghouls and myself, and get the hell out of this village while I was able.

CHAPTER 26

The childish part of me insisted that I head uphill to where I had placed my hunter box. The hunter in me demanded that I head in the direction where the winged creature had flown off with Dominus.

There was a greater chance that he was dead than alive. But even if there was the slightest chance that he was alive, it was my duty to bring him back. And if he was dead, I risked my own life by looking for his corpse.

Several things about this night changed me inside. For one, I wanted to become a stronger vampire hunter, but I discovered that in doing so, I needed to know more about these other undead creatures that emerged during the night. So many nasty beasts roamed at night, and I wondered why most people had never mentioned them. The most logical thought was the beasts had killed the ones who had seen them. Thus, allowing no testimonies to warn others.

Over time, I learned the asylums were filled with people who had seen things so bizarre that no one believed them. The more the insistent person attempted to prove the monster existed, the crazier the person sounded until relatives had no choice but to have the person locked away. And to be honest, the creatures I had seen this night I'd never tell a person outside of my immediate family for that very reason. Insanity accusations destroyed a person's credibility.

While I walked, I held the crossbow in my left hand and a stake in my right. A misty haze hung about ankle height all along the ground's surface. I hurried, running slightly stooped forward, hoping to make myself a smaller target, which was laughable, given my massive size. Of course my heftiness was in my favor because it would take an incredibly strong beast to hoist me off the ground anyway, and such an attempt probably would yank its arms or legs out of place when it tried to loft me upwards.

The sound of the rushing river increased, so I didn't have much farther to investigate. Dominus had been crass upon our first meeting, and there was a time or two when I really wanted to punch him. Okay, sometimes I ached to do much worse than that. But once that phase passed, I discovered he really had the best intentions for others, even if he didn't know how to express it.

Mist sprayed off the river as I neared the bank. I sighed, wishing it was daylight, so I had a better view. With all of the dark crevices and holes along the river's edge, finding a body at night was impossible.

Something thrashed against the ground several times to the right of me. I turned toward it with my stake ready. Easing closer, the thing crashed again. A long arm covered with rows of feathers. It almost looked like a giant bird's wing except for the hand at the far end. The last bit of life was apparently fleeting from this monstrosity.

When its strange wing slammed against the ground again, I placed my foot upon it and held it down. The huge body jerked slightly in protest, but there was no fight to escape or attack. Best I could tell, it had stopped breathing altogether.

Still holding my weight atop the wing, I knelt and examined its humanlike hand. Long razor talons like those I had seen on hawks and owls, lengthened outward. I set down the crossbow and gripped its wrist tightly. Stepping back I pulled on the arm part of its wing and flipped its body over. A stake was driven deep into her chest, right between her feather-covered breasts. A pool of blood formed a dark circle where its body had lain.

Dominus wasn't one to be killed easily, I supposed, but where was he?

Looking around, I distinguished lots of large rocks and old tree stumps, but wasn't able to see him anywhere. I backtracked through a long row of bramble and not the mountain road since I'd never passed him upon it. Based upon where the creature had fallen, I wagered he must have fallen nearby.

A large section of the bramble was bent over. The stems were broken and crushed. Lying atop the mangled thorny vines was a figure. I recognized the long coat. Dominus. He lay facedown and wasn't moving.

I hurried to him and took his hand. He was warm. His fingers moved. Relief flowed through me. He was alive.

I put my hands beneath his armpits and heaved him forward. He groaned as the briars snagged his clothes and bit into him.

"It's me, Dominus," I said.

He moaned and turned his head, trying to look up. He choked and hacked and spit out the wad of wet tobacco at my feet.

Once I freed him from the thorns, I sat down beside him on a large rock near the river.

"Are you okay?" I asked.

"I've been better." He placed his hand against his forehead and winced. "I must have hit a rock when that damned bird-woman dropped me. How long have I been out?"

I shrugged. I told him what had happened after the creature snatched him away into the darkness.

"Ghouls!" he exclaimed, rising to his feet. He staggered and placed his hand upon my shoulder to hold himself steady. "Boy, we gotta get back there."

"Why?"

"Unlike vampires, those flesh-eaters *don't* need an invitation to enter homes. They'll devour the villagers before dawn if we don't stop them."

"How can you kill them?"

"Fire. It's the only way I know." He patted his pockets. "Dammit, where're those matches. Ah, there they are."

I stood beside him and he leaned partway against me as we walked. He smelled of old tobacco, whisky, and something else.

Dominus chuckled and crinkled his nose. "Hell, I must've pissed my trousers when I fell, too. She had me quite a ways up there 'cause it was a long ways down. It's a wonder I didn't soil myself as well."

"Do you think the ghouls killed the vampires?" I asked.

"Depends."

"On what?"

"How badly they ripped the vampires to shreds." Still leaning against me, he held out his hand, and extended fingers as he counted. "There are several ways to kill vampires. One, a stake through its heart. Two, cut off the head. Three, fire but you have to burn them to complete ash. And fourth, dismember the body, which is what I suspect those ghouls were doing when you left."

"It seemed that way." I listened for the sound of large wings as we moved off the road and toward the village. "What was that winged beast?"

"Harpy."

"Never heard of it."

"Few people ever have. You've had the good fortune of seeing one of them *dead* after I struggled to stay alive."

"You think there are more of them nearby?"

Dominus groaned and touched his forehead again. "Lots of cliffs here. It's possible. Though highly unlikely. They're quite rare."

"So were ghouls, you said. There's at least a dozen of them in the center of the village."

"They're still rare," Dominus replied. "But you seldom see just one. They come in groups, but usually three or four. Not a dozen."

"Fire kills them. So how do we manage that?" I asked.

"We need to find something to make a torch with and hope the vampires killed several of the ghouls or injured them at the very least. I doubt the two of us can take on a dozen of 'em."

"A torch?" I frowned, trying to think how that might work. "Are we supposed to jab them with it? These things rushed the master vampire."

"We'll find a way. I take it that the dagger worked."

I nodded. "Yes."

"Better that you discovered that with only a few vampires, instead of inside a lair full of them."

"I agree."

We came upon a small pen with a calf in it. The boards nailed to the fence posts were narrow slats but tight and secure. I tugged at one slat with all of my strength. It didn't budge. I studied the small shelter connected to the pen. Dry hay bales were inside but fenced off from the calf's reach.

"What are you doing?" he asked.

"I thought about ripping off one of these to make a torch. We can use the oil in that hanging lantern to start it."

Dominus grinned. "I have a better idea."

"What's that?"

"You're not going to like it."

CHAPTER 27

"Bait?" I said. "You want to use me as bait?"

"Yep."

"Look at my size. There's no way I can outrun those ghouls."

"You think I can? It's all I can do to hold up my pounding head." A good size lump had grown above his left eye. It looked painful.

I sighed and shook my head. "Explain what you want me to do once more."

He pointed. "Sneak through that alley there, locate the ghouls, and then get their attention. They will chase after you. You lead them into this pen and slip through the side door of the shelter. The hay will be saturated with lantern oil. Once they run inside the shelter, I'll toss in a match and latch the door shut. You make certain the other door is secured, too."

Dominus loaded an arrow into the crossbow and handed it to me.

I gave him a curious stare.

"Shoot one of them to get its attention and then run like mad to get back here."

"What if it kills it?"

He chuckled. "Trust me, it ain't gonna kill it."

I ran through the plan in my mind again. Sounded easy enough, if I were one hundred pounds lighter. I never liked running. My feet were so large that I often tripped over them while running, which was the awkwardness of growing tall and large so quickly. I lacked coordination. With my clumsy footing in mind, the entire scenario didn't sound too promising. But I wasn't about to leave this village at the mercy of these creatures. I was willing to risk my life to save theirs.

I edged my way down the dark alley. Most of the storm cloud cover had passed, which allowed for a bit of the overall darkness to fade. I peered around the corner of the shop where I had fought and killed the three vampires earlier. Toward the center of the main road sat six ghouls. They were feasting on the three vampires' dismembered bodies. For some reason, their bodies had not disintegrated into dust. Perhaps they weren't fully dead.

The vampires had managed to rip six of the ghouls apart before succumbing to their own demise. I now understood why Dominus had said that fire was the only way to kill and destroy the ghouls. The strewn ghoul body parts were bloody, but they were still moving. Severed arms and legs flopped. Some hands were crawling, pulling the connected arms along behind them.

A couple of the ghouls ripped and tore meat from the vampires' arms and legs much like a person ate the meat off a chicken's leg. Two ghouls were tugging and devouring the entrails of one female vampire.

I held the crossbow and steadied my aim toward the ghoul that was the farthest away. I figured if I struck it, the others would follow its pursuit of me when it charged. I stepped out onto the main street and fired. The arrow struck the ghoul in the gut, bringing a loud howl of pain and a growl of instant anger. Its eyes fastened onto me as it yanked out the arrow and tossed it aside.

In a frenzy this creature's eyes widened and grew into large dark circles. The long tongue oozed drool mixed with blood. It chattered madly and leapt to its feet, running toward me. The other ghouls did as I had hoped. They abandoned their meal and ran in my direction.

I turned toward the narrow alley and tore into a sprint. I never imagined those beasts could run as fast as they were moving. My feet thundered as I clopped along. Near the rear of the shop, I turned and the tip of my large boot struck a rock, knocking me off balance. I dropped to the ground with a hard thud. I caught myself with my right hand, careful not to crush the crossbow in my left when I hit the ground.

By the time I pushed myself back to my feet, the ghouls squealed with excitement. They were less than a few yards behind me. They were gaining on me, and I still had a ways to go before I reached the pen where Dominus waited.

I glanced over my shoulder. They were closing in fast. I cursed beneath my breath with words that I had heard Dominus say but I didn't know what they meant. Anything to release my inner frustration.

My footsteps struck heavily as I ran, and I tried to pick up my pace, unsuccessfully. One ghoul leapt forward and grabbed at the back of my long coat. Its sharp claws snagged into the cloth. It flung its other hand forward and attached itself to the back of my coat.

I kept running as it clawed its way up my back. A low guttural sound came from its mouth. It pulled itself to the edge of my shoulder and its long wet tongue wrapped around the front of my neck. I grabbed its tongue and yanked the beast in front of me, snatching its claws from my leather coat. Before it had a chance to bite with its jagged teeth or sink its vicious claws into me, I turned and slung the beast toward the other five ghouls.

It squealed its protest, striking two of the ghouls pursuing me. The crash didn't deter or slow them, not even the one I had thrown. They ran on all fours, scampering like the vile hungry predators they were, panting, and grunting with their slippery long tongues hanging out the sides of their mouths.

At least they were running away from the village, but I wasn't certain that Dominus' plan would work. Mainly because I wasn't certain I'd get there before they dragged me down. While I might be able to fight off one or two, I couldn't keep six of them from overtaking me. And I didn't want to end up like the vampires. Being torn to shreds and devoured wasn't part of tonight's agenda.

The hay shed attached to the calf's pen was the largest structure in this area outside of the village, so it wasn't difficult to know which direction to head. As I came closer, I looked for Dominus, didn't see him, and I became concerned.

Another harpy? More vampires?

I hoped not.

But he wasn't within view.

Follow the plan, I told myself.

The small gate to the pen was slightly open. The calf was gone, so I assumed Dominus had released it. Otherwise, the ghouls might not follow me into the shed and slaughter the calf instead. I didn't know if they fed off of livestock or not, but since they were some type of demon, I guessed that the calf would hold their interest less than I did.

The hoarse hissings and gurgling sounds coming from the ghouls were unnerving. I kept running, focusing upon the gate, and hoping I made it through the entrance, into the shed, and out the other door without getting slashed or bitten by these frenzied beasts.

I pulled the gate open enough to squeeze through and headed for the open door. Dominus lay face down on the oil-saturated hay, right inside the shed. He was unconscious. I didn't have any time to waste or the ghouls would all be on me, and my young life and Dominus' were over.

The side door of the shed where I was to exit and secure was partly ajar. I dared a glance over my shoulder. The ghouls were fighting amongst themselves on which one entered the pen gate first. I kept moving, shoved my wide shoulders through the narrow door, grabbed Dominus by the arm, and pulled him out the other door.

Growls and maddening snarls snapped inside the pen. Apparently the ghouls had stopped their petty dominance struggle and gotten through the gate. Their dark eyes peered at me as they rushed into the hay shed heading for us. I shoved the door closed, pressing my weight against it. A second later, I bolted the latch into place. They screeched and clawed at the wooden door, unable to control their bloodthirsty behavior, ravaged by their never-ending need to satiate their hunger for human flesh. Their lust to get to me prevented them from even noticing the other door was still open. They could easily escape and charge around the pen toward us. I was thankful that the beasts weren't too intelligent.

I patted the pocket where Dominus had put the matches until I found them. I grabbed several before flinging myself over the fence and shoving the other door closed. I latched it. The desperate beasts lunged their weight against that door, trying to break through. Claws protruded through the cracks and holes. They hissed, snarled, and growled with such unearthly sounds. Even though they were on the other side where I couldn't see them, their aggressiveness still made me wary. I expected them to burst through the walls at any moment. They scratched viciously, desperately.

I struck a match against the rough door. The match burst into a large flame and slowly shrank. Loose pieces of hay stretched beneath the door, some of which had been doused with the flammable oil. I stooped and lowered the match, touching it to the hay strands. The flame flickered slowly, growing slightly, and a few seconds later, the fire grew even larger. The hay acted like a wick, sucking the flame toward the door, and allowing the fire to crawl beneath the door. Once the flames began rising on the other side, the dry hay ignited quickly.

The hungry cries from the ghouls changed into anguished high-pitched screeches of terror. They flailed against the doors and walls, trying to break through, but the wood held them as the fire grew inside. Flames licked from the edges of the wood-shingled roof. Their piercing shrills sent chills down my back and hurt my ears.

I crossed the fence and grabbed Dominus, lofting him over my shoulder, so I could get him away from the side of the burning shed. I set him down near the back of a shop and watched the shed. As the fire increased in size, the cries of the ghouls diminished.

I moved Dominus around to the front of the shop beneath the awning. After a bit of searching I discovered a wooden wheeled cart set at the rear of a building. I pulled it to the spot where the vampires had been dismembered and their entrails were strewn. The road was a bloody mess with an awful indescribable odor that tugged at my gag reflex. I held my breath and tightened my throat while pinning my chin to my chest, trying to suppress the urge to retch.

Grabbing the moving ghoul body parts, I tossed them into the cart. I came to what remained of Aron. His head had *almost* been severed from his shoulders, but not enough apparently to have killed him. His arms and legs had been ripped from his torso. I stared down at him and almost leapt backwards when he blinked and glared at me. He flashed fangs but his threat lacked any vehemence. He wasn't dead but his expression showed his displeasure. Not that I blamed him, given the circumstances.

I pulled a stake from my coat pocket.

His eyes glanced toward it and then back to me. "I did my best to stop them." His lordly tone was apologetic.

I nodded, having forgotten that the dagger still controlled him. I thought about releasing him from its bondage since he poised no real threat to me now. But what point did that serve? A moment for me to boast my victory or for him to curse me. Neither mattered now. The small village was free of the vampires, and I hoped this was the last of the ghouls. The irony was in me ordering a former aristocrat to servitude as his final act before his death. Although, I was guessing that he probably deserved a worse fate than what he was given.

I pressed the stake against his chest, directly above his heart and pressed the heel of my right hand upon it. "You did good."

I shoved my weight atop the stake. It sank deep. His eyes widened. A moment later his ash smoldered beneath me, and what remained of his two female companions were ash as well. I finished gathering up ghoul body parts and hurried back to the hay shed.

By the time I returned, the flames had risen high in the night sky. The roof was gone and the sides were nothing more than a burning skeleton of a small building. I wheeled the cart closer and began tossing the body parts into the center of the flames. The flesh bubbled and popped.

After I tossed the final hand onto the fire, I stood and watched the tall flames licking higher. The heat felt good against my skin. Dissolving boards cracked and fell inward, onto the huge fireball that had engulfed and was feeding off of the dry hay bales.

A strange sensation passed through my body and into my mind. Memories came to me like a rushing river bursting through a dam. Not memories from my past, but someone else's. Others. Knowledge from books I had never read. History. Death. Images, some delightful and others, horrifying, flooded my mind. I closed my eyes, processing the knowledge being gifted to me. Although some of the information might be considered by some as a curse to behold.

When I opened my eyes, I noticed something on the ground. Dominus' hat. I picked it up and dusted it off while listening to the fire crackling and popping.

I reflected upon the night's events. I had faced six vampires, killing three of them and cunning the other three into fighting for me, which led to their demise. That put my kill total to eight. For two nights' time that wasn't bad, and I already had two more than my father.

Placing my hand upon the hilt of my dagger, I knew I was ready to face the baron and kill him. I wanted to kill him while the pain of my mother's murder was fresh in my mind. Killing Baron Randolph might not end my father's tortured, agonized soul, or the ache of my loss, but I hoped it brought some closure in knowing the monster was dead and he could never harm our family again. But weeping an ocean of tears never cleansed a tarnished soul stained by the loss of true love. Even the passing of time didn't erase the pain. Lessened it, perhaps, but it never truly faded.

CHAPTER 28

After the fire settled a bit, and I was certain it wouldn't spread to anything else on the outside of the village, I returned to the shop where Dominus was propped against the wall. With a gentle hand, I shook his shoulder.

He tilted his head and squinted, trying to focus on me.

"Are you okay?" I asked, handing him his hat.

Dominus put on the hat and glanced around. "The ghouls?"

"All dead."

He reached his hand toward me and clasped my forearm. I pulled him to his feet.

"Quite a night of training for you," he said.

"I survived."

Dominus chuckled. "The vampires?"

"All dead, too."

"All six of them?"

I nodded.

His eyes widened. He looked impressed. "See? I told you that you didn't need me."

"It would have helped."

"Nah," he replied in his gravelly voice. "You'd learn to rely too much on me. What you've needed was a confidence boost and that's what you got tonight. Albeit, not intentional on my part. Trust me. The harpy was a surprise I'd never have expected through all of eternity."

"First one?"

"Hell! I hope it's the *only* one I ever have to deal with." He smiled. Laughter tugged at the wrinkles around his eyes.

I grinned. "So you didn't know a stake would kill it?"

He shrugged and picked up his crossbow, groaning in the process. "It has a heart. Piercing it surely would kill it. I figured it was the best hope I had. I reckon I was right, but I probably should have waited until we were closer to the ground. So that puts you up to what? Eight kills now?"

I nodded.

Dominus patted my shoulder. He took out a square of tobacco and bit off a new hunk. "Good. Now, I'm guessing you carried me all the way here? 'Cause I sure don't remember walking."

"I did."

"Sorry," he replied. "I got dizzy at the shed and don't remember anything else."

"I understand," I said with a slight shrug. "I'm ready to go after the baron."

"When?"

"Tomorrow night."

Dominus shook his head, chewing on the tobacco. "No. Not tomorrow."

"Why not?"

"Give me a couple of days to recuperate, Forrest. I'm not spry like I used to be. I have quite a few years on you. I need to be in top shape before we enter the lair of any vampire master. With my head hurting, I won't be alert enough. Promise me that you're not going to enter alone."

I shook my head and frowned. "You don't need to worry about that. I'm not a fool. I have better sense than to ever do that."

"Revenge can blind you to unforeseen risks."

"I realize that."

"You told me before I lost consciousness that the dagger had worked?"

"Yes."

"What happened before you came close enough to draw upon its power? Did he send any of his lesser vampires after you?"

I nodded. "Three of them."

"When you seek to use the dagger against Randolph, he'll send *dozens* of his lesser vampires after you. He'll do everything possible to keep you at a great distance. He's aware that you possess that dagger. The master here didn't know about it. Depending upon his age, he might not have even sensed it. But we cannot enter Baron Randolph's lair without a precise plan. It cannot be a spur of the moment venture. We need every step mapped out. I understand why you want the baron dead. And we'll need more than four people, too. The risks are too great."

I agreed. "May I ask you something?"

Dominus gave a simple nod. "Sure."

"After you kill a vampire, do you ever get an odd feeling?"

His eyes narrowed. "Like what exactly?"

"It's hard to explain. A surge of excitement rushes through me. After I killed this master, I could see a lot of images that seemed like memories, but not my own."

He grinned evenly. "You're a true vampire hunter, Forrest. Chosen at such a young age but your body grew so fast. Faster than your mind. Best I can make of it, and I've not quite received exactly what you're describing, but it's a way to increase the wisdom of your mind. It helps your mind mature faster."

"So, I'm absorbing the vampire's memories?"

Dominus shrugged. "His, and possibly some memories from any of the vampires he has made. Increasing your knowledge makes you a better hunter."

"I don't doubt that. I was only curious because I didn't know what was happening."

He chuckled. "Boy, we're not given a manual. Although there were times early on that I wished we were."

"Trial and error?"

"Don't forget dumb luck, too," he said, nodding.

"I've had my share of that."

"We all have, son," he replied. "I'd have had better luck hitting water and not a rock earlier."

"Let's head home."

He nodded. "Yep. We should leave before sunrise, or they might charge us for the hay and shed."

"Even though the vampires and ghouls are all dead?"

"Where's your proof?" Dominus asked. "There's something you need to remember whenever anyone ever hires you to slay a vampire."

"What's that?"

"Draw up a contract ahead of time. Make sure the magistrate signs it before you kill anything. Have a trustworthy witness verify all of your kills. Since vampires generally vanish after you properly kill them, you have no proof. Sometimes now, they *might* leave behind a brooch, necklace, or a ring that can identify them. That's a good thing, but if they don't wear anything like that, you have nothing if you don't have a witness."

"Where do you get a witness?"

"Well, when they hired me to kill the vampires in this village, one of the townspeople stayed with me after dark as my witness. Most villages and cities won't take the word of a hunter's witness should you have a traveler with you."

"Why not?"

"Avoids them from being hoodwinked. Some people who aren't hunters have been known to travel from village to village, demanding coin for professed kills even when they've never killed anything. So a lot of town leaders have written bylaws to prevent such things from occurring. I have a contract written up for hires, too."

"So, nothing we argued would be in our favor in the morning?"

He shook his head. "Nope. We, or rather *you*, killed all of these for free. Of course the training experience is invaluable."

"That's true. But even though they had hired you before, they won't take your word for this?"

"Here's another thing in their statutes. Usually, the person that acts as the witness gets a small percentage of the reward, which is why they want someone from their town. Prevents outsiders from getting all of the money. Now I don't mind that cut, but it can be a real pain ensuring that your witness stays alive during the hunt. If he dies, no pay." He laughed. "And most likely, no rehire if they ever need another hunter."

"Then I suppose we should leave," I said. "Since I don't have any way to pay them. However, I think killing the vampires and ghouls is worth more than what they have lost."

"No argument from me."

During the several hours it took to get back to my home, I worried that my father might be dead. I worried about Rose as well. Now that I was killing vampires, I feared for the wellbeing of those I held dear.

The sun was breaking the morning sky as we took the last turn in the road before I could see the cottage. I feared the worst. My chest ached and my stomach felt hollow. Finding my mother dead had been the most unexpected, horrifying experience in my life. I doubted that anything could be worse in life. But, it was too soon to lose my father, and I wouldn't put it past the baron to kill him, too.

Dominus stopped to lean against a tree. He glanced toward me in obvious pain. "What's troubling you?"

"Ah, I worry too much."

"About your father?"

I nodded.

He pushed off the tree and forced himself to keep walking. When we came around the bend, father was standing at the woodpile sharpening the wood ax. I was happy to see that he was alive, but surprised that he was outside working so early in the morning. After seeing him unharmed, a weight lifted off of me.

By the time we got inside the cottage, Dominus wasn't any better, but he didn't seem any worse. Exhausted and hungry. Father fed him and insisted he get some sleep. I set my hunter box right inside the door.

Jacques had not returned from his trip, and according to my father, he didn't expect Jacques to be back before the next morning.

I grabbed some cheese and stale bread, leaving Dominus in my father's care. I walked down the road, heading to Bucharest. I had never journeyed there alone, but I knew the directions to where I needed to go. I didn't know why, but Rose continued to be on my mind. The way that she had run off the last time I had seen her still bothered me. I wished to talk to her again. I needed to know that she was okay.

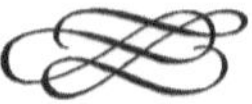

CHAPTER 29

*E*ven though I was tired from being up all night slaying vampires and ghouls, my mind refused to rest until I saw and talked to her.

While I walked, I studied the lines on my hand, remembering the warmth of her hands touching mine. I thought of the way she had looked into my eyes and how she had smiled when she did. I felt a rush inside, thinking about that.

I recalled the words that she had spoken when she had studied my hand. She had insisted that my eyes were filled with innocence, but she predicted that I'd eventually become cold and filled with pain, never resting or staying in one place. After last night, I knew she was correct. One didn't kill undead creatures without changing inside.

I didn't plan to remain in Bucharest after I killed Baron Randolph. I needed to move on and leave the hurt of my mother's death behind. Sadly, that meant I had to leave Rose as well. She was safer by not being around me anyway. But I felt a tear in my heart that I couldn't understand. The only explanation was love and affection, but I was too young, at least I told myself that I was, to feel that way. But my mind was growing. I looked at the city and the surrounding people with renewed confidence, my inner child shrinking with sudden manhood rising in its place.

Without my father, I made the journey to her shop in less than half the time it had previously taken. It's true his slow walking ability would have slowed me down, but I got to the shop even quicker because of my desire to see her. In other words, I didn't walk at my normal gait. I was almost running.

On the street outside of the shop were the same entertainers wearing strange makeup and doing their tricks. I hurried past them, careful not to make eye contact and ran down the stairs.

I shoved the door open and nearly screamed. The loud parrot welcomed me. I'd forgotten about the screeching bird. Believe me, the squawk was almost as bad as the wailing ghouls burning in the fire. But I'd still take the bird over the ghouls any day.

From behind the small table, Rose stood with excitement in her eyes. "Forrest?"

I smiled; relieved to see her.

She rushed across the room and embraced me. She clung to me. I put one arm around her back and my huge left hand on the back of her head. She held me for several minutes, and I wondered if she'd ever release me. In a way, I hoped that she never did. I had forgotten how good a hug made me feel.

Rose eased her hold enough to look up at my face. She smiled and looked into my eyes. But within seconds, sadness came to hers, and she frowned slightly. "What happened?"

She leaned back and took my hands into hers.

"When?"

Rose looked down, avoiding eye contact. "After we last spoke. I don't . . . I can't . . . even now, I can't say what I saw, but it was horrible and it reflects in your eyes and part of your innocence is gone now."

I nodded toward the table. "Perhaps we should sit down?"

She gripped my hand hard and led me to the table. After she sat down, she still refused to release my hand. I caressed the back of her hand with my thumb. Her eyes held pain and worry. I knew she didn't really want me to tell her, but she needed to know. She was torn inside, but she wasn't going to ask me again. She was fine if I volunteered the information or even if I didn't. At least, that's what I sensed from her.

"My father and I returned home that day," I said.

Her free hand covered her mouth as she waited for me to finish. Perhaps she could tell by the tone of my voice or by the pain in my eyes that my news was what she had seen.

"To find that my mother had been murdered."

Her eyes closed. Tears etched at their edges. She shook slightly. "I'm so sorry, Forrest."

"Is that what you saw?"

Rose nodded. "Do you know who killed her?"

"Yes. He's dead, but the person who sent him to kill her is still alive."

"Who?"

"You're safer not knowing."

She cocked a brow. The tears broke free and meandered down her cheeks. "And why is that?"

I almost told her, *'the same man who killed your mother,'* but then I remembered her father had warned me not to tell Rose that the baron had killed her mother. I had nearly slipped up. Telling her was dangerous because I sensed she was like me. She wouldn't rest until the baron was dead.

"I cannot say."

"Can't or won't?" she asked.

"To be frank, both."

"You're a hunter." She said it as a statement without any hint of a question.

I nodded. "You saw the hunter box your father had made for me when I had left."

She shrugged. "Father makes boxes for lots of different reasons. But you being an actual hunter explains a lot."

"What do you mean?"

"My readings of your palm. It explains a lot." She studied my eyes. Unlike our previous meeting, I didn't look away. I no longer feel intimidated or shy. "And, you've changed since we last talked. Not from your mother's death, but from something else."

I took her hand into both of mine, never looking away from her brilliant blue eyes. "Rose, everything you had said to me is true. I recognized that when you first said it that your reading was accurate. I had no doubts then and I don't now. I've accepted what I am."

"A hunter?"

"Yes."

"Have you killed any vampires?"

"Six last night, one of which was a master vampire. Two, the night before. And six ghouls last night." I wasn't trying to be boastful, but I figured there was no reason to lie to a fortuneteller. After all, she could tell, couldn't she?

She licked her lips and then she swallowed hard. "That explains the hardness growing in your eyes. It will only become worse if you continue the life of a hunter. You can stop, you know?"

I shook my head. "No, I've been told by several people that a true hunter cannot deny his calling. Doing so is death."

"Not doing so will kill your compassion and make you as cold-hearted as the undead. Is that what you wish, Forrest? To not be able to love?"

"No, it's not what I wish. It's what I am."

"Not fully yet, you're not. I didn't see that in you when we last talked, and I don't see it now, provided you'd be willing to denounce the calling."

I studied her eyes for a moment. Her insistence that I denounce my calling struck me as odd. "Why do you wish for me to decry what I am?"

She bit her lower lip and placed her other hand atop mine. "Because . . . I'm rather fond of you. You're different than other men your age."

I laughed.

"What's funny?"

If you only knew.

I shook my head. "It's nothing."

"Don't you want a normal life? Instead of this killing vampires?"

"It's far too late for that. I can't deny my calling and I won't."

Rose frowned. "What do you mean that it's too late?"

"In two days, I will kill a powerful master vampire." Confidence grew in my voice, being more a prophecy than a guess. "After which I will be forced to leave the city, possibly to never come back."

Sadness came to her eyes. "And why exactly must you kill this particular one?"

"Because he is the one who sent the man to kill my mother."

"You have proof of this?"

I nodded. "Yes. On my way out of the city that day, a different human servant of this master vampire approached my father and I. He gave me a message."

"What kind of message?"

I explained all of the events that had happened next.

"That still doesn't explain why you'd need to leave," she said sadly. "You'd simply remove an evil undead. I'd think people would praise you for such a feat."

"When he dies, great calamity will occur throughout Bucharest. Because of those consequences, I will be sought. The city council will want me dead."

"Why? Who is he?"

"Baron Randolph," I replied.

Her eyes widened, and she shook her head. "No. He can't be."

"You know him?"

Rose looked away. "I know *of* him. Everyone in Bucharest knows his name."

My mother had recognized his name when Jacques informed her of who had attacked my father. She had been shocked to learn that the baron was a vampire. So, I supposed what Rose was saying was true. Of course, people living in the city might know the baron with a different sort of reputation. It seemed unlikely that he'd display evil actions openly if he valued his prominence in the city.

She glanced into my eyes again. "Are you certain he's a master vampire?"

"He is. I have no doubt about it."

"If that is true, Forrest, why would he kill your mother?"

"It's a long story."

Rose waved a hand toward the shop, devoid of any patrons. "It's not like I'm going anywhere. Come now, Forrest, continue. Please tell me."

I explained how my father had been hired to kill Bodi, and then everything that transpired afterwards. By the time I had finished she sat dumbfounded. If she thought any differently about me, it was hard for me to tell.

She kept her hands entwined with mine. Finally, she smiled. "May I read the cards for you?"

I shrugged.

Rose released my hands and took her Tarot cards. She began flipping cards, placing them into different sequences, occasionally frowning or making an odd expression; depending upon what card she turned up. None of it had any real bearing on me because I didn't know what each one stood for, and even if she told me, I doubted it would make any difference.

She shook her head with a worried expression on her face.

"What is it?" I asked.

"Two days from now? That's when you plan to slay the baron?"

"I do."

"I'd advise against it," she replied.

"Why?"

"The cards indicated that you'll fail miserably. Please, Forrest, I'd delay, for at least a few days more."

"Do you have any way to predict when a better time would be?" I asked.

Rose picked up the cards and placed them into a neat stack. "I could check the crystal ball."

I gave a slight nod.

She stood and reached for the ball on the shelf, which was covered beneath a black cloth. She lit several candles to add more light to the corner. After she sat down, she leaned toward the glass ball and extended her delicate hands toward me. I wrapped my huge hands around hers.

Her eyes grew distant as she focused upon the ball. Spellbound. Watching her transformation made me uncomfortable. Her innocence and beauty shriveled, and were replaced by a darkness that she had predicted would befall me. I wondered upon what power she drew upon.

Her fingers tightened inside my hands. She swayed slightly and her eyes turned back with only the whites visible. She remained like that for nearly a minute before she violently shook and yanked her hands from mine.

"Do you plan to face the baron alone?" she asked.

"Of course not."

"How many will be with you?"

I shrugged. "I'm not sure yet."

She shook her head. "Forrest, you mustn't go."

"Why not?"

"You will be betrayed."

"By whom?"

"Unfortunately, such answers aren't given," she said, nodding toward the crystal ball, "but be assured that you will be betrayed. Please, don't go after him."

Rose reached for my hands, but I stood. "I will consider what you've said."

"You're leaving?"

I nodded.

"Why? Is it because I've given you bad news again? I—I can't control *what* I see or *how* the cards fall."

"No, it's not that. I'm needed elsewhere." I turned toward the door.

Rose lifted the hem of her dress and rushed around the table to get between me and the door. "Please visit for a while. Thanks to those tricksters outside, I seldom get a visitor anymore."

"I need to go, Rose. I've been up all night. I needed to know that you were okay."

I read the hurt in her eyes, more from her loneliness than anything else. As much as I wanted to stay, I did need to get back to the cottage. I hoped that Jacques had returned with the other werewolf. I agreed with Dominus. We needed more than four people before we entered the lair. Having another vampire hunter or two would be even better.

I tried to step around Rose, but she wrapped her arms around me tightly. I hugged her back. After a couple of minutes, I realized she wasn't going to release me. Still hugging her close, I picked her up and spun her around, exchanging places with her. After I set her down, I backed my way to the door.

"Forrest," she said.

"I'm sorry, Rose. I need to get home."

I opened the door while facing her. She pouted her lips. I gave her a gentle smile and shook my head. "Until next time."

Closing the door behind me, I looked to the top of the stairs where the odd entertainers called and catered to the passersby. I ignored them and hurried down the street to avoid them and hoped to be out of sight in case Rose emerged from the shop and came after me.

I doubted she would pursue me.

While she had insisted something horrible had happened when my father and I had been in the shop previously, she had never actually told me what had happened ahead of time or what she had *seen*. In fact, she didn't even tell me when I had returned and insisted I reveal to her what had happened when I had returned home. My skepticism spurred suddenly. Had she seen anything at all? Or was she as deceitful as the festival folks in the street outside of her shop?

CHAPTER 30

*L*ate in the evening, after I had slept fitfully for several hours, a knock came at the cottage door that awakened me. My dreams had been of a darkened lair where I'd never been before, but possibly a place I'd enter in the near future, or simply this den was from the memories of a vampire that I had already killed. It was difficult adjusting and sorting through memories that weren't mine. But gleaning any useful intelligence was much better than nothing at all.

I placed a hand on my dagger and eased the door slightly open. It was Jacques. I pulled the door wider, inviting him and his two guests inside.

"Cousin," Jacques said with a broad smile. He squeezed my shoulder firmly. "I'd like for you to meet Zsolt and Rusk."

Jacques went around the room, making the introductions to my father and Dominus.

Zsolt was a husky man, slightly shorter than myself, but his eyes held every bit the coldness that Rose had predicted mine would eventually become. It chilled me to look into his eyes and to think that one day my eyes reflected the same. There was an instant when I took to heart what she had forewarned.

He was fair skinned with eyes of blue. His hair was blonde as was his short-cropped beard. He was hardened with two deep scars that slashed across his left cheek. He was a hunter, if the hunter box he carried signified anything. He wore a silver cross around his neck. His tall hat and long coat was similar to Dominus'.

Thick black sideburns covered Rusk's cheeks. Long black hair coiled down his back, much prettier than most girls, but I'd never make such a comment aloud in his presence. His eyes were odd, brown with rich gold speckles. Thick black wiry hair protruded from the neck of his shirt. And like Jacques, the backs of his hands were covered with bristly hair. If this man wasn't a werewolf, I'd fight the baron with my bare hands.

With only the six of us, I didn't know how much that aided us in our pursuit to kill Randolph, but it was definitely better than four. Not knowing their strategies or their kill numbers, I hoped they'd share that information with me. I had learned a lot from Dominus, and I needed to learn from other hunters as well. While there wasn't one definite strategy, sharing our tactics bettered all of us. At least, I thought so.

Father lowered extra chairs down from our loft. We formed a near circle where we could sit and see one another as we talked. Energy pulsed amongst us. The hairs on my neck and arms bristled. I liked being in the company of other hunters. We had two werewolves, three of the Chosen, and my father, the self-appointed hunter.

Even though it was preliminary—our hunt to kill the baron—excitement rose inside me when I should have been nervous due to my actual age. But I no longer mentally felt like an eight year old. Dominus had been correct. My vampire kills had boosted my knowledge, thrusting my mind forward to catch up with my outward appearance.

I wanted to believe my calling was a blessing, but in many ways, perhaps it was right the opposite, a curse, if I took everything into its proper account. I had been robbed of my childhood without a choice and without my consent. But my loss was for the better good of society —if the force that had chosen me needed any validation for their reasoning.

Jacques looked at me with a quizzical grin. "I take it that your trip last night faired well?"

I nodded and gave a slight shrug. "As best I could hope."

"I thought so. I could tell by your eyes. You seem more confident."

"The boy's being overly modest," Dominus said. "Due to a mishap, I was incapacitated. He singlehandedly killed all six vampires and a half dozen or more ghouls."

Zsolt's eyes brightened with curiosity. He spoke with a Hungarian accent. "Ghouls? Where'd you cross those?"

"Glodrim," Dominus replied. The lump on his forehead was the size of a goose egg and dark purple.

Jacques couldn't keep his gaze off of me. "So how many kills do you have now?"

"Eight," I replied softly.

"In two days," Jacques said to Zsolt with strong pride in his tone.

"Impressive," Zsolt said.

My father saddened and looked down at the floor. I didn't want him to know I had surpassed him with my numbers, which was why I had tried to shrug it off as of no importance. Of course, if I hadn't told the number, I knew Dominus was itching to state it aloud. Since I considered him my trainer, I imagined my number of kills reflected good for him as well.

"We have a common enemy," Rusk said. "When Jacques told me that you needed a group to kill Baron Randolph, I didn't hesitate to join your conflict."

"Nor I," Zsolt said. He looked to my father. "You're the one who was taken into his lair as his prisoner?"

Father nodded.

I shook my head. "He kept him alive just to torture him."

"I see. What do you remember of the place, John?" Rusk asked. He took out a yellowed piece of parchment paper, a dark pencil, and flipped a wooden food tray for solid support so he could draw. "I'd like to try to map it out."

"Not a lot, actually," my father said. "I was kept in one large sepulcher with stone caskets lined around the walls. And when I escaped, I was too worried about getting out alive that I don't remember much about my surroundings. I ran up several sets of spiral stairs."

Zsolt said, "So you were fairly deep underground?"

"I believe so," my father replied.

"Is there anything more you can tell us?" Rusk asked.

My father frowned and stared at the floor. He was silent for a long while. I knew he was trying to remember. He was always deep in thought whenever we had held discussions when Momma was still alive. He was adamant about trying to recall the exact details. That was just his nature. So for him to tell everyone that he didn't remember meant that he wasn't lying. If he truly remembered, he'd have told us. I wondered if he was blocking the memories because he had told Momma and I about Bodi's torturing him and his escape.

Rusk appeared slightly frustrated. "I'm not trying to pressure you into remembering."

"Then don't," he replied.

"But," Rusk said, "we're going into a very dangerous situation."

"I realize that," Father said.

"Possibly a hundred vampires reside with the baron," Rusk said, never pausing. "The odds are greatly against us."

"Would he have such a legion?" I asked.

Rusk nodded.

"I'm new to all of this," I said. "But vampires need to feed. How often?"

"Daily," Jacques replied.

"I expected they'd need to. How does this number of vampires feed without the residents of Bucharest discovering them?" I asked.

"I took you through the slums," my father said.

I nodded. "And another lair is hidden inside the building ruins, run by another master. Right?"

Father nodded.

"Each master holds a certain amount of territory," Zsolt said. "My guess is both lairs feast upon the poorer citizens in the slums. The two masters probably have a truce between them as long as their boundaries are not crossed."

Rusk said, "Which is why Baron Randolph has always opposed renovating that area of the city. Whenever business proposals are made to better the slums, those he holds influence over promptly vote down such movements. And if masters aren't taking their victims there, the river ports bring hundreds of new people into the city each week, giving the vampires victims that would go unnoticed by the city. Ship captains are used to losing crew members at port dockings, too, so they recruit new workers at the next stop."

Jacques glanced toward me. "Vampires can feed upon humans without killing them or turning them. They use compulsion to keep the victim from remembering and only take necessary amounts of blood to sustain themselves."

Rusk turned his attention back to my father. "Has anything come to mind about Baron Randolph's lair?"

"Sorry, no." My father propped his elbows upon his knees and rested his head in his hands, staring at the floor. "It's all a blur. And the more disturbing parts I've blocked from my mind, to be honest."

"Perhaps," Zsolt said. " I can help you."

"How?"

Zsolt removed a pocket watch from his coat. The gold watch was attached to a long chain. "John. Please look."

My father lifted his head and glanced at the watch.

"Focus on the watch," Zsolt said. He lowered the watch on the chain and swung it back and forth. He looked at me and shook his head. "Only your father should focus on it. It's best you look away."

"Why? What are you doing?" I asked.

"Hypnosis. Everything we hear and see is recorded by our subconscious. By getting him to fully relax, there's a good chance that he will find what is currently hidden from him."

I turned my attention to Jacques. My cousin nodded and gave an approving smile.

"John," Zsolt said in a soft calm voice. "Focus solely upon the watch. Relax. Drive away everything except the watch and the sound of my voice."

My father's eyes moved left to right, following the watch's movement. Zsolt's voice held a lulling ability, and soon my father's eyes grew heavy, as though he were about to drift off into sleep.

"John. Relax. Close your eyes."

My father obeyed.

"Focus. Let your mind drift back to when you were in Baron Randolph's den. You are there now. Alone. No one else. No vampires. Just you. You're safe. Take a look around. Tell me, what is it that you see?"

"Two pillars support an archway made of red brick and white mortar."

"Good," Zsolt said. "What else? Where are the stairs?"

My father leaned back in his chair and folded his hands over his stomach. He frowned slightly. "Directly in front of me."

"Okay, what's to your left?"

"Caskets."

"How many?"

Father was silent for a few moments, as if he were counting. "Six."

Zsolt smiled. "Good. To your right, are there more?"

My father nodded. "Six more."

"Okay, take a look around the room. Are there any more?"

"One at the far wall directly opposite of the stairwell."

"Is this one any different than the others?"

Father nodded. "Yes. It's embellished with gold trim. And it seems set higher than the others, on a platform."

Zsolt flicked his eyes toward Rusk. "The baron's."

Everyone else nodded in agreement.

Zsolt leaned forward, getting closer to my father. "John, I need you to ascend the steps. Remember, you're alone. No one else is there. No vampires."

A nervous expression claimed my father's face.

"It's okay. No one else is there. Go up; count the steps to the next level. How many steps?"

After a few seconds, my father replied, "Twelve."

"How is the stair layout? Where does the next set of steps ascend?"

"I can turn to the left or right. A narrow door is to the right side. Maybe enters into another large chamber or a tunnel? I'm not sure. The stair platform is inside a square room, but I need to walk around the column that houses the stairs to get to the next set."

Rusk drew a rough layout of what my father described.

"Ascend to the next level. What do you see?" Zsolt asked.

"It's the same. Another door to the right. Twelve steps."

"Good. Now to the next floor."

A few moments passed. "The same . . . except—"

"What?"

"No side doors and no more steps. I'm at the surface level. There are two large doors. Nothing else. I push them open. The graveyard is before me."

"Which cemetery?" Zsolt asked.

"The one nearest the cathedral," Father replied.

Zsolt thanked my father and slowly brought him out of the trance. When Father looked around, he seemed somewhat baffled, not remembering what had occurred during the time that he was under this *hypnosis*.

"Now, shall we get down to our strategics?" Zsolt asked.

I looked him in the eyes and said, "Before we do that, what is your grievance with the baron?"

"There are many, Forrest," he replied. "Like you have lost family members, so have I and fellow hunters that were like brothers to me. I'm willing to sacrifice my life, if need be, to see him dead."

"And I," Rusk said, nodding. "Have had many a Wolven brother and sister tortured until dead by the baron and his undead minions."

"This cemetery where the underground lair is hidden is possibly connected with the buried cellars and long tunnels that cut beneath the city," Rusk said. "From what John mentioned, there are side doors at each turn of the stairwell. These we do not want to enter. Seal them if they can be closed."

My father looked confused. "What doors?"

Jacques placed a gentle hand on my father's shoulder and whispered something in his ear. My father's brow rose, acknowledging understanding, but perhaps not completely because he still appeared uncertain of what they were talking about.

Rusk continued, "They may only be tunnels to other places in the city, but then again, they might well be filled with more vampire sepulchers, containing more caskets. Some of the tunnels could lead for miles. There could be armies of the undead down there."

"Is there any guarantee that the baron's casket is three stories down?" I asked.

Dominus straightened in his chair as he studied us.

"I believe so," Rusk said.

Zsolt shrugged. "When John first went under hypnosis, his reaction to the master's chambers had made him quite nervous. There are thirteen caskets, which is symbolic in many respects. It is a common number used in various religions throughout the world. I believe it holds quite a significance for the baron."

"In what way?" I asked.

"Prominence. Most people in other cultures consider the number *twelve* as completeness. Being the thirteenth places him one above the rest," Zsolt replied.

Dominus cleared his throat. "So even if we don't draw the attention of any vampires from the other adjoining rooms, we will enter a room filled with thirteen vampires?"

Rusk and Zsolt nodded.

"I must assume," Dominus said, "that these twelve vampires nearest the baron's caskets are powerful in their own right."

Jacques said, "I agree. Baron Randolph will keep his best vampire warriors near his place of rest."

"Or his mistresses," Rusk said.

"Don't forget about Bodi," I said.

Rusk turned toward me. "Bodi?"

I nodded and explained who Bodi was.

"Do you wish to be the one to stake Bodi?" Rusk asked.

My throat tightened.

Actually, no, I didn't want to do that at all. I hoped that once the Baron was killed, Bodi turned to ashes, which seemed merciful to me. But if someone had to stake him, I supposed I'd rather it was me. I replied with a slight shrug.

My father shook his head. "No. Forrest shouldn't be the one to do that."

"Why not?" Zsolt asked.

"He's the youngest one in our group, and he was friends with the boy. Others of us have hardened in mind and spirit over our lives. We've experienced harsher things. I have no idea how this will affect Forrest this early in his life. It might be too much for him to handle."

"I'll be fine, Father."

"No, son," he replied, pointing a firm finger at me. "It's not your place. Besides, I was hired by Bodi's parents to slay him. I failed the first time. I won't again."

His hurt and self-disappointment softened his eyes. But whether or not either of us wanted to admit it, the reason behind Momma's death could be traced to the night when Father had tried to slay Bodi, only to be attacked and nearly killed by the baron. So, in that light, my father had more reason to justify his actions.

Dominus stood and frowned. He took a few moments, looking at each of us seated around the circle one at a time. "You see, folks, *this* is why I've spent most of my hunter days alone. No bickering. No who's going to do this or that. I'll lay it all right out before you, okay? Kill any vampire that you're within reach of. No designation on who kills whom. That will simply keep all of us out of focus, and some of us might get killed. I prefer the tidy little endings when I walk out the victor. How about the rest of you?"

Rusk gave Zsolt a perplexed stare. They nodded. As did Jacques and I. Father remained indifferent.

"Good," Dominus said, sitting back down and straightening the lapels of his overcoat. "I'm glad the issue is settled."

I tried not to grin and was partially successful. Six of us were about to go against, at the very least, *thirteen* vampires. That meant we should kill two each with one of us killing a third. Somehow the ratio sounded too easy. I didn't expect our invasion to go smoothly. According to Rose, someone would betray me during the attack. I ruled out Father and Jacques. Dominus, I was pretty certain was dependable. Rusk and Zsolt, however, I didn't know anything about either of them really. They were strangers. People we were entrusting our lives.

"When should we plan to enter and attack?" Rusk asked.

Jacques said, "Tomorrow night?"

Zsolt frowned. "Will that be enough time to prepare?"

"What more do we need?" Rusk asked.

Dominus lit his pipe, slightly amused as he looked at both of them. "How many stakes are you each carrying?"

"Six," Rusk replied.

Zsolt shrugged. "Usually no less than eight. Why?"

"You're dealing with a master and his top dozen vampire protectors, plus whatever other surprises we might happen upon down inside those catacombs. I have a dozen with me. I think Forrest has about that many. But we should probably carve out a few more dozen to take with us."

Jacques nodded. "Not a bad idea."

"I agree," Rusk said.

Someone knocked on the door. I glanced nervously toward the door and then to Father and Jacques. Both held questionable expressions like I did. It was late, close to midnight, if not later. I started to stand, and Jacques shook his head and rose to his feet to answer it. After he turned toward the door, I stood anyway. If we were about to face any physical threat, I didn't want to be caught sitting down.

CHAPTER 31

Jacques opened the door slightly. "Yes?"

The lady replied with a strong accent, "Ah, we're a looking for Rusk and Zsolt. Were told . . . to meet here?"

Jacques pulled the door open wider, and he glanced back toward Rusk. A horse whinnied outside.

Rusk hurried to the door, greeting her.

"So sorry," Rusk said, turning to face us. "All caught up in getting prepared for our attack, I completely forgot. This is Volya and her brother, Hoval. They will accompany us into the lair."

Dominus' brow narrowed as he evaluated the couple.

The woman stood wearing a long dress bordered with delicate lace with a matching bonnet. She wore white gloves. Her dark hair was pinned neatly beneath. In her right hand she carried a small leather satchel.

"Our apologies for our lateness," she said. "We came upon unexpected delays."

Hoval was tall and extra slender, almost a skeleton covered by tanned skin. His sunken eyes held a hollow look. He wore a brown tailored suit with a light shirt and a black bowtie. He held his hat in his left hand, and a wooden box in the right. It didn't look quite like a hunter's box. If it was, it was the smallest one I'd seen so far.

Dominus cocked a brow as he looked from Hoval to me. He flicked his gaze back to her. "You two don't appear to be hunters. What is your purpose for wanting to join our fight?"

She smiled and held her satchel with both hands at her midsection. "You choose to fight a master inside his den, no?"

He nodded. "We do."

"Then you need shielded by a blessing."

"What kind of blessing?" he asked, frowning.

"A master," Hoval said, "is strongest in lair. You need protection to block his . . . mind control."

"Hell, boy," Dominus said in his gruff voice, "No offense, but *any* vampire could snap your frail body in half."

With nervous eyes, he faced his sister, almost pouting.

Volya's eyes focused on Dominus. "And what power do you take against vampires? How many vampires have you killed?"

Dominus' jaw tightened. "Lady, I've killed well over one hundred vampires. Probably closer to two hundred. You learn to act quickly or you die. What power, you ask? Well, nothing other than my hunter instinct, and every thing holy. What else is there? The undead are cursed apart from God."

"You are Christian?" she asked.

"Don't know that I'd be considered such. I'm certainly not on the list of God's appointed saints, but I know how to deliver these undead directly into the pits of hell. I don't think He's been too disappointed with that."

She studied his eyes for a few moments. "You ever kill master vampire?"

Dominus nodded. "Several."

"In their lairs?"

Dominus thought for a minute before finally shaking his head.

"See? You know not what you face."

"And what makes you an expert on vampires in their lairs?" Jacques asked.

"We shield you from the master's compulsion," she replied.

"With what? Magic?" he asked.

Volya nodded. "Yes."

"Well, hell," Dominus said. "That settles it. We'll just send you and your brother down there first. Problem solved."

Her eyes grew cold and her jaw tightened. "You mock us?"

"Ma'am," he said. "I've killed all of my vampires without magic."

"You said you use holy . . . Are you talking relics?"

"Holy water, bible, blessed salt, and a cross."

"And yet, you are not Christian?"

"No ma'am, I am not."

"Then are these things not magic in their own right?" she asked.

Dominus took a long draw on his pipe. Fury was rising in his eyes. He released a long stream of smoke. "Are you a Christian?"

Volya looked insulted. "I am not!"

"Good to see we stand on the same side then," he replied.

"We do not," she replied in a low hissing manner. "I have question for you."

Dominus raised both hands and nodded. "Shoot."

"Huh?"

"Ask it!"

"If you don't believe in the power behind these holy relics, why do you think they work?"

"Hell, I don't know. Perhaps it's because *they* believe? Or they fear the outcome of what their eternity is beyond the grave so severely that they believe they are cursed and holy objects act on that belief. I don't think it's magic, but it has worked every time."

She acquiesced a nod. "Some of what you say . . . is truth. But what happens when you face a vampire who has no fear of what others consider holy? One that has no faith in cathedral objects?"

"I've yet to come across one."

I thought about the point he was making, which was something I had wondered about since I first rummaged through my father's hunter box. My family was not believers in the cathedral, but I had watched the items used—the cross, holy water, salt—and they worked against the undead. Was it the vampire's faith, if one could call it that, which allowed the blessed items to work? I wondered. With so many religions around the world, I questioned if these same objects held any power against a vampire that didn't believe in the cathedral and its teaching.

The arrival of these two heightened my skepticism, especially with Rose's warning. Rusk had not even hinted of their arrival to us or to Jacques, who he had spent a lot of time traveling back to our cottage with. When we were talking numbers and odds of success, I'd have thought that was a time when Rusk's memory should have been nudged enough to remember two more would be joining our group. Dominus seemed overly cautious of them, as did I.

Rusk motioned for Volya and Hoval toward him. He showed them what we believed the lair setup to be like.

Dominus glanced at me. "I think it's time I retire for the evening. Let them work out the specifics."

"We can tell you the plan tomorrow."

Dominus laughed. "You can make all the plans for your expectations, but once you arrive, trust me, it all goes out the window. It all boils down to one thing: Kill or be killed. The basic plan is always the best one."

He stood and walked to the ladder that led up to the loft where we had made him a cot to sleep. I needed to find more thick furs and quilts to set up places for the others to sleep through the night.

Dominus had some valid points, but I worried that perhaps he wasn't taking the situation seriously. I did. I believed the fight against the baron would be one of the hardest I'd ever face. It might actually become my premature death, despite the lines etched into my palm.

While Rusk and Zsolt explained the details to Volya and Hoval, I got my father to help me find enough materials to set up beds on the floor for Rusk and Zsolt. Jacques volunteered to help. Volya and her brother insisted that they sleep outside in their covered wagon.

I wanted to talk to Jacques and Dominus alone, without the other four hearing our conversation. I was uncomfortable about the overall situation.

By the time I got to the loft where my bed was, Dominus was snoring. I rolled onto my bed and stared at the ceiling. The small fire in the hearth allowed light to dance upon the ceiling. My mind was too preoccupied to drift off quickly. I thought of Rose and her warning. I didn't like sleeping under the same roof with two complete strangers with two more outside.

CHAPTER 32

The following morning after breakfast, Jacques, Dominus, and I began carving stakes from an ash tree Father had cut down. Rusk and Zsolt helped the gypsy siblings with other tasks they deemed essential to us invading Baron Randolph's lair. They were inside the gypsy covered wagon, which essentially was a small room set upon wheels. The spotted horse ate oats from an attached bag beneath its mouth.

Father was asleep inside. He had stood watch throughout the night until I relieved him about two hours before sunrise. I had the feeling that he didn't trust the other four any more than I did.

Dominus and Jacques took sharp hunting knives and were smoothing out the long pointy ends of their stakes.

I stepped closer to them and whispered, "Do you trust them?"

Jacques paused with his work and cocked a brow. "Do you not?"

"You traveled with the two for several hours. I expect that you spent the day before talking to them?"

Jacques nodded. "I did."

"Did they seem trustworthy?" I asked.

"I had thought so."

"And you don't now?"

"Rusk is like me, a werewolf. I sense the pack bond between us without any power struggle for dominance over me. He stressed his hatred for vampires because he had been held in bondage to the same vampire I had."

"Then why didn't he tell you about these two?" I asked.

Jacques frowned. "I've asked myself that last night and all this morning."

Dominus cleared his throat and whispered in his deep voice, "If you ask me, they have something more they wish to gain from this attack."

Jacques turned and faced him. "I had thought maybe the same thing."

"What's your opinion about them, Dominus?" I asked.

"I agree with Jacques about Rusk. He seems on the level, but then again, he never told us about the gypsies. I've been around people who worked magic in New Orleans, but those practiced a different type of magic, much darker. And whatever they're doing, they're certainly not including us in it."

"What about Zsolt?" I asked.

"Typical hunter. Young and boastful, but he doesn't seem to have faced any true challenges. I doubt he'd have survived what you did the night before by himself."

The compliment made me feel good, but now I worried about how well Zsolt could handle himself once we were at the baron's chamber inside the lair.

"Now the brother and sister," Dominus said, "I don't care for either of them and wonder what their true hand is on this."

"I wonder about them, too." Jacques nodded, setting his freshly sharpened stake onto the pile with the rest of them. "We have two dozen stakes in addition to what we carry on our persons."

"That should do," Dominus said.

I grabbed a burlap sack and began setting them inside, carefully lining them so I could bundle them by wrapping the remainder of the sack around itself to make carrying the stakes easier. The rear door of the wagon opened. Rusk and Zsolt stepped down the crude portable steps attached to the wagon.

"What's been going on in there?" Dominus asked. "You decide to get more sleep while the rest of us work?"

Rusk grinned and chuffed a small laugh, but Zsolt looked insulted.

"Actually," Volya said, stepping down the steps of the wagon. She held several golden medallions attached to narrow leather bands that formed necklaces. Her brother did not emerge. "I work to bless these pendants for us to wear when we enter the lair."

"And that was necessary to do without us present?" I asked.

Her eyes flicked to Dominus. Her jaw tightened. "Yes. As some do not share our belief."

"Now, lady," Dominus said, taking a step toward her. I placed a gentle hand on his forearm.

"All the same," she replied, looking nervously at him. "I made one for you as well."

Volya walked to each of us. Since she was much shorter, we had to bow slightly forward so she could slip the leather necklace over our heads. While bowed, she kissed our foreheads and chanted something in a language unfamiliar to me. When she got to Dominus, he removed his hat, staring her in the eyes as he bowed toward her. She was hesitant and uncertain, but after a few seconds, she slipped the band over his head, kissed his wrinkled brow, and repeated her chant. When she finished, and he had put his hat back on, he took her tiny hand into his.

While slightly bowed forward he kissed the back of her hand. "Dear lady, my humble apologies for my rude behavior last night. I don't warm up to people I don't know right away, and when I'm exhausted, I can be one cranky old man."

Volya's eyes softened, as she detected his sincerity, and she slowly slipped her hand from his.

She smiled. "Thank you."

He gave a single nod and winked.

Her face reddened, and she looked to me. "Your father? Where is he?"

"Still asleep," I replied.

She pointed toward the door. "Do . . . you mind if—?"

I shook my head and smiled. "Not at all."

Volya offered a small curtsey.

After she entered the cottage, we glanced at Dominus with odd expressions. Had he been bewitched?

"What?" he asked, somewhat defensively. "Why are you looking at me like that? Look, we're heading into the baron's lair. A strong master vampire. We have to be on the same side, regardless if we don't all agree on the same things. She and I won't ever see eye to eye on our beliefs, but I mustn't allow *that* to keep contention between us. Who knows if I'll need her to protect my back or the other way around?"

Jacques smiled. "I agree, but . . . that was a sudden switch of attitude."

"My mother always insisted I treat a lady like a lady," he replied. "And she was kind enough to include me in her blessings, which tells me a lot about her, especially since she didn't have to."

Volya stepped back outside of the cottage. Her eyes causally looked toward Dominus. She blushed and quickly turned away.

Jacques said to her, "Could you get Hoval to join us? We need to discuss the best time to set our attack."

"Yes," she said, nodding. She hurried to the wagon to get him.

I went to awaken my father.

A few minutes later we met at the front of the cottage, standing in a circle. Jacques and Rusk stood side by side.

Rusk asked, "Is everyone comfortable about invading Baron Randolph's lair tonight?"

"At what time?" Zsolt asked.

"Midnight?" Jacques asked.

"Sounds good to me," Dominus said.

Zsolt nodded.

A thought dawned upon me, which I could only explain as being from hunter instinct and not a direct thought of my own. It was an impulse that I knew I couldn't shrug off and ignore. It was guidance from a higher plane. I glanced at Dominus. "Do you always hunt vampires after midnight?"

He shrugged. "Ever since I found them during the Civil War, yes."

"Why?"

"That's when they are on the prowl," he replied. "And when I can easily find them."

I nodded. "Exactly. But aren't they also at their strongest? We know where Baron Randolph's lair is and what his chamber room looks like. What happens if we attacked during the day, say around noon, when the sun is at its strongest? Wouldn't that be when he's at his weakest?"

I was surprised at what seemed a major revelation, and so was everyone standing around me. It made perfect sense. Attack the vampires when they least expected it.

Jacques and Dominus marveled, nodding their heads. Both walked to me and clasped my shoulders.

"I never thought about that," Dominus said.

"Nor I," Jacques said. He glanced toward the sun's position. "We're three hours from noon. We'd best get moving."

CHAPTER 33

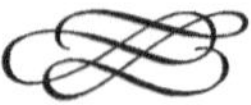

We entered the cemetery about a quarter past noon, much to Dominus' disappointment. He grumbled something about high noon, but I didn't understand his translation. The sun was bright and the sky cloudless. Hoval parked their wagon near the center of the cemetery and tied the horse to a low tree branch.

We stood in a circle, each hunter holding his box, and the werewolves holding a stake in each hand. Volya held a lantern in one hand and an odd stick in the other, which I guessed to be a wand. She had never said. Her thin frail brother had the rolled burlap sack with the extra stakes slung over his shoulder. He looked strained and stressed trying to support the bag's weight. He also held a lantern. He and Volya had agreed to carry the light since we'd be preoccupied with our weapons.

The pendants we wore, she told us before we left the cottage, were most powerful in her presence. I wondered if that were true, or if she simply led us to believe it so we fight harder to keep her alive.

Like at Glodrim, I had stakes tucked at each forearm, two at my back, one inside each boot, and several inside my deep coat pockets. In my pockets were vials of holy water, a cross, crushed garlic stored in small glass globes, and the ax with a claw on one end. I had the blessed dagger tucked in its sheath on my belt. I also had two more daggers fastened on the other side of my waist. I never knew when I might need an extra knife.

Dominus loaded his crossbow with a gleam in his eyes.

Excitement rose inside of me before we opened the doors. Other thoughts passed through my mind. The largest one, of course, was wondering who in our group was going to betray me. I fought to thrust it aside because I didn't need any distractions to prevent me from successfully killing the baron. Not that I'd be the one who actually killed him because I agreed with Dominus. Kill any vampire that you came into contact with, and that was acceptable to me. But deep inside I hoped that I'd be the one who drove a stake through that bastard's heart.

Rusk stood before the double doors and looked over his shoulder at us. In a near whisper, he said, "Ready?"

We all nodded.

He pulled the doors outward. The rusted hinges creaked, and we all tensed, holding our weapons ready. What we had hoped to achieve was entering the catacombs silently and reaching the third level down without being noticed beforehand. Although the creaking sound wasn't excessively loud, the noise seemed magnified because of my apprehension. I often wondered why whenever I had tried my hardest to be quiet that was when I unintentionally made the most noise. It never failed.

A cool musty, earthen breeze mixed with the scent of death and decay blew from the opening. For nearly a minute we stood watching the stairwell that vanished down into the darkness. Rusk motioned Volya ahead of him, so we could use the light of the lantern to see the steps on our way down. Rusk stood behind her, followed by Zsolt and then Jacques. Dominus was in front of me. My father followed me. Hoval was at the rear with his lantern. While they offered light for us to see the stairs, they were also exposed, making themselves the most vulnerable to attack. As far as I was concerned neither of them were equipped with ready weapons, but I doubted stakes would even help them.

Hoval's frailness wasn't a subject of any debate, and Dominus had been more than ready to state the fact the previous night, which had hurt the young man's feelings. But denying the truth didn't change anything. I knew from Glodrim that vampires were stronger than they appeared in size. The female vampire that had boosted me off the ground was a third of my weight and much smaller in stature, but her stern shove had left me immobile for the better part of a minute. Enough time for her to lunge on top of me as she tried try to bite me. I couldn't imagine the damage she'd have done to Hoval.

In single file we walked down to the first turn in the stairs. Like Father had mentioned, there was a door that opened into a narrow tunnel. Volya hesitated as the lantern lit the side of the wall beside the doorway.

I tightened my hands around my stakes until my fingers ached. I half expected something to rush toward us, but the only sound was our slow steady breathing. The tension increased around us, but none of us made eye contact with one another. We watched the door.

Rusk finally nudged Volya's shoulder. She stiffened at his touch but then advanced past the doorway on tiptoe and made her way around the column to find where the stairs descended. For a moment her eyes met mine. I read her fear before she turned her attention back to the stairs and took the first step downward.

I didn't like knowing she was afraid, especially not after her argument with Dominus about faith. She had seemed to indicate her magic was strong, and now I questioned her true purpose for coming.

She held the lantern in her left hand, slightly pulled back to her hip, and extended the crooked stick with her right hand. It wasn't sharpened and was incapable of piercing anything. I wondered exactly what she planned to do should a vampire rush at her.

At the bottom of this set of steps, Volya turned, allowing Rusk, Zsolt, and Jacques to step beside her. I peered down and saw the man, standing at the doorway that led into another tunnel. I recognized him. He was the human servant that had given my father and I the message on the day Momma died.

Anger rushed through me. I pushed my way past Jacques and Rusk before they even noticed I was running. Jacques then tried to grab my arm but missed. The human servant realized who I was. He spun and ran into the dark corridor. I went after him without any hesitation.

A lantern moved up the tunnel behind me. I didn't think it was Volya as she was too apprehensive about the doorways. One of the others must have grabbed her lantern and headed after me.

Other than the faint light behind me, complete darkness filled the tunnel ahead. I kept running. This man was not going to escape me. His footsteps thudded hard, and he sucked huge gulps of air as he ran. I knew where he was in front of me. The only real advantage he held was that he knew the tunnel and where it led. My rage blocked me from even caring.

The tunnel reeked of sewage and dead animals. There might have been outshoots that led to other rooms, but I kept my attention on the man ahead of me. His ragged breathing indicated he was about ready to collapse. His pace slowed so I chanced reaching out and grabbing for him. I caught the back of his shirt with my left hand and yanked him toward me. My big clumsy feet entangled with his, and we dropped hard to the brick floor.

He fell partially beneath me, face first, and my weight atop him brought a painful grunt from him. He gasped and groaned, trying to breathe. I panted, too. Sweat rolled off of me, but I didn't move off of him, nor did I loosen my grip on his shirt collar.

The lantern carrier turned out to be Jacques. He knelt to the side of us.

"Are you mad, Forrest?" he asked. "You have no idea where this tunnel leads or how many vampires might be hiding down here."

I tightened my hand around the man's collar and pressed my weight down on him, smashing his face against the dirty bricks. "I don't care. This is one of the baron's human servants. He's the one that gave us the baron's threat the day Momma died. If we let him go, he will warn Randolph. We cannot risk that."

"So what exactly do you plan to do?"

"The exact same thing the baron had the other servant do to my mother."

"You can't," the man said.

I pushed myself partway up and buried my knee into the small of his back. He groaned.

"Watch me," I replied.

"If you kill me," he said, "Baron Randolph will awaken. He will feel my pain. Right now he sleeps."

I pressed the point of my stake to the side of his throat. "I don't trust you."

"Did I lie to you before?" he asked. "I didn't. You know that I didn't. I simply did as my master bid. I gave you his message."

Jacques placed a hand on my shoulder. "Listen to him. If he's telling the truth, Randolph will know that we're here."

"And if he's lying, he goes free and might run to warn the baron."

"Forrest," Jacques said, lifting the lantern so I could see his face. "If you kill him, it's not the same as killing a vampire. He's still a human. It's murder. The body doesn't dissolve into ash."

I swallowed hard. Tears heated my eyes. Slowly I eased the sharp stake away from the man's throat. "What do we do with him?"

"Let him up," Jacques said.

I rose to my feet, grabbed the man's collar, and yanked him to his feet. I didn't lessen my grip though.

Jacques looked at the man. "Why have you chosen to be the baron's servant?"

Fear widened the man's eyes. "I have no choice."

"We all have choices," Jacques said. His voice deepened. "I'm giving you a choice right now."

"To do what?"

Jacques raised the lantern with his hair-covered hand and offered it to me. I took it.

"Whether you face your death, or flee."

Jacques yanked the medallion from his neck and shoved it into his coat pocket. He flexed his entire body, releasing a series of harsh growls as his bones, muscles, and sinews snapped and crackled. Then he released one long howl. The servant yanked free of my hold and sprinted away into the dark tunnel.

In werewolf form, Jacques snarled and ran after the servant. Less than a minute later, a bloodcurdling scream echoed through the tunnel. I held the lantern up, trying to see, but Jacques carried the man deeper into the darkness where I couldn't witness whatever he did to the man. The echoing sounds didn't sound pleasant, and I didn't know that I had the stomach to watch. My curiosity after hearing the slashes and tears and the man's whimpering made me wish I were much farther away.

Even if what the servant said wasn't true about his pain and death awakening the baron, I didn't think the terrorizing sounds had gone unnoticed.

I turned and headed back toward the stairwell to join the others. When I reached the others, Volya and her brother stared toward the door where I emerged with a heightened sense of terror. I handed her the lantern.

Rusk, however, was only seconds from turning into a werewolf. His eyes held the wildness of a wolf. Perhaps it was hearing Jacques change, I don't know. Rusk held his medallion in his hand while he took huge gulps of air, closing his eyes like he was trying to fight the rising beast inside.

After he calmed, he placed a gentle hand on Volya's shoulder and motioned for her to continue. We headed down to the next level, minus one of our party. I wasn't certain when Jacques might return to join us, but after the echoing disturbance, I wouldn't have been too surprised to see the baron awaiting our arrival.

At the bottom of the steps we only had one more set of stairs to descend. Volya hurried past the door this time, anxious to get to the lower floor where the baron's chambers were supposed to be. We rounded the column and as Volya stepped upon the first step, something emerged from the side door and grabbed Hoval, yanking him into the corridor.

"Volya!" he screamed, but his voice faded down the tunnel.

"Hoval!" she turned and ran toward the tunnel.

Dominus stepped between her and the door. He shook his head. "Let me check for you. Stay here."

He reached down with his left hand, grabbed Hoval's lantern off the door, and stepped into the tunnel with his crossbow ready to fire.

CHAPTER 34

*V*olya stood at the threshold, holding her lantern, and desperately watching. I stepped beside her with a stake in hand.

Dominus fired his crossbow. A few seconds later, Hoval ran through the door, clutching his throat. Blood seeped through his fingers. Volya set her lantern on the floor and hugged him tightly.

"You killed it?" Zsolt asked Dominus.

He nodded.

"Good."

Dominus pulled Hoval free of Volya's grasp. He took a bottle of holy water and uncorked it, handing it to her. "Put this on his bite to boil out possible infection."

She looked at the bottle with skepticism but when she noticed Hoval's pleading eyes, she poured it. Steam boiled from the bite mark. Her eyebrows rose.

Hoval fought screaming, and Zsolt gripped the young man's elbows to prevent him from running away. When she was able to pour the holy water without any bubbling on the flesh or her brother suffering pain, Zsolt told her to stop.

"He's okay," Zsolt said. "He'll be fine."

Tears crested in her eyes. She went to Dominus, placed her hand on his forearm, and rose to kiss his cheek. "Thank you. You saved him."

Dominus smiled for a moment and then he pointed toward the stairs. He whispered, "We need to keep going."

"It's doubtful that he's not expecting us," I said.

Rusk nodded. "Watch out for one another, but as Dominus stated last night, kill any vampire that comes at you. We're not keeping count. We just want to all walk out of here alive."

Zsolt said, "Agreed."

My father remained silent. With all of the distractions, I hadn't really taken a moment to evaluate him. For one, he was my father and in my mind, one of the strongest men alive. But we stood only twelve steps above the room where Baron Randolph resided. Father was pale and his haunted eyes were filled by obvious terror. Had the things he had tried to forget resurfaced because of the hypnosis?

"Father, are you okay?" I whispered.

He replied with a slight shrug. I almost wanted to leave him at the top of the stairs, but with Hoval being attacked at the door, it was too great a risk for Father to remain up here alone.

Volya was midway down the stairs with everyone else following in proceeding order except for Jacques. She paused at the final step. Candles flickered inside the chamber room. Lanterns hung in each corner of the room.

While I was thankful to see a well-lit room, I was surprised to find all of the heavy casket lids shut. No vampires were waiting outside of these coffins made from heavy carved stone. I wondered if the thickness of the stone had prevented sound from getting through. Of course Jacques' disruption wasn't even on this floor, and a lot depended upon how soundproof the walls and floors were, too.

Zsolt and Rusk headed to the casket closest to us. They tried to slide the heavy stone lid and couldn't budge it. Rusk motioned for Dominus to help. I walked over with him since I was the largest one in the group.

Dominus shook his head. He made a hammering motion with his

hand. Zsolt placed his mallet on top of the lid. I slid my stake into my pocket and placed my huge hands to the side of the lid near the top and shoved. The stone rattled and scraped against the sides of the walls. We moved it far enough to glimpse inside.

A female vampire lay with her arms crossed over her chest. Her alabaster skin nearly glowed beneath the flickering candle flames. Her pointed nose and thin lips gave her a distinguished appearance almost like royalty. Her high cheekbones and flowing black hair enhanced her beauty even more. She seemed too beautiful to stake.

If she breathed, she showed no signs of doing so. I wondered if she even had a pulse. Was she undead or really dead?

Zsolt grabbed the hammer and his stake and eased to the side of the stone coffin. His brow furrowed slightly and his eyes softened. I could tell he found it as difficult as I did to stake someone so lovely, but I kept reminding myself that she was a sleeping monster.

Rusk frowned at him.

Zsolt took a deep breath, leaned over the coffin and placed the tip of the stake slightly above her left breast. And one solid quick strike, he drove the stake through her heart. Her eyes flicked open for a brief second before she collapsed to heated ash.

"Fools!"

Volya screamed.

On the far end of the room, Baron Randolph stood, pointing a stern finger. Bodi stood to one side of the baron with the cross-shaped scar on his cheek. My father trembled when he looked at them. In what seemed like lost time, eleven vampires rushed toward us. Their stone coffin lids were cast aside before I even blinked.

I grabbed my father and pulled him behind me. I shoved a hand in each of my side pockets and drew out stakes. Dominus fired his crossbow, dropping one vampire into dust before she noticed his weapon. Two wild-eyed female vampires exposed fangs and rushed Dominus. They ripped the crossbow from his hand and rammed his back against the brick wall. I turned to pull one of them off but was struck firmly in the back by a large male vampire. I was falling toward an open casket, falling fast, and had only a moment to twist to my side so I didn't slam my forehead against the solid rock casket wall.

The entire right side of my body ached, but I managed to roll onto my back. The vampire hissed and lunged for my throat. I thrust my left forearm beneath his throat, pressing him away from my neck. Without knowing where to aim, I speared his lower chest with the one stake. He clutched it and pulled back. Taking advantage of his ill thought move, I plunged the second stake through his heart. I scrambled to help Dominus, who had somehow managed to hold back the two females, but before I could reach him, another vampire tackled me.

Sharp claws sliced through the back of my heavy coat, ripping into my skin. I winced and shoved off the floor. I rose and turned, slamming my thick fist into its jaw. Its neck snapped and the momentum of my punch spun its entire body around. He dropped to the floor. Dust pillowed up like a brown cloud around him.

He wasn't dead, but he struggled to move. I ran to Dominus and yanked away one of the females. She had bitten into his shoulder, and he was bleeding. It didn't seem severe, but I didn't have time to inspect it.

Dominus nodded his appreciation, reached into his pocket, and then he smashed a globe of holy water against the side of her face. She reeled backwards as her flesh blistered. She screamed. He came at her and flung the blessed salt over her blistering skin, making her screech in agony. This combination of weapons seemed his forte.

Snarls erupted behind me. I turned, expecting to see Rusk but it was Jacques. He ran to the vampire whose neck I had broken and tore into its back. Immediately following Jacques entrance, Rusk howled and began his transformation.

During all of commotion, I had lost track of my father. Glancing around the room, I finally noticed him. He was in the center of the sepulcher where he had pinned a female vampire to the floor. She gnashed her fangs and kept slapping away the stake as he tried to stake her. He still appeared to have the advantage.

My attention turned to Bodi. He stood beside Randolph and when he looked into my eyes, his mouth dropped slightly from recognition.

His tiny fangs were visible. Sadness came to me. Remorse, too. I wished I could turn back the calendar and rescue him.

Ignoring everything else around me, I stalked down the center of the sepulcher floor, staring into the baron's eyes with all of my fury. I seethed. If ever I hated anyone, it was this very moment and this pompous bastard.

I started to rush toward him and noticed the narrow gap in the floor where a layer of the brick foundation had collapsed. One misstep could drop me several feet or a hundred feet below, depending on the depth of the hole. His gold embroidered casket was also on a platform several feet higher than the floor where the other twelve caskets rested.

Baron Randolph studied me for a moment. His eyes peered sternly into mine. He attempted to lure me, but his power seemed weaker than the first time he had tried that. His eyes widened slightly. "You seem . . . stronger. But it's no matter, really. You will become a new servant to this master."

I ignore the statement.

"Are you responsible for this?" I demanded, pointing my finger toward Bodi. "Are you the monster who turned him?"

Randolph sneered in a condescending manner. "And if I am, peasant, what is it to you?"

"It is your death," I replied.

"Kill me and you kill the boy," he said.

"He's already dead."

"Why would the boy concern you?"

"He was my friend in school. That's why. It takes a horrible monster to rob a child of his life."

The baron gave a haughty grin. "Robbed him? He is blessed with living forever."

"As what? A walking child corpse? His parents are brokenhearted over losing him. They hired my father to remove Bodi from this horrid lifestyle, so you tried to kill my father."

Baron Randolph shrugged. "But I did succeed in having your mother killed, did I not?"

"You've caused enough pain in this world."

"You wish to finish me?" he laughed.

My hand slipped to the dagger. I wondered why it hadn't already taken control of the baron. I was a lot closer to Randolph than I had been to the master in Glodrim.

"You think your silver trinket will aid you, boy?" Randolph asked. He motioned his hand toward the right side of the room. The rocks were set in such a way that I hadn't seen the hidden door. From this door stepped . . . Rose.

$\mathcal{I}$ stared in disbelief.

Tears streamed down her cheeks. "I'm sorry, Forrest."

I frowned and flicked my gaze toward the baron. He smiled.

"You seem surprised," Randolph said.

I didn't reply. I looked back at her. So many emotions struggled deep inside of me. I felt my shoulders soften.

"I tried to warn you, Forrest," Rose said. "I told you *not* to come here."

"You betrayed me but led me to believe someone else in my party would do that." My hand went to my dagger.

"You don't understand, Forrest. I was trying to warn you. I have no control over my being here," she said, sobbing.

"Forrest," Randolph said. "All you had to do that night was let me finish what I started. Let me kill your father, and you wouldn't have to lose everything you cherished in this world. Now, look around you. This little gathering of yours will end horribly for you."

"And why did you want him dead?" I asked.

"Because he had discovered what I am."

Sounds behind me suddenly seemed louder. Through my shock, I supposed that I had blocked out everything else. I dared a glance back.

Although we had killed several vampires, dozens more had come into the room from the stairs. I wanted to turn and help them.

Rusk and Jacques were the only ones not being detained by vampires. They were slashing and ripping their way through the vampires, but not having much success decapitating any of them.

"They have their orders, Forrest," Randolph said. "Not to kill anyone until I give the command."

"What do you want?"

"Yield your will to me, and they live," he replied.

I leveled a harsh glare toward him.

Randolph attempted to draw me but failed. "There are rules in war. You needed to abide by them and obey."

"There are no rules in this war. Not this time. Not anymore."

Anger flared his nostrils.

I looked at Rose. "Why did you do this, Rose?"

"It was not me."

Baron Randolph took her left hand into his and then he grabbed Bodi's with his other. As he stood with his arms outstretched, he was quite vulnerable, but the only way I could even get to him was to leap across the gap in the floor and run up several steps to reach him. I could never get to him fast enough.

"She's under my control, boy," Randolph said. "She does whatever I ask. She's the reason why your magic no longer has a hold on me. Oh, I sensed it the night I was at your cottage, which is why I needed to find someone capable to counteract the magic. You and she seemed to hold an affection for one another."

I shook my head. "You're mistaken."

She winced. Tears streamed down her cheeks.

"Am I?"

I nodded.

He released their hands and steepled his fingers together. "There is a grave lesson in all of this for you."

My jaw tightened. "And what is that?"

"Never threaten the man who allows a roof over your head and a place for you to hunt. I warned you that your malevolence toward me was a deadly mistake. You have no power over me, as you so believed. I am the victor. I *always* shall be."

I drew the dagger, gazed at the baron, and laughed. "You believe that Rose has the power to undo a gypsy witch's spell? She's a fraud. She cannot predict the future. You're foolish to think she has any power over the magic that blesses my dagger."

"Then, dear boy, why not use it then?" he asked.

I shrugged and flung it.

The dagger drove deep into Rose's right shoulder. She wailed and staggered back away from the baron. I turned toward the dozens of vampires behind me, reached into my side pockets and hurled every glass vial of holy water and garlic juice at the ceiling above them. Glass shattered, showering harmful liquids upon the vampires. Some fled. Others dropped to their knees.

Dominus leapt for his crossbow.

I ran toward the baron, jumped the gap, and landed upon the bottom step. He was knelt beside Rose. Before he noticed me, I kicked him in the side of my head with my boot. The impact slung his head hard to right and knocked him to the ground. I held a stake in my hand.

Bodi looked at me, saw the stake, but didn't approach. I motioned for him to move back.

I ripped a sleeve from Rose's dress and wadded it up. Setting down the stake, I took the hilt in my hand and pressed the cloth to the side of the dagger's blade. In one swift tug, I yanked out the blade and shoved the cloth down over the stab wound.

She screamed.

After her scream ended, I said, "Hold that tightly to stop the bleeding."

Snatching the stake in my right hand, I came for the baron. I held the dagger, but I sensed no power flowing from it like I had at Glodrim. I came at Randolph, ready to stake him, but he turned and flailed his long nails across my chest. He ripped through the coat and sliced deeply. I winced.

The baron came at me, clutching both of my wrists. Although he was much smaller than me, he was incredibly powerful. He shoved me back, causing me to stumble over my own feet and fall. I fell a few inches from the ledge of the gap in the floor. He battered my wrist against the brick floor until the dagger dislodged from my fingers and dropped down into the deep hole.

He leaned back with a look of triumph on his face and laughed. Bodi stood at the ledge, looking down.

"You see, Bodi," Randolph said. "Your father will always look out for you."

Bodi looked at him, at me, and then back down into the trench to where the knife had vanished.

The baron cocked a brow at me. "My messenger gave you the message that you and I were even, did he not? And yet, you just won't let well enough alone."

"We are far from even," I said, gasping.

I glanced toward Rose. She was no longer sobbing and lay quite still. Maybe she had lost consciousness. I hoped that she wasn't dead. I looked for Bodi and didn't see him.

The baron sneered and placed his hand firmly around my neck. "But you are so wrong, you foolish impetuous boy. I shall make you one of mine. Since you treasure your *friendship* with Bodi, how would you like to become his brother for all eternity?"

He pressed harder and flashed fangs. My pulse throbbed behind my eyes. I blinked, trying to clear my vision. He was so incredibly strong.

Something blue glowed above the baron. I thought I was seeing colors because of how severely he was choking me. In a flash the blue was gone. The baron stiffened, releasing his hold around my throat. I gasped hard. Bodi leapt off of the baron's back and onto the casket lid.

Baron Randolph reached behind him, trying to pull my dagger out of his spine. I slowly pushed myself to my feet.

"How?" he stammered. He gazed toward Bodi. "*Why?*"

I walked toward Rose and knelt beside her. She was breathing, but barely.

Still fighting to get my breath, I reached into my coat pocket and brought out another stake. I grabbed the baron around the throat in the same manner he had mine. I squeezed tightly and forced him to his knees.

Bodi sat on the casket lid. His eyes peered at me, like he was lost and a little sad.

I pressed the stake against the baron's chest.

Bodi nodded.

I cocked a brow at him, questioning him without saying a word.

He nodded again. He knew if I killed the baron, he died too, and he seemed at peace about it.

"Then rest in peace, my little friend," I said to Bodi.

His small mousy face smiled.

I glared at the baron and spat in his face. "*Now*, we're even."

His eyes showed more fear than they had the night he had stood outside our cottage. The magic of the dagger held his body paralyzed where he couldn't fight or resist, or even protest. I gave him a grim smile with slight satisfaction as I shoved the stake through his heart and almost through the other side. He crumbled to ash, as did little Bodi, and so did the other vampires in the room. Death was instant for them, but I didn't feel I had true justice. But in a way, we had received exactly that.

CHAPTER 36

I picked up my dagger from the pile of baron ash and returned to Rose. She was breathing but still not awake. Power gushed through me, similar to the few moments after I had killed the other master vampire in Glodrim, but much more powerful. I placed my hand upon Rose's bleeding shoulder.

The power surged down my arm and through the palm of my hand with a glowing, radiant heat. Rose's body jerked. Her wound stopped bleeding. When I removed my hand, there was no mark where the dagger had pierced her. Placing my hands beneath her, I lifted her, and jumped the gap in the floor with her in my arms.

I looked at the rest of our hunting party.

Dominus was worn out, bleeding from several bite marks on his shoulders. His left hand was bent and twisted quite severely. He limped, gathering up his crossbow, arrows, and stakes scattered across the floor.

Rusk wore his medallion and had returned to his human form with slash marks all across his torso, but the cuts were knitting themselves shut. He knelt beside Zsolt and shook his head. Zsolt's throat had been ripped out. There was no surviving that mortal wound. Apparently the baron hadn't had the power over his children as well as he thought he had.

Hoval lay still on the floor beside Volya, staring at her face and caressing her cheek. Her eyes were glazing. He wept, but silently. Dominus noticed and hurried to her, setting his equipment down on the floor. In spite of his twisted arm, he lifted her to him and cradled her in his arms.

"Dear lady," he said, shaking his head and then kissing her forehead. "This is not meant to be."

But it was. Loss came at heavy costs whenever we fought our enemies.

Volya tilted her head slightly, recognizing his voice, but her eyes were already blinded by her impending death. As hardened as I had viewed Dominus to be, I never thought I'd see the man in tears. He dropped to his knees, holding her, and sobbing. I turned away.

Jacques had few cuts on him. He was with my father. Father had several bruises and lacerations on his face. He was slow getting to his feet, but he was alive, for which I was grateful.

I sat down on the edge of a casket, holding Rose in my arms. We had won, but we had also suffered losses. Rose's eyelids fluttered. She stared up at me with her brilliant blue eyes.

"I'm sorry, Forrest," she said.

"Why did you do this?" I asked. "Why did you betray me?"

She shook her head. Her moist eyes surfaced fresh tears. "I didn't. Not intentionally. I told you that you'd be betrayed, remember?"

"Quite well."

"I also told you that I didn't know by whom. I told you the truth."

"And yet, you came?"

Rose reached up and touched the side of my face. "Forrest, I came for other reasons, none of which was to betray you. Honest."

"So tell me."

"After you left, I decided to see what else I could learn, and I discovered something about the baron that I had not known before. He . . . he had killed my mother. I came here to kill him. For two reasons, actually. One, to avenge my mother. And the second reason was so, you . . . didn't have to. I didn't want you to begin transforming into what I know you'll become. I thought by killing him that I could spare you that."

"You cannot change my destiny, Rose."

She nodded. "I realize that now. But when I snuck in to find the baron, he found me first and compelled me. He found out about my feelings for you and used that against us."

"He tried to."

Rose cried. "While you may not believe I can use magic, you are incorrect. He forced me to block the magic on your dagger."

"I said those things to distract him, Rose. I didn't mean them."

"They hurt just the same, but not as badly as you throwing the dagger at me and stabbing my shoulder. *Why* did you do that?"

"To break his hold over you. I guessed that enough pain should sever his compulsion control over you. Once that was broken, you were free. After you lost consciousness, your spell lessened or dissolved, granting back my dagger's power."

"Did it work?"

I nodded.

"So you killed the baron?" she asked.

I hesitated in answering. Something had occurred to me that I had almost missed. The dagger never granted me the control over the baron. It was Bodi. When he had retrieved the dagger, he held the power over Randolph. Not I. Chills shot through me. Had the child chosen to, he could have had every one of us slaughtered by the vampires. Instead, he granted me the right to stake the baron. He wanted to be free. Why exactly, I wasn't certain. But from the moment we had noticed one another, he still regarded me as his friend. Perhaps he remembered all the times I had protected him from those who picked on him at school. Perhaps he remembered me as his true friend, and real friendship stood solid through almost any tribulation.

"The baron is no more," I replied. I looked to Jacques. "It's time we leave."

He nodded.

Dominus carried Volya up the stairs. His broken heart weighed on his face. Hoval followed behind him.

Rose pressed her face against my chest and closed her eyes. I couldn't wait to get out of these catacombs and see the sunlight once more.

CHAPTER 37

Several days passed and I, along with my father and Jacques, were traveling by horse and wagon into a bordering country. As we rode, I reflected upon the aftermath of our battle against Baron Randolph.

Zsolt . . . Rusk had buried him in the catacombs where the baron had died. Afterwards, Rusk returned to Ploiesti. He never discussed any future plans for slaying vampires, and I didn't press him for such information. I doubted our paths ever crossed again.

Hoval had taken Volya's body in their covered wagon to bury her in the cemetery where their family members were buried. According to Hoval, Volya had sacrificed her life by casting a powerful protective spell over all of us, apparently after she had witnessed Zsolt's gruesome death. She had given her life to save the rest of us.

Dominus had said his goodbyes in a few words. He told me, although I had figured it out myself, that I didn't need any further training. He had been a hardened man when I had met him, but his eyes held greater rage as he was leaving. I wasn't sure how Volya's presence had affected him so quickly, but he seemed to have taken rather fondly to her. Perhaps her death angered him in that he had not been able to keep her safe. I don't know. But I guessed he'd spend a long time taking his anger out on any vampire he happened upon, making them suffer before he finally staked them.

Jacques had set the bones in Dominus' wrist and wrapped it with tight cloth. They also boiled his bite marks with holy water. Dominus didn't show any pain at all while the process was being done. He told me that being bitten didn't turn someone unless they had ingested the vampire's blood. But, if the vampire was still alive, a bite could turn someone into a human servant who had not partaken of the vampire's blood. Regardless of either, infection could set in, so it was advisable to cleanse any vampire bite with holy water.

Before Dominus left the cottage, he opened his hunter box and handed me a pistol when Jacques wasn't around.

"Use only silver bullets," he had said.

"Why?"

"They won't kill vampires. I know. But they hurt them and slow them down. Also, not every werewolf is like Jacques and Rusk. Silver bullets can kill werewolves. Trust me, the time might well come when you'll need this."

And after that brief conversation, he had traveled on down the road. I hated seeing his departure. In spirit and our calling, we were brothers. But to me, he was more than that. He was like a second father, and I sorely missed him.

My father ended up trading our cottage for a young horse and covered wagon. We said our goodbyes to Bucharest and decided to travel into another country that Jacques indicated had a severe vampire infestation.

As we rode away on the wagon, I kept my gaze on our former cottage. Memories flooded through me. Some good. Others, not so much. A boy never really became a man until he had left home for good. As we left, my childhood innocence and grief for the loss of my mother remained behind. Some things, like the scarring cuts on my back and chest, I'd keep with me until the end of my life. I'd always be reminded of Baron Randolph each day when I dressed, as he had left the worst scars.

Thinking of his demise, I shook my head. I rubbed my chin and cheeks. Short dark stubble was growing on my face. Manhood had arrived.

Jacques handed me a round box that Dominus had hidden at the front of the wagon. Lifting the narrow lid, I saw the leather hat inside. A narrow belt around the hat held six silver bullets; three on each side, and a small corked bottle was also strapped onto the leather belt. One bottle held holy water, and the other one contained garlic powder— Dominus' special combination. I put the hat on my head. It fit.

Jacques remained with Father and I, more as emotional support due to the loss of Momma. Father was hard-faced and seldom spoke or smiled. I distanced myself from him. I figured when he was ready to talk to me, he would. Healing from loss differed from person to person.

Instead of all of the calamity occurring after Baron Randolph's death, the city officials decided to start renovating and rebuilding the buildings in the slums. While that was good for the poor people, it only moved the other lair underground where Randolph had reigned.

As much as I wanted to see Rose before leaving, I knew better than to go. I had made the vow that after I killed the Baron I was leaving Bucharest for good. She knew my ultimate goal. I didn't want to add to my grief by seeing her again. Deep inside I longed to be with her, but such was too dangerous. Not for me, but for her survival.

With the other lair untouched, I doubted I could justify staying out of Bucharest for too long. Those vampires needed exterminated like the preying vermin they were. But I'd return later, once my pain over Rose faded, and I estimated that might take several years.

I am a vampire hunter; one of the Chosen, and sadly, my losses in life have always outweighed the gains. Sorrows had already come, and more waited over the next horizon, which would make me wiser, and yet, I became ever colder inside. No one ever adjusted to misery, not even I. The only good I'll ever have is in removing the growing pestilence of the undead across the land. I'd never kill all of them, but I'd die trying.

THE END

AUTHOR'S NOTE

Forrest Wollinsky's first appearance is in Succubus: Shadows of the Beast. He was such an interesting character that I knew he'd have a book of his own. However, while writing this novel, I know several more will follow this one. Thanks so much for being a part of this adventure. Please leave a review. Reviews help others in their search for a story to take them into another world. And, they also encourage me to continue writing. Thanks!

ABOUT THE AUTHOR

Leonard D. Hilley II grew up a quiet, shy kid with an inquisitive mind. Learning to read at an early age, he fell in love with books. He read every book he could get his hands on and stacks of dark comics about ghosts, monsters, and creepy things that stalk the night.

Like a lot of boys, he caught beetles, wooly bears, butterflies, and had an ant farm. When he was ten, his interests in science increased even more after seeing a professor's insect collection. Soon he set out on his quest to build his own collection. He also learned to rear butterflies and moths to obtain perfect specimens. He learned botany, gardening, and set his goal to become an entomologist.

At eleven, he saw Star Wars. His imagination soared. Soon after, he discovered Roger Zelazny's Chronicles of Amber. Six months later, he had written the first draft of a novel. A novel he later discarded, but the characters stuck with him. Years later, these characters came to life in Shawndirea, which Hilley intended to be a novella for Devils Den. The characters, however, refused to be ignored and took the opportunity to unveil Aetheaon in their first epic fantasy. Lady Squire: Dawn's Ascension was quick to follow.

Shawndirea was Hilley's farewell to butterfly collecting, and those who have read the novel understand why. He has taken Ray Bradbury's advice to heart: "Follow the characters." He does. He follows, listens, and take notes—often never knowing where they're going to take him, but he's never been disappointed in the results.

Hilley earned a B.S. in Biology and an MFA in Creative Writing to combine his love of science and writing.

Sci-fi Titles: Predators of Darkness: Aftermath, Beyond the Darkness, The Game of Pawns, Death's Valley, The Deimos Virus.

Epic Fantasy: Shawndirea (Aetheaon Chronicles: Book One), Lady Squire (Aetheaon Chronicles: Book Two), Frosthammer (Aetheaon Chronicles: Book Three), Shadowfae (Aetheaon Chronicles: Book Four), and Devils Den.

UF/PR: Succubus: Shadows of the Beast (Nocturnal Trinity Series: Book One), Raven (Nocturnal Trinity Series: Book Two)

YA UF/Paranormal: Forrest Wollinsky Vampire Hunter: The Beginning; Forrest Wollinsky: Blood Mists of London; Forrest Wollinsky: Predestined Crossroads.

www.ingramcontent.com/pod-product-compliance
Lightning Source LLC
Chambersburg PA
CBHW051843180726

48284CB00007BA/2028